Keeper of Trust

The Carly Sisters Series

Mary Kay Tuberty

MRP
Mantle Rock Publishing
www.MantleRockPublishing.com

©2016 Mary Kay Tuberty

Published by Mantle Rock Publishing
2879 Palma Road
Benton, KY 42025
www.mantlerockpublishing.com

Printed in the United States of America

All rights reserved. No part of this publication may be reproduced, stored in a retrieval system, or transmitted in any form or by any means—for example, electronic, photocopy and recording— without the prior written permission of the publisher. The only exception is brief quotation in printed reviews.

ISBN 978-0-9968807-9-4 Print Book
978-1-945094-00-2 Ebook

Cover by Diane Turpin. DianeTurpinDesigns.com

Published in association with Jim Hart of Hartline Literary Agency, Pittsburg, PA

for Dave and Mary Jo
Dan and Nancy
Jim and Kitty
Laura and Scott
Julie and Tom

The Keeper of Trust story, Book Two of The Carty Sisters Series, grew out of family lore, the author's imagination, and the letters Anne and Julia Carty received from their family in Blackwater, Ireland. The letters are included in the tale just as they were written some one hundred and fifty years ago.

Mary Kay Tuberty

Acknowledgements

I owe supreme gratitude to:

My Carty and Duff cousins, nephews, and nieces, scattered throughout the world, with whom I share these amazing, courageous ancestors.

The folks of Blackwater, Ireland, whose culture and traditions make up such a strong part of our heritage and who have so graciously supported the Carty Family story.

My brothers and sisters: Susan and Jerry Spann, Betty and Tom Pisoni, Tom Duff, Pat and Janet Duff, Ellen and Stan Poniewaz, Mike and Joyce Duff.

My husband, Larry; children; and grandchildren: Jessica, Chris, Alex, Kyle, Nicole, Jack and Gaby.

My Thursday lunch group: Barbara, Debbie, Jeanine and Mary Ann.

Special thanks to:

Jim Hart; Hartline Literary.

Kathy Cretsinger, Diane Turpin, and Monica Mynk; Mantle Rock Publishing.

Praise Be To God!

Chapter One

St. Louis, Missouri;
August 12, 1866

"Good morning, Mrs. McNulty." Julia stood at the long, wooden, bakery counter, behind trays of currant rolls and fresh biscuits sprinkled with cinnamon.

"I have a message for you, Julia. Your sister sailed out of Cork on the same ship as Bridget Rice's brother. She will arrive here on Friday."

"Ma'am?" Julia inched a few steps toward her customer.

Lizzie? Could it be?

"Ah, that magnificent cinnamon smell tempts me." Mrs. McNulty's pale, lined face peeked from layers of cloth wound about her head and shoulders. Only her soft blue eyes, beaming with eagerness in the direction of the sweet rolls, betrayed her youthfulness. She backed toward the wall, to the rows of neatly stacked bread.

Julia placed a hand on Mrs. McNulty's arm. "Shall I wrap a loaf or two for you?"

"Molasses bread. The two end loaves, please, and I'll thank you for it." She lifted the lid of her weathered straw basket and produced two frayed towels.

Julia folded a towel around each loaf and arranged them in the basket. The moist bread, her own favorite, could crumble

7

if not handled with care. "We referred to it as brown bread back home. What county are you from?"

"Galway, the most beautiful place ever." Mrs. McNulty's eyes misted. "Have you visited there?"

Julia chuckled. "I had never even seen Cork, until I sailed from there."

The face of her dear, little sister danced before her eyes, as she tied a ribbon around the basket in a firm knot. Could it be true? After all these months of waiting?

"You mentioned my sister, Mrs. McNulty. Were you referring to Lizzie? I am perplexed, you see, because on two separate occasions, my sisters and I sent passage money home for Lizzie and my brother, Michael." Julia drew her face into a grimace. "When months passed and the children did not come, we were so disappointed. We have written countless letters to our parents, but received no word of explanation. Sure, we had given up all hope."

"'Tis your Lizzie, I do believe. The word is from Bridget Rice. Her brother, Brendan, reports that she is in Boston and will arrive here day after tomorrow." Mrs. McNulty pulled a handkerchief from her sleeve and patted the perspiration from her forehead and chin. "The heat and humidity are oppressive this afternoon, are they not?"

Julia appreciated Mrs. McNulty's discomfort. Walter and Mary Dempsey, the bakery's owners, had painted the entire place—walls, doors, shelves, counter, and floor—a shiny, brilliant white. The small hearth at the side wall and the display window in the front offered the only relief. With the strong rays of the sun pouring in through the window, the heat radiated off the sparkling whiteness all about. Mrs. McNulty, draped in yards of woven cloth, must be sweltering.

"Did Bridget mention anything of my brother, Michael?"

"No, dear, I am afraid Bridget named only Lizzie. I'm sure she will provide the particulars when you deliver goods to the mission this afternoon." The young woman placed two coins in Julia's hand.

"Thank you for bringing the wonderful message, Mrs. McNulty." Julia waved as her customer headed for the door.

She walked back to the counter. "Lizzie. Oh my! Our little Lizzie." Julia jumped into the air, her shoes reaching halfway to the countertop. Her cheeks warmed, as Mrs. McNulty giggled behind her.

"I wished to have a go at Mr. Dempsey's latest innovation." Mrs. McNulty stood before the open door, her arms spread wide. "I don't understand it at all, but I feel a slight breeze."

"I'm not sure my explanation will be correct." Julia pointed toward the square metal contraption installed high in the outside wall at the back of the shop. "The vent draws a flow of air through the room each time the door opens."

Mrs. McNulty took another moment, indulging herself in the breeze that on this summer day could only be warm air. At last, she stepped out the door. "Good day, Julia."

"I thank you kindly for coming." Julia held the door open as Mrs. McNulty descended the steps. "God go with you."

Mrs. McNulty disappeared into the crowd, along the busy city thoroughfare.

"Our Lizzie is coming! She will be here on Friday." Repeating the words in a strong voice brought Julia a measure of satisfaction. When a man walking along in the road slowed his steps and inclined his head in her direction, she quieted.

She closed the door softly and glided the few steps to the bakery counter. How long had it been since she left Ireland. Lizzie had been a mere ten when she departed for America, some six years ago. Would she even recognize the little girl who'd be near to a grown woman now? Had her long, curls remained blond or changed to her sisters' varied shades of brown? Did her once chubby cheeks now show the signs of hunger she had just seen in Mrs. McNulty?

"Time to close up, is it not?" Mary Dempsey, Walter's sister and her employer, burst through the archway that led to the back of the bakery building carrying several wicker baskets. Short and sturdily built, Mary moved without a wasted step. And yet, behind her energy, ready grin and kindly words lurked the mind of an excellent businesswoman.

With her blue dress guarded from soiling by an ample white apron, Mary presented an impeccable appearance. The perspiration-dampened curls peeking from beneath her cap offered the only evidence of hours spent at work in a stifling baking room.

"I've received wonderful news, Mary! My sister Lizzie is coming. She will be in St. Louis day after tomorrow." Julia reached out for the baskets. "Is it not thrilling?"

She placed the baskets on the floor and pushed them against the wall. Taking Mary's hand in hers and guiding her other hand to her own waist, Julia drew the shop owner along for a few awkward shuffles.

Mary gasped, but once they left the wide archway area, she relaxed into the dance. They made a slow circle around the shop, gathering their skirts close to avoid catching onto the fireplace grate or any shelves in their path.

Julia sang *Sally's Courtin'*, an old, old tune—her dear grandmother's favorite. Mary hummed along, as they whirled about, gaining speed. They drifted by the shop window and glided along in front of the bins of fresh bread at the back wall.

Passing the front door for the third time, Julia's energy spent and Mary's breathing unsteady, they drew to a halt. Though her feet stilled, Julia twisted about and waved her arms from side to side. "I find it difficult to take in. Our Lizzie is coming. A true gift from God, it is."

"I have heard so much talk of Lizzie in these past years...I consider...she is my own sister." Mary's breaths remained uneven, but her warm brown eyes twinkled. "How wonderful... it will be...to welcome her here."

"Aye, what's all the commotion? Has Bossy sprung loose and rung her cowbell through the shop?" Walter Dempsey filled the archway that led to the back of the bakery building. He pulled off his white baker's hat. Even without it, the broad-shouldered man loomed over them, a full head of curly brown hair topping his wide, smiling face.

Julia searched Walter's eyes until she detected a glint of humor there. "'Tis not the neighbor's cow, Walter. It is my little sister Lizzie. She will be here on Friday."

She glanced over at Mary. A mistake. They both dissolved in giggles.

"Sorry, Walter." Mary inhaled, and then blew out a long breath. "Miss Julia and I will compose ourselves."

"I do apologize for the ruckus in the shop." Julia followed Mary' example, drawing in deep breaths, expelling the air slowly. "It is all my doing. I allowed my excitement to gain the better of me."

"Ah now, your sister's coming is grand." Walter placed the tray he'd been holding on the counter. "And sure, a bit of noise is no worry to me."

"Will you make one more allowance for me, then?" Julia cast a questioning eye from Walter to Mary. "I must run back to the dressmaker's shop and tell Kate."

"Tell Kate what?"

Julia's younger sister stood before her, arms extended, fingertips brushing the wood molding at either side of the archway. Kate's simple green dress, created in her dressmaking shop at the back of the building, perfectly fit her small, neat frame. Her dark blue eyes blazed with intensity and wariness.

"Oh, Kate, our Lizzie is coming! Mrs. McNulty just brought us the word. Lizzie is in Boston. She will be here on Friday." Julia rushed toward her sister, arms outstretched.

Kate stiffened as she drew near.

She halted and took a step back. "Is it not grand?"

"Lizzie's coming?" Kate's brilliant eyes dulled, as if a cloud had passed before them. "I cannot believe it. I have worried so over her. Has Michael come out with her?"

"We know only that Bridget Rice's brother Brendan sailed with Lizzie. He did not mention Michael." Julia gripped Kate's shoulder. "Lizzie will be here in two days. Are you not happy, Kate?"

"I'm not sure. I cannot grasp the meaning of it." Kate folded her arms. With her head lowered, she strode toward the front door. Spinning her petite frame around, she returned to them, her heels striking a steady pat, pat along the wooden floor.

The shop bell chimed and Mrs. McNulty re-entered the room. "Excuse me, Julia. Oh hello, Walter, Mary." Her eyes rested on Kate. "I left my parasol behind."

Kate swerved in Mrs. McNulty's direction, her face glowering now.

The young woman crept closer to Julia. "What is it? Has something terrible happened? Sure, and I believed I would interrupt a celebration."

"Nothing is wrong, Mrs. McNulty. We are thrilled about Lizzie coming. Kate and I wonder about our Michael, is all."

Kate resumed her pacing. "Our parents possessed no funds at all last Christmas." She faced Mrs. McNulty. "Twice, we sent them the passage for Michael and Lizzie. I'm thinking they spent our hard-won money to pay the taxes on that dreadful farm. Now Lizzie is coming? Why not Michael? There is no sense to it at all." She moved toward the door, again. "They're up to something. There's the truth of it." She pressed her fists to her waist. "And then, after we all begged our parents not to, they committed Lizzie to that awful Hogan's—"

"Kate, please, Mrs. McNulty doesn't need to hear this." Julia placed herself in front of her sister. From the corner of her eye, she saw Mary withdraw a small cake from the window display and wrap it.

"I will just retrieve my parasol and head on home. I do wish you all well." With a quick bow to Walter and Mary, Mrs. McNulty started for the exit.

As Julia held the door, Mary passed her the package.

How thoughtful of Mary to make such a gesture. And, what was Kate thinking, burdening Mrs. McNulty with their troubles?

Julia placed the cake in Mrs. McNulty's basket beside her earlier purchases. "Here's a nice dessert for your family. Thank you again for bringing us the grand message."

"Thank you, Julia, Mary. My children have not tasted a fine treat such as this in many weeks." The young woman stepped out the door, holding her basket in front of her, as if guarding a valuable prize. Julia could hear her singing, as she moved down the street. If only Kate would be as easily placated.

"Of course, we will learn no answers until Lizzie arrives." Julia took her sister's arm. "Think about Lizzie, Kate. We have waited so long, and in two days, she will sit down to supper with us."

Had Anne happened by the shop, she would know how to calm Kate. If only God had blessed her with the same patience her married sister possessed...well, she must try. She captured Kate's small hands and covered them with her own. The poor dear. While everyone throughout the city suffered from the unrelenting heat, Kate's skin felt icy cold.

Pulling away, Kate stepped toward Walter and Mary. Brother and sister stood at the counter, similar perplexed expressions spread across their faces. They likely wished they'd escaped back to the oven room or out the door with Mrs. McNulty.

Kate's wide sleeve latched onto the tray Walter placed on the countertop, sliding it to the edge. She flinched, as if stung, when the tray clattered to the bakery floor.

13

"Oh my." Julia lunged for the tray. She lifted it and set it back on the counter. Several rolls remained untouched, none the worse for the spill. She and Kate knelt, Mary held her apron wide, and they tossed the spoiled rolls into it.

In one sweep, Walter untied the bow of Mary's apron and folded the cloth, biscuits, and the bit of dust they had collected into a bundle.

Julia ran to the cupboard and pulled out a mop, still damp from her earlier cleaning. She scrubbed the small patch of floor vigorously, and then hid the mop away again. When she rejoined the little group, she stood quietly, eyes cast down.

"Imagine, four Carty sisters here in America together. God is good." Kate leaned forward and rested her head against Julia's shoulder.

Smoothing the strands that escaped from Kate's bun, the darkest brown of all the sisters' hair, Julia whispered to her. "Let us give thanks Lizzie will soon be with us."

"One less child to worry over." Kate pressed her hands together. "'Tis a blessing, indeed. I've no call to be cross." She brushed wrinkles from her skirt. "Now, I must finish my work, so I will be free to visit with Lizzie on Friday."

She lifted her shoulders. "Mary, Walter, forgive me for creating a disturbance right out in your shop. Oh my. I must have frightened poor Mrs. McNulty. I will apologize to her, I promise you. Such a display is disgraceful. It will not happen again."

"Not to worry, Kate." Mary patted her cheek.

Walter winked at her. "No harm done, my dear."

"I do not deserve such understanding, but I thank you for it." Kate's eyes still held a pained expression. Holding her sleeves in check, she rushed through the archway and down the hall toward her seamstress shop at the back of the building.

"That tiny smile is worth an apron of ruined goods." Walter adjusted the bundle under his arm. "I do wish we could help Kate overcome her sadness and anxiety. "She will certainly miss

Keeper of Trust

your good cheer, Julia. Will young Lizzie take on your role and bring comfort to Kate, when you've gone off to marry Corporal Tobin?"

"I've no immediate plans for leaving."

"I detect a tiny grin, my lass." Walter waved his free hand in front of Julia's face. "You cannot pretend with me."

"You know Martin is still attached to the Army. We will make no plans until he is discharged at the end of the month and gains proper employment." Julia batted Walter's hand away.

"Now, Walter, no more teasing," Mary shook her finger at him.

"You are right about Lizzie, though." Julia gazed out the window. If only she could look out across the ocean. The memories, once so strong and sharp, could fade at times. "Even at only five or six, Lizzie was the peacemaker. We all endeavored to please her. She and Kate possessed an uncommon bond. I pray her presence will render Kate more comfort than I have provided."

Julia placed a hand on her hip. "I will instruct her to be high-spirited and perpetually noisy." A little more impudence had slipped in than she intended, and she forced a serious tone into her voice. "Lizzie is a sweet natured girl. You will delight in her company."

"I am sure we will, Julia," Walter said. "We've enjoyed coming to know each of the Carty sisters. And, we are grateful for the fine assistance you have given us."

"The Carty girls are beholden to you and Mary, Walter. Since we arrived in St. Louis, each of us has basked in the warmth of your home and blossomed under your care."

Walter responded with an absent minded wave of his hand, and then faced his sister.

"Well, Mary dear, I wager plans are already underway for a 'Welcome Supper' for Lizzie? Will you soon be deciding on a special dessert I must prepare?" He squeezed her elbow and then followed Kate's path, heading through the archway toward the rear of the building.

"Aw, go on with you." Mary took up a ladle resting on the counter and shook it at him. "I've not even given it a thought."

Chuckling as he moved along the hallway, Walter called back over his shoulder. "I am happy for you, Julia. I look forward to meeting your Lizzie."

Julia wrapped an arm around Mary. "I should not have whirled you about the shop in the worst heat of the day." She led her to the chair resting against the back wall, just beneath Walter's infamous air vent. Adjusting Mary's cap, which had slipped to the side of her head, she tucked back the escaping curls.

"I am capable of a grand spin around my shop and a good laugh, girleen." Mary gave Julia a gentle push and rose from the chair. "And now, back to things of importance. Our little sister will arrive day after tomorrow. We will not admit a thing to Walter, but a menu must be drawn up for her special supper." Mary picked up a tablet from the desk at the back wall "The roast beef stored in the cellar will not be large enough to serve our group. Do you remember Lizzie's favorite dishes? Let's decide, and I'll make up a list for the market."

"Our family back home has tasted few fine meals these past years, Mary. Lizzie will take pleasure in whatever dishes you choose." Julia retrieved the smaller of the two baskets she had shoved aside to make room for their waltz. She approached the table displaying day-old rolls, goods sold at half-price, and transferred what remained there into the small basket. "These biscuits will certainly provide a fine addition to the evening meal at the mission."

"The news of Lizzie's coming troubled Kate, but she was pleased, was she not?" Mary lifted a sturdy, wooden container from the drawer behind the counter and emptied the money inside into two small canvas sacks, separating coins from the few bills. Her lips moved slightly as she worked.

Julia nodded, as she collected the emptied trays and placed them on a table in the hallway.

"Perhaps her poor troubled mind will be relieved of some of its bitterness…" Mary lowered her head. "Oh, dear…," her eyes met Julia's. "I should not have said such a thing. I am sorry."

"It is no more than I've been thinking. And you and Walter are family. We welcome your guidance. I, too, pray Lizzie's coming will ease the turmoil that has taken hold of Kate's mind." Julia placed the larger basket on the counter. As she filled it with the long loaves of bread, the wonderful doughy, yeasty scent made her stomach rumble. Had she eaten since breakfast?

"Kate has not been the same since our parents sent her to work in that Hogan's Emporium back home. Her tales of the mistreatment she suffered there are appalling. And, she worries so about the young ones still in Ireland. Since Jimmy died, and then our little sister Maura, we have all been troubled."

"You know, I love Kate. I am concerned for her, is all." Mary secured the openings of her cash bags with a heavy twine. "She strives to obtain enough sewing work to keep her helper Ellen occupied. I applaud her efforts. I do not want Ellen to be forced to work in that wretched garment factory again, but perhaps, Kate takes on too much. She is a generous, caring girl, that's sure."

"It is growing late, Mary. It is my doing, of course, with the waltzing about the shop and all. With your permission, though, I would like to take the news to Anne."

"Of course, you must tell Anne. You should leave now. She will be thrilled to hear of your Lizzie's coming, will she not?" Mary fixed Julia with a steady appraisal. "Now, why is a look of worry growing across your eyes? Surely, Anne's reaction will not be a cause for concern?"

"No, not at all. Lizzie's coming moves us one step closer to our goal of reuniting our entire family in St. Louis. And it is Anne who has been here the longest, working and saving for passage money. Anne will be thrilled."

"And Martin?" Mary placed her strongbox in the drawer and stuffed the money sacks in her deep apron pockets. "Are your thoughts on Martin and your wedding plans?"

"Martin's discharge is imminent." A rush of warmth crept across Julia's face for the second time that afternoon. "His strong sense of honor, rather than anything to do with Lizzie, is my concern. He insists it is his duty to obtain a respectable position before we can talk of marriage. With hundreds of able men pouring into the city each week, all vying for work, it is a difficult time to be searching for employment. I cannot imagine how long his quest will take."

"Jobs are hard to come by, it is sure," Mary said. "Still, the experience Martin gained, purchasing Army supplies during the war years, should hold him in good stead. And, one less sister to bring to America should prove of some help."

"I will soon have the opportunity to discuss these matters with Martin. You do remember he is coming for supper tonight, Mary? He is invited still, is he not?"

"Of course, he is. We will hold good thoughts until then." Mary held the larger basket steady while Julia secured the latch.

"I do thank you for delivering these goods to the mission. You work mornings at the church office and afternoons here in the shop, and now, here I am sending you out in this dreadful heat again."

"You and Walter are so good to me, I intend to help in any way I can."

Julia took up the bulky baskets then paused. "And now, here's another Carty girl on her way to St. Louis," she called out to Mary. "Perhaps your sisterly pursuit of a wife for Walter will have one more chance at success?"

Mary lifted the hem of the fresh apron she had only moments before tied at her waist. Flinging the cloth at Julia's heels, she shooed her along the way with the swats. "Get by with you."

Julia held the baskets in front of her, feigning a need for protection. Mary's giggles betrayed her attempt at a stern expression.

"I will hurry right back, Mary." Julia left Dempsey's and crossed the street.

She could already picture Anne's happy smile. There would be no worries with her visit to her sister's home. And, thanks to the Dempseys' generosity, she and her baked goods would be welcomed warmly at the mission.

But the walk back to the bakery…her arms stiffened. Martin almost always met her along the way home, when invited for supper. Would it be a happy walk, this evening? As she climbed Anne's back steps, a tingling in her feet rose steadily toward her knees. Had Martin been successful in securing a position? Would he, at last, deem himself worthy to discuss their marriage?

Chapter Two

Julia tugged at the cumbersome basement door of St. Vincent's Church until it swung free, and stepped into the still scorching sunshine of the August evening,

She raised her arm to block the glare from the sun. Martin waited at the top of the stairwell. As she climbed the deep, uneven stone steps, he rushed forward, arms outstretched.

"Good evening, my dear. How are you faring?" Martin slipped the empty baskets from her arm. Her breath caught when their fingers brushed. Did he feel the same shiver at the touch of her skin? Alas, his face, serious and thoughtful, held no indication of a strong emotional surge.

She peered up to him, standing erect two steps above her. Had he grown taller than his five feet, nine inches? His uniform, fitted smartly to his slim frame, remained crisp in spite of the unrelenting heat. With the baskets slung over his left arm, he extended his right one at a precise angle, as though ready to salute her.

"I apologize for keeping you waiting, Martin. It has proved an eventful day, and I bear such wonderful news." If only, he would greet her with a hug or kiss. A tiny touch of her cheek or a pat on the arm would suffice. Why did it matter so? He had never been demonstrative. He did love her, she knew. His steel blue eyes bore his devotion deep into her soul, softening her foolish misgivings. A surge of warmth rushed through her.

Martin guided her into the quiet thoroughfare, a far cry from the clopping of horses and rumble of wagons of her earlier walk. With many of the city's residents already home from their workdays, only a few people hurried along, keeping to the side of the road. An occasional carriage rolled by, but no delivery trucks or wagons. She drew in a fresh, easy breath. How fortunate they were this evening. They would be allowed a few moments of private conversation before they reached Dempsey's.

"I have something to report myself." Martin linked his arm with hers, as they ascended the steepest section of the hill. "But, you must proceed. I can see by the glow in your eyes your tale will not wait. I worry you will burst into pieces, if you do not reveal what has excited you so."

"My sister Lizzie has reached Boston. Bridget Rice's brother arrived today, and he reported Lizzie sailed with him. She will arrive in St. Louis the day after tomorrow." She grinned up at Martin.

Though this earth shattering news did not elicit a hug, he did smile warmly at her. Surely, deep in his heart, he was pleased. "It is a grand development, indeed. I know you and your sisters are overjoyed. I am happy for you."

"Oh, I am thrilled." She twirled away for a moment, but moved right back to Martin.

He removed his hat, allowing his abundant, wavy brown hair to tumble free. One swipe of her hand and she could capture a strand of that thick, dark mass and judge the softness of it for herself. Foolish girl. She held her hands behind her back. Hopefully, he had not become aware of her designs on his hair.

"I am puzzled." Martin inclined his head toward her. "I understood all along Michael would come out next."

"We are all in a quandary over Lizzie's coming with no word of Michael. Anne and I plan to visit Bridget's brother tomorrow. He may have more information. Otherwise, we will be forced to wait until two days pass and Lizzie arrives to explain it all."

Her fingers ached to touch the hand now resting on her arm. Would Martin think her too forward? Moments slipped away. Julia looked up, startled. They had already attained the steeper portion of the hill. Only two short blocks remained until they reached the summit, turned the corner, and crossed the street to the looming bakery building. She inched closer to him.

He led her along a short stretch of road, less than a block long. Tall buildings on both sides soared high above them, blocking the sunlight. How she loved this small patch. Here, they could linger for a few brief moments and exchange private words.

She touched his arm to slow their steps. "And you? What have you to tell?"

"Perhaps, we should save my news for later. Before we reach Dempsey's, I must say something even more important." In the dim shadow of the tall buildings, he wrapped his arm around her shoulder and drew her to him.

The streets all but deserted, they stood alone. Silence descended all around them. Could Martin hear the bump and pound of her heart? Her eyes sought his, finding tenderness. Linked together, their hearts in unison, their thoughts bound together, could she ever pull away?

"With your soft blue eyes shining in anticipation of your sister's coming, and your entire being trembling from the joy of it, you are the most beautiful girl I have ever seen."

Julia gasped. In the years she had known him, Martin had never said such a bold, beautiful thing. She must continue to breathe.

"I love you. You know that, do you not?" Martin brushed her cheek with his fingertips, the touch of his hand exquisite in its gentleness.

The distinct fragrance of rose petals drifted to Julia, though none remained this late in the summer. She placed her hand across her heart, pounding out a symphony chorus now.

"Yes, I know it." And here, she had complained about his lack of affection.

"Do you love me?"

"I..."

Even with their slowed steps, they had moved out of the shady area and toward sunlight. Several people walked past the bakery just ahead.

Martin edged away from her.

Here, in the most wonderful, breathtaking moment of her life, a momentous question had been placed before her. She grasped Martin's arm firmly. She must halt his steps. Seconds passed. At last, the people moved on, and they were alone once again. She rose up on her toes and whispered in his ear.

"I love you with all my heart."

Though Martin's sober, serious countenance had returned, a hint of his brilliant smile remained. She giggled.

Inside the building, Martin held her arm, and with shoulders touching, they made their way through the shadows of the darkening shop. He bent his head close to her. "I will not be able to stay and walk out with you after dinner. I have only two hours until I must return to the post." His voice dropped to a whisper. "With any luck, I will secure the entire evening free tomorrow. You and I will set out for a long excursion. We have many things to discuss." Martin moved away and the delightful moment of closeness ended.

They advanced toward the bright rays streaming through the archway from the dining room. Julia blinked. Was the room more enchanting than ever tonight? The rich cream walls, the gleaming chestnut hardwood floors, and soft, gold-flecked draperies, created by Kate and her assistant Ellen, had surely jumped from the pages of a fairy tale. Wall-mounted gas lamps glimmered and candles flickered on the ivory cloth covering the long dinner table. Did the place hold an extraordinary glow, extending a special greeting for Martin and her? Or, were her thoughts encased in a fluffy cloud, incapable of sound thought or observation.

The Dempsey folks, a varied yet impressive group, moved into the room from all entrances. She lowered her head. It would not do for everyone in the room to guess her state of love.

"Good, evening," Mary bustled in from the kitchen and placed a bowl of steaming potatoes on the table. "Come, sit beside Walter, Martin. Julia, take the place right beside him."

"Hello, Walter." Martin greeted his host and extended his hand across the table to Eddie and George, the bakery helpers.

"Sure, it is grand to have you with us," Walter said. "You'll have an opportunity to talk with Eddie and George about their boarding house. With your days of army living almost at an end, you are likely seeking a place to live."

"It is a comfortable place," Eddie nodded. "If you are interested, I will speak to the landlady for you."

"I would appreciate it." Martin's smiled toward Eddie, then Walter. "The house where my brother Patrick stays is unsanitary. It would be grand if we could find a place together."

"Sorry to be late everyone." Red-haired, blue-eyed Ellen, Kate's helper and a long time boarder at Dempsey's, entered the room from the back hallway. "Hello, Martin. It's good to have you here." She patted Martin's shoulder and then walked around the table and sat across from Julia. "Our last customer just left the shop." She turned to Kate, who came in right behind her. "I would say she left happy with our work, don't you agree?"

"It was your fine work, Ellen." Kate slid into a chair beside Julia.

Julia squeezed her sister's arm. What a relief to see her smile.

Grace, another Dempsey boarder, rushed out from the kitchen with an enormous platter of chicken. She appeared pale

Keeper of Trust

and thin, her hair mussed and her expression dour as always. But, something was different this evening.

Julia dragged her attention away from the scent of apricots and chicken wafting her way from the platter before her. Grace moved about the room with a new confidence, a startling change, indeed.

Cara, who kept the place clean, walked in behind Grace with a steaming bowl of vegetables. Mary followed them into the room, bearing a large basket of bread.

The girls arranged the dishes on the table, clinking and scraping them against one another as they were moved and shifted. Julia pushed her shoes together hard, to keep them still. She stole a glance at Martin. Was there a hint of a smile on his face?

Julia bowed her head, as silence descended over the room and Walter offered the thanksgiving prayer. She followed along, pouring her heartfelt gratitude into her words. At the "Amens" around the table, she squeezed her hands in her lap. *Thank you for Lizzie's safe crossing, dear God. Please protect her along the rest of the way.*

Walter passed the platter of chicken to Martin. "Tell us about your job search. Are positions as scarce as reported in the newspapers?"

"I've approached the new water treatment plant, and I spoke to a fellow at the Omnibus Company—"

"James Duff mentioned new openings at the railroad." Eddie's hands maneuvered a hefty bowl of corn and a serving spoon. "It is possible those posts would require moving out west."

"Will you pass the butter along, Julia?" Ellen spoke out from her place across the table. "I did not mean to interrupt the men's conversation," she giggled, "but I see the tablecloth rippling around Julia. I'm thinking she is bouncing with impatience to tell us about her sister. That is, of course, if her attention can be drawn away from our Mr. Tobin and his job prospects."

Laughter erupted around the table, when Martin's face turned red.

"Yes, Julia," Mary said, "did you have an opportunity to speak with Bridget? Did she provide new details?"

"Bridget was waiting for me at the mission. She confirmed—"

"I am sure Anne will wish Lizzie to stay with her," A look of worry had settled over Kate face.

Julia placed her water glass on the table. "It is all right, Kate. You raised a question I have been avoiding, a worry I pushed to the back of my mind all afternoon." The subject could not be pushed aside forever. "Anne did not mention a word of it, when I took her the news about Lizzie. She has been planning all along that Lizzie would live with her." Casting her gaze down the long table to Mary, Julia swallowed.

"Would it not be grand to have Lizzie work as your shop girl and live with us in the attic room? If that would be agreeable to you, of course, Mary?" Julia clenched her hand into a fist and pushed down hard into her knee. Had she been too forward? Hopefully not. "Lizzie is a wonderful girl. She would be a great help to you here."

"It would be splendid to have Lizzie's help." Mary nodded vigorously. "The place has not been the same since Anne left us to become Mrs. James Duff. You girls have all attempted to assume a portion of her duties, but I know it places a hardship on you. We need a permanent shop girl. Of course, if Lizzie works in the shop, she must live here at Dempsey's."

Walter slapped his hand on the table. "You've been working yourself to the bone, Mary. This is the finest idea yet. And, Anne is a sensible girl. She will not object to the arrangement."

"I'm not so sure, Walter." Julia picked up her fork, and then rested it back on the table. "Since James bought their house, she has been planning the children would come there."

Keeper of Trust

"Why don't we talk this over with Anne?" Mary asked. "Perhaps we could all go tomorrow. Our Anne is the dearest girl in the entire world. We will work it out."

"Well then, I'll leave that question for tomorrow and tell you what I remember of the young girl who will arrive in our midst in two days." Julia tilted her head, thinking back.

"How long has it been?" Martin asked. "Was Lizzie a baby when you left Ireland? A young girl?"

"Six years have passed since I left Lizzie behind in Blackwater. In my own memory, I see a girl of nine or ten." She stopped.

"You are the better one to tell us about her, Kate. It has been only a little more than a year for you."

"I hold naught but fond memories of Lizzie." Kate held a spoon upright. "Were you still home with us when she picked wild flowers all over town and placed a few in each church pew?" She pressed the handle of the spoon into the white tablecloth, drawing imaginary lines, again and again. "Lizzie will be sixteen next month. She is a wonderful happy girl, a little like Julia, but calmer, with a gentler humor." She sent Julia a sheepish grin.

Everyone around the table looked toward Julia, their expressions guarded, but Kate had no need to worry. A bit of teasing would not disturb her tonight. She smiled at her sister and waved away their concerns. Walter and Martin broke into hearty laughter, and the merriment traveled around the table.

"Tell us more about Lizzie." Ellen leaned toward Julia. "Does she resemble Kate and Anne, petite and dark haired?" She turned to Kate. "Or, is she more a match for our lithe, downy haired Julia?"

"Lizzie is near to Julia in height." Kate propped her thumb beneath her chin. "Though no one in Ireland could secure enough food to grow stout, Lizzie is a big girl with a larger frame than the three of us."

Julia brushed her fingers along the tablecloth. The lines of worry around her sister's eyes and mouth softened as she spoke. The spoon had fallen away from her hand and rested atop the ridged, creased tablecloth beside her now relaxed hand. Did she dare to hope her sister was letting go of her apprehension over Lizzie's coming?

"I remember once Mother attempted to teach her to sew." Kate giggled. "It proved an impossible task. The project cast the entire cottage into disarray. Pins, needles, and scissors strewn all about. Precious scraps of cloth ruined, some slipped surreptitiously into Lizzie's apron pocket." She broke off a tiny piece of a roll, and they waited while she chewed.

"The young ones managed to escape out the back door ahead of the looming explosion of wrath. And yet, the lesson ended in laughter." A frown crossed Kate's face. "Can you imagine laughter from our serious, sober mother, Julia?"

"I remember my own tedious sewing lessons." Julia groaned. "Like Lizzie, my sewing ability was limited. Kate held all the talent."

"Lizzie will not work in your dress shop then, Kate?" Grace patted her lips with a white linen napkin.

"Perhaps not." Kate took up the pitcher. Beginning with Mary, she moved around the table, adding water to each glass. "Though Lizzie never became a seamstress, she did enjoy the housework and even the farm chores. In the last few years I lived at home, she became an excellent cook. Our mother never did any cooking, you see. She directed from her chair. But under her supervision, Lizzie mastered the task. She will love the bakery."

"I look forward to sampling her fine cooking." Walter waved his empty plate in the air.

"Our Michael wrote of how Lizzie wished to come here," Kate said.

Julia bumped her water glass against her plate. Kate twisted from one story to another. What would come next?

"I doubt she longed for the journey. I feel sure the desire was his more than Lizzie's. Perhaps, he convinced her she wanted to come. Michael is single-minded about America, you know, and he can be persuasive. I only wonder why she has come alone. We all thought Lizzie and Michael would travel together." Kate stopped, and for a moment, silence fell over the room.

"Are you certain Michael is not coming?" Martin addressed Kate. "People are jammed together on those ships. It may be that Bridget's brother never encountered him."

"We'll soon know." Julia said.

"Well then," Mary rose, "our Cara has prepared a wonderful treat for us. I'll fetch it."

"You sit, Mary." Cara jumped from the table and headed for the kitchen.

"Ah, Cara." Julia hurried after her. "Is it your orange sponge cake…?"

In moments they were back at the table. "Place your magnificent creation here on the side board, Cara. You cut it." Julia placed a slice on each dessert plate Kate handed her and passed them around. "I cannot wait for a taste. You are a wonder at these cakes, Cara."

"Aw, 'tis nothing…a recipe my mam handed on to me."

"I will be stopping at the post office first thing tomorrow," Walter accepted the first slice of cake from Julia, "if anyone has a letter to mail."

"I would appreciate your mailing a letter for me." Martin walked to the coat rack in the corner and searched his pockets. "I wrote to my Uncle Joseph in New York to tell him of my discharge."

"Coffee, Julia?" Grace stood behind her with the coffee pot.

"No thank you, Grace."

"Will Martin take coffee?" Grace pointed to his cup.

"No, he does not drink coffee."

"Of course, Julia would know." Ellen sang the words, quietly, a smirk across her face.

Martin returned to his place. "Why are you blushing, Julia. What have I missed?"

"It is only our Ellen being silly, Martin." Julia wrinkled her nose at Ellen. "Don't worry, her turn will come. We've all been saving our most potent taunts, as her just reward."

"Ah, I've no hope at all." Ellen drew her arm across her face in a dramatic gesture.

Martin blinked at Julia, and when she only shrugged, he turned to Walter, questioning with his eyes.

"I live here, Martin, and I will never understand them." Walter scraped the last crumb from his plate. "Do not even attempt it."

"You can be proud, Cara," Julia spoke above the laughter around the table. "Your cake was magnificent. I believe every morsel has disappeared." She jumped up from her chair and began to clear the dishes away.

"You always take the lead in insisting I retire to my room to rest." Mary took the plates from Julia's hands, as they reached the kitchen. "Sure, Martin says he must return to his base right away. Show him out and spend what little time he has left with him."

Kate nearly pushed her through the kitchen doorway and out to the dining room. "You two will have much to talk of tonight." With a broad wink, Kate pulled the sliding door shut behind her.

Julia raised her arms. While she worried about her, Kate could in a moment such as this, revert to the caring, generous girl she once knew.

"Goodnight, Walter. Please give Mary my compliments for the grand meal." As Julia moved into the room, Martin stood at the table, holding his cap in his hand.

He must have heard their conversation. He took her arm and they pressed on through the shop and out the front door.

"I must say goodnight and hurry off." Martin stood with her on the bakery steps. "If I secure time away tomorrow evening, I will come and fetch you. We will take a long walk and continue our discussion."

"That will be grand," Julia said. "I will be waiting."

"Good night, my dear." He trailed his hand along her cheek, and then moved away.

"Good night Martin." As she touched her fingertips to her face, he turned back to wave. Then he disappeared from sight.

"I assumed Anne would be as shocked as you and I, when I told her about Lizzie." Julia perched on her bed in the attic room, later that evening. "She said she felt all along someone would come."

"I do not believe it." Kate sat on her own bed, brushing her hair and smiling. "Anne must have spent too long in the sun today. We had all given up hope, and that's the truth."

Julia gathered her courage. "During my visit today, Anne offered me a parcel of letters she received from home over the years."

Kate's warm expression turned grim.

"I realize reading the letters from home upsets you, but bear with me. I have a purpose here. I'm looking forward to Lizzie's arrival, but I do not feel I know her as you do. I try to picture her as a girl of sixteen, but it is impossible. I thought I would find small bits in the letters that mentioned her." Julia took up a letter. "Listen to this one, written just after Anne arrived in St. Louis." Kate closed her eyes, but since she did not complain, Julia pushed on.

> *Your sister Lizzie often asks Mother will Anne ever come home to her again. Her interrogations cause your mother and I to shed a tear. Kate is living with your Uncle Martin. She was going to school for the last twelve*

> months, but is now obliged to stay at home in consequence of an increase in their family. She says if Julia goes to you in the spring, she must go also.

"Here is another mention of Lizzie, written just a few months later," Julia said.

> My dear child, as to Lizzie, she is not the size of Kate. Small as she is, she threatens to go to you for a new coat.

"The letters make only the barest mention of Lizzie." Kate's words were barely audible.

"Yes, you are right. I thought I would discover more about Lizzie." Julia rose from the bed. "Well, here's another mention of her."

> My two dear children, if it is in your power to send anything, it never was so wanted, but we would not like you to pay a pound to send a pound. Lizzie asks you to send her the price of a new dress.

"Here they are asking you for money again." Kate pounded her fist into the mattress.

Why had she not skipped that part of the letter? Taking a few deep breaths, Julia moved on.

> Dear Sisters, after Kate is with you, I expect to be soon with you, with the help of God. Lizzie says you never speak one word about her.
> I remain your affectionate brother, write soon. M. Carty

Kate's face broke into a grin. "That Michael, always Lizzie's protector. Actually, he was guardian to us all. I do miss him."

"Here's my favorite." Julia positioned the sheet below the flame of the candle. "It is brief, but it was written in Lizzie's own hand."

> *Enclosed I send you this note that you may see by it how I am improving at school. I hope to see you in America yet, and when I go there I will be able to write a proper letter home to my Mother. Maura and I are lonesome after poor Jimmy. Maura and I send our love to you,*
> *Lizzie Carty*

"Ah, it was written while our Maura still lived. Our precious little Maura." Kate sighed.

Julia tapped Kate's knee with her finger. "Here is the last letter I could find that mentions both Michael and Lizzie. It must have been written last fall, when they were planning to come together."

"I've had far and away enough fine words from Blackwater." In an instant, Kate's wistful expression turned bleak. "I never wish to hear from any of them again." She threw herself face down on her bed.

"You cannot mean it. Please, just listen to one paragraph of this letter. Julia shifted closer to the candle, and read aloud.

> *Dear Anne, if the passage was entered before Christmas it would save a great deal. I am sure there will be many going in March for there is no one in this country has half a crop of anything they sowed. It is a happy news for Michael and Lizzie to be leaving this unfortunate country and all I can do is to pray for you all for your kindness to them and I hope when they are there they will not forget you a day, or a year.*

"I give you my word, if you do not stop reading those foolish, senseless messages from home…" Kate rolled on her back and held a pillow down over her face.

Julia reached out and pulled the pillow away from Kate.

"I will not take another breath until you stop." Kate pressed her lips together.

Julia raised her sister's shoulders and placed the pillow beneath her head. Chills washed over her. Such an anguished, desperate tone. She folded the fragile letters. She and Anne had read them so often, sitting together here in the attic room, longing for everyone at home. Each word from their dear ones soothed her. If only, they would bring the same comfort to Kate.

"There now, the letters have been hidden away." Julia pushed the box under her bed. "Please calm yourself. We do not wish Lizzie to arrive only to learn you have stopped breathing."

The beginning of a smile crossed Kate's face.

"I will have many opportunities to come to know Lizzie again."

"Yes, I suppose you will." Kate's voice held a touch of weariness.

Julia blew out the candle and rested her head on her pillow. "Goodnight, Kate." What an ominous end to an otherwise magnificent day.

Chapter Three

Julia sat at the small, battered oak desk shoved in a corner of the St. Vincent's Parish office. She pushed stray curls into her cap without a pause in her work, becoming distracted only when Kathleen the housekeeper peeked in the doorway.

"Father Burns sent me to let you in, Julia." Kathleen slipped into the room, dangling a gold key from a chain. "Since you are already in, I suppose you remembered your key. Father said you would forget."

"Thank you the same, Kathleen, but Mary reminded me. I came in early today, because I plan to leave as soon as this work is finished." Julia spread her arm over the stacks of paper strewn across her desk. "With the priests away this morning, I have worked without interruption. When will they return?"

"Late afternoon. They are attending a meeting of St. Louis clergy. Father Burns said to 'lock the door when you leave.'" Kathleen whirled around and disappeared from the room, the hem of her long grey dress trailing behind her.

"Thank you, Kathleen." Julia called out to the retreating footsteps. She bent her head again to her work.

Julia wrote several letters for the pastor. She placed two generous contributions from the morning mail into an envelope, locking them away until Father Burns could deposit them at the bank. After writing checks for the mission, she arranged the invoices, vouchers, and envelopes in a stack for Father Ryan to review the next day. After an hour, she released a slow breath. Now, a quick dusting and she'd be on her way.

She took up the long-handled feather duster, and gave a hurried swipe to Father's desk and her own, and attacked the tall, narrow windows and the bookcase. Good enough for now, though the windows could use a good scrub. Perhaps tomorrow. Today, a visit with Anne took precedence. Shutting the office door, she locked it behind her. She dropped the key into the small, blue satchel Kate made for her.

As Julia hurried toward the stairway that led to the outside door, a young, frail-looking girl made her way up the steps. Did she need help reaching the top?

Julia held out her hand. "May I help you?"

The stranger shook her head and avoided Julia's arm. "Will Father Burns see me?" The girl's voice quivered.

"Oh, my dear, I am so sorry." Julia stepped back. She is so young, likely the age of Lizzie. And also as her sister appeared, her clothing was disheveled and frayed from her harsh journey. "Father is away from the building this morning. May I help you?"

"No. I must see the Father." She leaned against the stairway, dangerously near the edge.

"I'm sure he will speak with you as soon as he returns, but that may not be for several hours." She must somehow prevent her visitor from collapsing right in the hallway. They were a good distance from anyone who would hear her call for help. "May I take you downstairs to the mission for lunch while you wait?"

The girl lowered her head. Her thin, ragged shawl slipped away, revealing brown, stringy hair and a worn, patched dress. "I am a tad hungry, and that's the truth of it."

"Come with me. I'm Julia Carty. What is your name?"

Oh please God, let her remain upright, until we reach the kitchen.

"Ceil. Ceil Brown."

"Are you new in the city?" Julia placed a hesitant hand under the girl's arm.

"My own sister is in Boston, waiting to come." Reversing their direction, Julia guided Ceil along the narrow hallway that led to the mission. Lizzie could be in the same situation as this poor young girl, hungry, likely out of money, alone. How lucky she was to have her sisters awaiting her in St. Louis. How fortunate they all had been to receive help from Walter and Mary Dempsey when they arrived in the city.

"I came yesterday morning." Ceil allowed Julia to grasp her arm firmly now. "My mam said to 'go see the Father'. I prayed the priest could help me find work."

"It is not far." They descended a steep stairway. "How long has it been since you've had a meal?"

"Two days." Ceil swayed a little. "I purchased something on the train, but my money ran out, you see."

"Well, you've come to the right place." Julia rejoiced to see a light shining though the doorway ahead. A few more steps and we will be in the kitchen. "My friend, Bridget Rice, is in charge here at the mission while Father Ryan is away. She will care for you, until he returns."

As they entered the cheerful room, Bridget moved about, pouring coffee. The smiling blonde stopped to engage in conversation with a sturdy young man with thick red hair that jumped out at all angles. The differences in the two seemed striking, until Julia moved closer. Their similarities—warm smile, curly hair, and blue eyes that sparkled as if with a secret—captured Julia's attention. This young man must be Bridget's brother.

Bridget waved to them. "Julia, we were just speaking of you. Come, meet Brendan. He has a message from your sister."

"This is Ceil Brown." Julia stepped closer to Bridget, leading Ceil along with her. "She is hoping Father Burns will help her obtain work. I've assured her you will care for her while she waits." Julia placed herself between Ceil and Bridget. "She is hungry," she whispered.

"Of course, you must have a meal, at once." Bridget took Ceil's arm. "A plate of warm food will revive your strength, my dear, and the priests will help you, when they return." Patting her shoulder, she led Ceil off toward the kitchen.

Julia turned her attention to Brendan. "Welcome to St. Louis. Are you recovering from the harsh journey?"

A wide grin spread across Brendan's face, and his bright blue eyes shone. "Ah, I am grand. A bit of rest and my dear mother's cooking have restored me already.

"I know it is your sister you'll want to hear about." He held out a chair for Julia. "I believe the word is all good. Lizzie appeared well, when I spoke with her back in Boston. Sure, she's weary, God bless her. We were all exhausted."

"Did you and Lizzie even know one another?" Julia asked.

"I had not made her acquaintance before our voyage." Brendan's curly hair bounced as he spoke. "One of her traveling mates is sister to a classmate of mine. Imagine our surprise, when in the course of our conversation, Lizzie and I discovered we had grown up on the same small lane in Blackwater." He paused a moment and made a long, study of Julia's face. "With my being away at school for many years, I do not believe we have ever met."

"I do not think we have." Julia advanced a step. "I am happy to make your acquaintance now, as my sisters will be."

"Bridget mentioned the Carty sisters and the Dempseys in many of her letters. Sure, I look forward to coming to know all the folks from home who've settled here." Brendan placed a hand across his heart. "Nothing for it, but the longing for Ireland is so sharp."

"When you come to know more of the people here, you will see we're all a bit lonesome for our homeland." Julia touched his arm. "The pain of it eases with time, but it does not disappear. We will, none of us, ever forget."

Julia's body trembled. "Did Lizzie travel alone, Brendan? Was my brother Michael with her? Did you speak with him at all?"

"I am sorry to disappoint you." Brendan's eyes reflected understanding. "Lizzie was in the company of other young girls. We had but a few minutes to talk. Though we came on the same ship, people were packed in, with men and women restricted to separate areas. I did not encounter her until we waited in line to enter the terminal at Boston.

"Lizzie made no mention of Michael. I assumed she came alone." Brendan grasped her hand, which still rested on his arm.

"She asked me to tell you she could not wait to be reunited with her big sisters." He stood and covered his mass of red hair with his cap. "I wish I could provide you with more information."

Brendan's easy manner and the familiar tone of his voice stirred memories of Julia's father and brother. That quality would soon fade, as it had for Martin, Walter, and the young men who resided in St. Louis for a time. The longing for the grand old place and the dear ones left behind never would diminish.

"I appreciate what you have told me." Julia walked to the exit with him. "I will share every word of it with my sisters. We are so happy Lizzie has come. It will be necessary to wait until tomorrow for the rest of the story.

"And, it is grand to hear you will remain in St. Louis, Brendan. Mary Dempsey asked me to invite you to join us for supper one evening soon. We look forward to having you." Julia waved as Brendan disappeared along the busy street.

Julia moved to the kitchen, finding Ceil seated at a table, surrounded by mission workers.

"Eat everything." Mrs. Brown placed a heaping spoonful of beans on Ceil's plate, while the girl chewed slowly.

"Father Burns will find work for you." Mrs. Kerry bobbed her head.

"I see you are being well cared for, Ceil." Julia tied the ribbon of her bonnet. "I'll likely see you again tomorrow. Good luck with your search for a position."

"Thank you for your help, Julia." Ceil grinned. "This wonderful meal has restored me. I am near recovered."

"Sure, you look and sound stronger, already."

"Not to worry, Julia," Mrs. Brown said. "We will see to our girl here."

Julia called farewell to Ceil and the kitchen workers and moved toward the door. On her way at last.

❦ ❦ ❦

The minute she stepped into the shop, Mary waved her over. "Julia, I'm happy you are back." Mary took coins from one customer and slipped them in her pocket. Without a hesitation, she filled another's basket. Several other women milled about, waiting.

Julia washed her hands, and moved behind the counter while drying them with a towel. For an hour, she and Mary wrapped bread and rolls and filled shopping baskets or canvas bags. They only spoke the words "Thank you" and "Come soon again."

"Now that everyone has gone on their way, I'll find Grace and ask her to take over out here. We must come to some agreement with Anne about Lizzie's living arrangements." Mary headed for the hallway and then stopped. "Do you believe Anne will be steadfast? Will she be upset, if I offer an alternate plan?"

"I do not know, Mary. Let me run to ask Kate if she will accompany us. We'll have time to talk along the way." Julia hurried toward the back of the building.

Minutes later, she emerged through the archway again, just as the front door swung wide and banged against the far wall. In the entry stood Mrs. Flynn, her favorite customer and a friend to them all.

A tiny, pretty lady, Mrs. Flynn appeared well dressed, as always. Each time she came to the shop, Julia observed a strange or unusual twist to her finery. Today, she wore a pale blue frock, dotted with delicate purple and green flowers and decorated at the neck and sleeves with subtle ruffles. Her rough leather boots, the likes of which might be found on a soldier or huntsman setting off on a day's hike across the mountains, offered the only exception to her grand appearance. Whether her outrageous accessories were meant to provoke attention or bring smiles, she had outdone herself today.

Still framed in the doorway, Mrs. Flynn struggled to balance a large bag, similar to a long pillowcase. While she positioned one hand at the top of the sack and used the other to brace the bottom, it threatened to buckle at the middle.

"Allow me to assist you." Julia rushed forward and attempted to take the bag, but Mrs. Flynn resisted. In the shuffle, the packet slipped between their hands and dropped to the floor.

Mary came out from the kitchen just as the large parcel landed on the floor with a thud. She stepped back into the hallway. "Walter, come help us, if you will."

"What have you brought, Mrs. Flynn?" Julia tugged at the top of the sack, trying to keep it upright.

"'Tis meat." Mrs. Flynn closed the door, shoving the package in ahead of her.

"Why are you bringing us meat?" Walter's voice boomed through the hallway. When he moved into the room and lifted the package from the floor, he laughed. "You know, Delia Flynn, folks generally come here to buy our goods, not bring things in."

"Well, here's the story, Walter." Mrs. Flynn attempted to wipe her hands on the corner of the bag.

Julia produced a basin hidden beside the hearth, and filled it with water. She moistened a clean cloth and took basin and rag to her friend.

"My Tim's brother arrived last evening with a load of meat. He operates a farm north of the city. He also butchers for the neighboring farms. Ever since...it...happened, you know, everyone looks out for us, showering us with kindness and with goods. Our cellar is filled to the brim. We did not wish the food to go to waste, and on his way to work this morning, Tim delivered a parcel to the mission."

Julia squeezed Mrs. Flynn's shoulder. Nearly two years had passed, since her seventeen-year-old son Barry died in the service of the Union Army. The family had been grieving, and even with the passage of time, they found the loss difficult to bear.

She held the basin while Mrs. Flynn dipped the cloth in the water.

"Thank you dear." She handed the cloth back to Julia and dried her hands on her skirt.

"I met Bridget on my way home from the mission. She told me about her brother and your Lizzie. I knew a Welcome Supper would be in the offing. So, here I am with a fresh supply of meat for the celebration."

Walter's eyes grew wide. "You carried this heavy sack for two blocks? And, in this heat?"

"Ah, go on with you." Mrs. Flynn dismissed Walter with a smile and a wave.

"Give Tim and his brother our thanks." He bowed toward Mrs. Flynn. "With meat still scarce in the city, this is a generous gift. I would have fetched it, you know."

"Will you come to our party for Lizzie?" Julia lowered her head. Sure, she knew the answer, but she could not refrain from extending the invitation.

"Ah, thank you for asking, my dear." Mrs. Flynn bobbed her head toward Mary, then Walter. "I would love to be here with you, but my Tim is not ready to venture out in company. He takes himself to work and puts in his hours at the foundry, you know, but he is capable of no more. He barely finishes his supper these days, before falling into an exhausted sleep. Perhaps, in time, he will recover enough to go about, but not just yet."

Mrs. Flynn glanced at Mary and then back to Julia. "But look at the two of you. You appear ready to bolt through the door. Have I interrupted an important outing?"

"We are on our way to see Anne." Julia peered through the archway. "We must wait for Grace to take over here in the shop before we set out." She stepped closer. "I took Anne the news last evening on my way to the mission. Oh, Mrs. Flynn, you can imagine the happiness that burst forth from her, when I told her about Lizzie's coming—"

"I will leave you girls alone to discuss Anne's happiness, while I store this meat." Walter swung the package over his shoulder, as if it were a feather pillow. With a wave to Mrs. Flynn, he disappeared along the hallway.

"May I wrap some bread for you?" Julia headed behind the counter. "After such a fine gift, we cannot overlook your needs, Mrs. Flynn."

"Two loaves, please, and six of your fine cinnamon biscuits, as well. I'll be having Tim's brother for supper tonight and then breakfast tomorrow. He will set out for home at daybreak." Mrs. Flynn took out her coin purse, but Mary shook her head firmly.

❊ ❊ ❊

Only Julia and Mary arrived at Anne's door that afternoon. "I wish Kate had come." Mary followed Julia up the steps.

"Kate did wish to visit Anne, but she insisted she must push ahead with her work so she will have free time to visit with Lizzie tomorrow." Julia rapped on Anne's back door.

"Come in, come in." Anne held out her arms to them, her face bathed in smiles.

Dressed in a soft blue garment Julia had seen her wear to church many times, Anne appeared ready for an outing. A white apron, made of a serviceable material but adorned with tiny embroidered flowers, covered the dress. With her hair in a neat bun, her sister looked every ounce the young housewife. And lovely as always.

"Shall we call on Bridget and her brother?"

She had guessed correctly. Anne dressed to visit Brendan Rice this afternoon.

Julia entered the kitchen with a heavy, purposeful step. This all important visit must not begin with Anne's dissatisfaction. Perhaps, her happiness over Lizzie would overcome this small disappointment.

"Brendan came to the mission today. I have already seen him and talked with him."

"That is grand." Anne's eyes brightened, warming her face. "Did he have news of Michael?"

"No information about Michael." Julia held Anne's hands and swung her arms between the two of them. "He said Lizzie traveled in a party of four young girls and she made no mention of our brother. Brendan and Michael have never met, so he would not have recognized him on the ship. He reminded me that he has been away at school for many years and he is a good bit older than Michael."

"And was he acquainted with Lizzie?"

"He came to know her." Julia placed a package of baked goods, a gift from Mary, on the table. "Apparently, he is a friend of Lizzie's companions. He explained the connection, but I am not sure of it. Lizzie will sort it all for us, when she arrives tomorrow.

"The important thing is Lizzie is well. When I spoke to Brendan this morning, he assured me of her good health.

He is a fine, friendly fellow. When you meet him, you will discover how similar to Bridget he is with his warm, outgoing personality." Julia placed her arm around Anne's shoulder and looked into her eyes. "Have I disappointed you by meeting with Brendan already?"

"Of course not. I am not as temperamental as all that. We will have more time now, for our own visit." Anne placed the teapot on the stove, and Mary arranged cups, napkins, and silverware on the table.

As Julia set out the baked goods, she took a moment to look around the cheerful kitchen. This room, and indeed the entire house, had been in a sorry state when James purchased it. The former drab green walls bore water damage and peeling paint everywhere. The warped floors and cracked windows added to its desperation. Now level, stained floors, and shiny new windows took their place. With smooth, cream-colored walls, similar to those in Dempsey's dining room, the place appeared attractive and substantial. How blessed Anne was to have a capable, hard-working husband.

She studied her sister closely. Anne did not seem upset over her visit with Brendan. Still, something felt amiss. The last few times she had been in her company, Anne appeared her normal, even-tempered self. The pretense surely took a determined effort.

When the tea had been poured and they gathered around the kitchen table, Julia cleared her throat. "Anne..." She stopped and coughed. "We must talk about Lizzie." She drew up her shoulders. "I know you and James worked hard to prepare this fine home for our family. The rooms you've set aside for them upstairs are beautiful."

"Yes, they are grand." Mary patted Anne's cheek.

"James finished the paint on the front bedrooms this past weekend." Anne lowered her head a little. "Either room would be perfect for Lizzie or Michael—"

"I am praying Lizzie will assume your former position in the bakery, Anne." Julia's voice trembled. "Since you left Dempsey's, Mary has made do without a permanent helper. We've all tried to take on some of the work, but you know better than anyone, it is not the same as a dedicated shop girl."

Julia took a breath. "Our dear Mary, here, has not said a word, but she could already have hired a new girl. Kind as she is to us Carty sisters, I believe she has been holding the position for Lizzie."

"Is that true, Mary?" Anne spilled a few drops of tea on the tablecloth, as she attempted to refill Mary's cup. "You must be working night and day." She set the teapot down and pulled Mary close to her. "Forgive me. I have been so engrossed in my home and my new life here I've neglected my dear friend."

"Ah, 'tis nothing. I am fine. The shop moves along well. Since Julia no longer has work for the Union Army, she has given us magnificent help each afternoon." Mary reached out to take Anne's hand. "We do need a full time shop girl, and I would love it, if your sister could take over the position. Each of our Dempsey girls has helped while Julia works at the church, but they are all busy with their own occupations. We do miss your good work, you know."

"I could come in and help, until—"

"With this huge house to keep, hah." Julia banged her fist on the table. "Do not even think of it, Anne."

"We are faced with a problem, Anne. If Lizzie assumes the shop duties, Walter and I would wish her to stay at Dempsey's." Mary looked from Julia to Anne, a question in her eyes.

Julia studied Anne's face. "For nearly eight years, you saved every penny to bring our family to America. Even after coming to love James, you resisted marrying him until we were all here. Here you are, settled in with your grand husband, ready to receive the first of the family to arrive since the wedding."

Anne sat back, her face thoughtful, her eyes narrowed.

"Now, Mary and I come to ask that Lizzie stay, not with you, but in Dempsey's attic room." Julia held her breath. Silence slipped into every inch of the room. A mouse—if such a creature would have been allowed in the immaculate Duff household—could have been heard scurrying about.

An amused expression inched across Anne's face. "I have been considering the matter myself. Working at Dempsey's would be a grand opportunity for Lizzie. And I know you need a permanent helper, Mary. I cannot thank you enough for holding the position for her."

"You've already considered this?" Mary clapped her hands against the sides of her face.

"Actually, there is another consideration. James and I have been discussing it, since we learned of Lizzie's coming. His brother Ned is our only guest at present, but the two back bedrooms upstairs have been restored. They are ready to let. The truth of it is, if we have three gentlemen boarders, it may be unseemly for Lizzie to live here. So, my dears, wipe those worried looks away—"

"Anne Duff! You allowed us to squirm here, while all along you expected Lizzie would live at Dempsey's." Julia giggled. Her worries had been without cause.

Mary and Anne laughed with her.

"It has not been without some disappointment that I pushed aside my dream of Lizzie coming here to live. Still, I've made my peace with it." Anne rested her chin on Mary's shoulder. "Once again, the Cartys thank you and Walter. Our little sister is fortunate to be offered a home in your cozy attic room and a position in your bakery. Lizzie is a fine girl. She will provide you with the help you need in the shop. I know it."

"It is difficult to imagine…that little girl we left behind…" Julia held her hand to the back of Anne's chair. "About this high…and soon she will be here, working in the shop."

"I must add something." Anne rose from her chair. "When Michael comes, there is a room upstairs ready and waiting. I'll hear no excuses for him not moving in here."

As Julia cleared the table and carried cups to the sink, she sighed with relief. This delicate situation could have stirred a morsel of hurt between them. Who could ever have predicted the discussion would end with Anne smiling broadly and Mary dabbing away tears?

"Let us not forget, Lizzie will be here tomorrow." Julia placed the teapot on the stove with a bang. Tomorrow. Ah now, she had chosen the right subject. Mary's tears disappeared and her expression filled with purpose.

"I agree, Julia." Mary tapped her spoon against her cup, as she moved to the sink to help. "We have much planning and preparing to do before Lizzie's grand arrival tomorrow afternoon."

"You and James will come for supper, of course, Anne. And please extend the invitation to his brother Ned."

"This talk of menus and arrangements is a fine thing," Julia moved away from the sink, "but we must bid you farewell and return home." She hugged Anne. "Please come by the bakery about noon, tomorrow. If I am able to finish my work at St. Vincent's in time, I will accompany you to the riverfront to meet Lizzie."

Along the way, Julia wished to run and skip. Instead, she practiced the calm, mature posture and demeanor her sister projected. She must learn to comport herself in respectable manner, if she intended to become a married woman anytime soon. As she took Mary's arm and they hurried toward the bakery, her heart fluttered. Would Martin choose this night for their all important outing? What, would be decided?

Chapter Four

While the girls finished the supper dishes that evening, Martin's voice drifted in from the dining room. "I apologize for missing your fine meal."

"No apologies necessary." Mary cleared her throat. "Shall I warm a plate for you?"

"No thank you, Mary." His smile sounded in his voice.

Julia scrubbed the silverware with a soapy dishrag then dropped the pieces in the tub of steaming rinse water beside her. She held herself still, pretending calm, as if she heard none of the conversation. In the next moment, Martin entered the kitchen.

"Good evening." He acknowledged each of the girls. Were his hands twitching? How unusual for the calm, sure Martin. "Would you mind if I whisk Julia away for a bit?"

"You two go right on out," Ellen said. "Our work is all but finished."

"Will you come for a walk with me?" He shifted his feet and pushed his hands in his pockets.

"He seems anxious to speak with you." Kate whispered in Julia's ear. She released her from her muslin smock and led her away from the sink. Amid teasing from all the girls, the giggles led by none other than Kate, she and Martin set out together through the side door of the building.

With the sun about to set and cool breezes rustling the trees, a perfect late summer evening unfolded before them.

"Will we begin right where we left off?" Julia clamped her hand over her mouth. She should have waited. His declaration of love, proclaimed just before they entered Dempsey's last evening, excused her poor manners. Her heart had fluttered and her concentration wandered ever since. Even the joy of Lizzie's coming could not compete with the thrill of hearing Martin proclaim his love for her.

"My apologies. I should have allowed you to speak first." She waved her hand. "It is your story to tell."

Martin remained silent. Ah no, when would she learn to hold her tongue? Had he changed his mind? Would he take back his loving words, now only a day old?

"I found a job for myself." Martin took her arm. Rather than circle the perimeter, their custom, he guided her along a narrow path toward the center of the park, between rows of somewhat wilted white and yellow daisies. After only a few steps on the flower path, he eased her in a new direction. They ventured on, their pace slower. His arm quivered through the thick cloth of his Army jacket. Was nervousness the reason for this uneven conversation?

"Of course, it is not the position I intended. I will be driving for the Omnibus Company." Martin gazed down at her for a moment.

"Martin, that is wonderful. I am amazed you found a job so soon." She smiled encouragement in answer to the question in his eyes.

"While I navigate the long routes around the city, I will have the opportunity to speak with many different people." His posture straightened and his voice gained confidence. "Also, my schedules will vary. I will be required to work some evenings and weekends, leaving a portion of my daytime hours free to search the city for a more lucrative position."

"Will it not be a difficult task to secure yet another one? The city seems in such turmoil over new businesses, scores of immigrants arriving, and such. Walter talks of little else."

"That's the very reason I've taken this position." Martin guided Julia into an area of the park dense with trees and shrubbery.

"What sort of company or manner of work will interest you? Will it be similar to your army tasks?" She clutched the narrow cuff of her sleeve. Dare she even consider where this conversation was leading?

"A large company, I suppose. I would like to work as a purchaser. I'm thinking a manufacturing company or even a hospital, ordering supplies and equipment. My army experience prepared me for that type of job. I may even be able to advance at the Omnibus Company." Martin released her arm and stood quietly for a moment. Then, he stepped close again.

"Meanwhile, if I succeed at this driving position, we will make our own plans in earnest. You have not changed your mind about marrying me, have you?" Martin's expression changed. He appeared pensive. Was he unsure of himself? Of her?

"Of course, I have not changed my mind." Julia faced him. The leaves around them appeared a little less brown now; the pink flowers looked a little pinker. "You know I love you. I believe I have loved you since the day we met."

Julia shuffled along for a moment, rolling a pebble beneath her shoe. "Why have you never spoken of any of this? Why have you never said the words 'I love you' until last evening? You sometimes spoke of a life together and a home of our own, but until tonight the word marriage never came up." She stilled her feet. Had she gone too far? "I am glad we are speaking of it now. It feels wonderful to hear these words spoken."

"I did not know how to approach you." He pulled off his cap and slapped it against his arm. "I am such a simpleton. I have lived with men all my life, Julia. You are the first girl I've had a real conversation with."

"But, you must have known I love you. I have been devoted, since we met."

He held her hand between his own. "I apologize for my awkwardness. I know I hold my feelings inside. I worry I will say the wrong thing, and then I say nothing. You deserve so much more than my silence."

"You are not awkward. You are wonderful. I will attempt to be more forward, and if you do not speak and I am left wondering, I will ask. I, too, suffer the constraints of my upbringing." She grinned up at him. "You know, a gentleman will not want someone who is too forward."

"You could never be too forward for me, Julia." He slowed his steps. "Have patience with me. I fear I will often need a little push. I love you so. Please never forget that."

Julia blinked. "Forbearance and a shove…I will attempt it."

"I've kept you waiting all these years."

"You were in the army when we first became acquainted, nearly five years ago. A war raged on around us. You were required to report back to your post early each evening." Julia's glance probed deeper. She could not pull her eyes from him. Had the long wait come to an end at last? "These past months, since the close of the war, afforded us the first freedom to spend time together and come to know one another."

"You are such a beautiful girl. Surely, fellows pursue you all the time." Martin released a strand of her hair from its pins and allowed it to slip through his fingers. His touch, gentle and tender, set off an explosion of shivers racing though her. "You have opportunities to meet young men every day, at the church, the mission, and the bakery."

"Sure, I've had a grand time, working with the volunteers at the mission." Julia laughed. "There have been courtships, and waltzes, and marriage proposals all the long day."

"Julia!" Martin's sober expression returned.

"I am but teasing." Was a small grin threatening to break through Martin's seriousness? Emboldened, she touched his cheek. "The majority of poor bedraggled young men who find their way to the mission are hungry and weary. Finding food, work, and housing weigh more on their minds than dancing with me." A chuckle escaped her. "It is kind of you to say I am pleasing. I do appreciate hearing it. And I've another truth for you. I have not ever met a finer man than you, my dear. I love only you."

"Patience does not come easily for you, I know." Martin held her arms, placing her squarely before him. "It is grand of you to wait for me to settle my course. Since I will soon be free of Army restrictions, I do not wish to postpone the beginning of our new life a moment longer than necessary."

"Your words are drawing forth a blush." She ran her fingers along her warm cheek.

"I wish to talk to you, not just on a Sunday afternoon outing or the occasional stolen evening, but every day." Martin's steel blue eyes penetrated straight to her heart. "I wish to spend an evening with you, not in the park or on a porch, but inside our home with a fire blazing. After this month, I never wish to leave you and return to an Army barracks again." He stepped back. His hands dropped to his side, gripped in tight fists.

She stifled a grin. He was nervous. "Oh, my dear."

He spoke softly. "I love you so. Will you marry me, as soon as I gain confidence that I will make a go at this position?" Martin exhaled slowly. "Will you, Julia Carty? Will you be my wife?"

Julia studied into the face of the man she had for so long held dear. He mustn't hold doubts or concerns. She willed her deep feelings into her voice and expression.

"I love you with all my heart. Be confident in that love. My devotion is deep and lasting. And yes, my dear, I will marry you."

"I love you, too." Martin swept her up in his strong arms. He kissed her then, brushing her lips with strength and tenderness all at once.

Her knees grew weak. The crunch of footsteps faded, along with the buzz and chirp of the park's critters. She and Martin floated on a soft, magical cloud all their own. If only she could capture this enchanted moment and preserve it for a lifetime.

And Martin's cheek, resting against her own...how could she separate herself from him? But daylight faded with each passing moment, and they must leave.

She moved a proper distance away. Such emptiness...it happened far too quickly. Her arm linked with Martin's, they retraced their steps, following the path toward the dim light of the outside world.

The once beautiful colors of spring and early summer burned to dull green and brown. The trees, hedges, and wildflowers looked worn and weary, beaten down by the unrelenting heat of the scorching summer days. Tonight, however, this little park beamed with perfection. Its beauty brought to mind the sweet pastures and groves of her childhood.

Strolling along in unison, Julia gripped Martin's arm with all her might. Had mere moments passed? Had it been an hour since they entered the park? She longed to be wrapped in his arms again, but how could they? If they continued to talk, could they retain some of the magic?

"Will your new position be difficult? Driving the large Omnibus and controlling the horses seems a monumental task. On a few occasions, I was allowed to drive a small cart pulled by one horse back home. My father sold them off eventually."

"It is a heavy, cumbersome wagon, often holding as many as twenty passengers," Martin said. "You are right. I am a bit concerned about that myself."

"Did your family have horses back home?" Julia slowed her steps.

"Of course, I grew up with horses. Before he died, my father raised them. Then, when I attended the military academy, it became my assignment to drive a large carriage pulled by

Keeper of Trust

four horses and filled with students. I experienced no trouble." Martin's jaw twitched as he spoke. "A few years have passed since I attempted such a thing. I've taken to observing Omnibuses and their drivers around town. Suddenly, they appear larger than I envisioned before I accepted the position."

"You will handle the job in fine fashion." Julia twirled around in a circle. Such a fine future for them now: Martin's grand success, their marriage, and the joyous life ahead.

"I promise you, it will not be long." He entwined his fingers through hers and placed her hand in the generous side pocket of his Army jacket.

For the second time that evening, his fine touch brought a lovely, fresh quiver bursting through her.

"I lived at a boarding school from such a young age with my Uncle Joseph as my only family, and later, in an Army barracks. I scarcely remember my time with my family back in Ireland. My dream all through the endless, dreadful war has been for a home of my own, and for you to be my wife and live there with me." Martin squeezed her hand.

She dug her thumbnail into her palm. Was she dreaming?

"Our time has come, Julia." Martin's face broke into a magnificent smile. "We have been awarded an opportunity to begin a new life. With you at my side, we will dream together."

"Would you consider going out west, at all?" Here she was, speaking before thinking again. What had caused her to say such a thing? Concern flickered across Martin's face again, and Julia lowered her head.

"I did not realize you still considered going out to your uncle in Oregon." Martin's brows furrowed.

"Ah, pay me no mind. It is a whim of mine, is all. Though I would love the adventure of the long journey, it is a foolish notion." Julia's footsteps became forceful. Was she beginning to react like Kate? "Besides, we seem to have lost all touch with Uncle James. Since receiving a letter, shortly after her arrival in St. Louis, Anne has not heard another word from him. And, with her settled with James, she would not think of going to Oregon. I am not even sure I would wish to leave her, or my other sisters, or the Dempseys."

"I suppose we could consider moving out west, if I do not gain a more satisfactory position here in St. Louis. Will that satisfy you, my beautiful butterfly?"

"Though my foolish tongue still flies away from me at times, I am no longer a young, fluttering butterfly. The war and my family's sorrows have driven every childish notion from me." If only she could feel the confidence of her strong words.

"I meant it only as a compliment, my dear," Martin said. "You know I've studied the Lepidoptera some. When a butterfly matures, its wings grow strong and it soars to new heights, colorful and beautiful as ever. The butterfly transformed."

"Thank you, Martin. While I may have wished for a grand adventure out west, my one thought now is to live wherever you are." If daylight remained, he would see the blush burning across her cheeks. He would also notice the wondrous expression of happiness building since they left Dempseys' kitchen. That joyful look must have grown a hundred times over with his talk of love and marriage.

"Lizzie's coming is a sign we must move ahead with our plans." Martin's thoughts seemed linked with hers. Would they now think and feel and speak as one? "I look forward to coming to know your sister. It will be grand to have her here for our wedding." He squeezed her hand, still held in his pocket. "Once I am confident I can manage the job, we should talk to Father Burns and set a date. Do you agree?"

"'Tis a wonderful idea. I suspect he will not be at all surprised." Her cheeks warmed again. "I suppose I have mentioned your name to him a time or two."

"Let's keep our intentions between us, until we've consulted with Father Burns, then," Martin said.

"I must talk this over with my sisters."

"Your sisters, of course." Martin rubbed his fingers along the front of his jacket. "All of them?"

"Well, I believe I should. I have already shared some of last evening's talk with Kate, and once Lizzie arrives, she will live in the attic room with us. It will be difficult to keep anything from her. And, Anne, of course. She and I have never kept secrets from one another."

"Whatever you say, my love." He rubbed the back of his neck. Did he agree only to make her happy?

"Have you spoken with your brother about our marriage plans?" She raised an eyebrow. "Did you write to your uncle in New York?"

He gave her a sheepish grin. "I must admit, Patrick and I discussed it. I also wrote to Uncle Joseph. I arrived here as a young orphan, and my brother remained back home with relatives. Loneliness overwhelmed me. Uncle Joseph was such a wonderful guardian to me, conscientious about his duties, but kindly. I felt I should let him know."

"Perhaps we could agree to tell only family, until you are comfortable in your new position." She pinched her lips together with her fingers. "I believe I could hold my tongue that long. Will that satisfy you?"

Martin rewarded her with a wide grin. "Once we have set the date, I will shout 'I love Julia Carty' from the housetops."

Chapter Five

The sun blazed high above the city, as the noon hour approached on Friday. Julia finished her thorough scrubbing of the counter, as the bell above Dempsey's door jingled. Anne entered the bakery, all starched and purposeful, wearing a wide, satisfied smile.

"'Tis grand to see such a fine married lady in our shop this morning." Mary entered from the back hallway and placed a tray of fresh bread on the spotless counter.

"Good afternoon, Mary, Julia." Anne stretched out her hand, preventing the door from banging shut behind her.

"You do look wonderful, Anne." Julia stepped away from the counter and hugged her sister. Trim and fit as always, Anne had fastened her thick brown hair into a neat bun and covered it with a proper blue bonnet. Her Sunday best dress, lilac with pale stripes of gray swirling through the skirt, fitted her petite frame perfectly. An extra spark enlivened her steady blue eyes this morning. Excitement over Lizzie's arrival, no doubt.

"You have been so busy at St. Vincent's, I worried you would not be free to accompany me." Anne punctuated her greeting her with a very un-married-lady-like bump in the hip.

"It is all Mary's doing." Julia took hold of Anne's hand and swung her in an abbreviated loop. "When I extended her invitation for Lizzie's celebration to the two priests, Father Burns insisted I rush right off to meet her at the riverfront. I will be required to spend some extra hours tomorrow catching up on my work. For now, I am right and ready, and we must be on our way."

Anne hugged Mary. "Thank you for allowing Julia to leave you alone here in the bakery."

"We will not be long at all." Julia started for the door. "Once we collect Lizzie, we will hurry right back to help with supper preparations."

"Ah, go on with you. Hurry along, and give not a thought to the shop." Mary guided them to the exit. "After the many years you girls scraped and saved to acquire the passage money for Lizzie, you deserve these happy moments. 'Tis a grand day for the Carty sisters. I only wish you could persuade Kate to go along."

"I just talked to Kate." Julia retrieved her shawl from the coat rack in the corner. "She wishes to go, but she is busy with a dress order that must be finished by tonight. Kate strives to earn a reputation for being dependable. She feels her responsibility keenly. What a conscientious girl."

"You do not need a wrap, you know," Anne pulled the fluffy shawl away from Julia's shoulder. "It is a sweltering St. Louis summer day. The sun is already quite strong."

"Oh, I know it. I suppose I am just silly with excitement. We have been thinking this day would never arrive. Now, the time has come." Julia removed the shawl from her other shoulder and hung it away.

She linked her arm with Anne's, and they headed outside. "Kate and Lizzie will have time enough together, once she is installed in the attic room."

When they moved down the steps, Walter waited, his carriage in readiness.

"Aye, I know you girls always wish to walk on your own," he tipped his hat to them, "but we did hear Lizzie was weary. I will convey you to the riverfront to fetch her."

As Julia and Anne approached the carriage, he jumped down to assist them. "Also, her trunk has not yet arrived. We may be able to collect it."

"It is fortunate we all love you so and will tolerate your tyranny." Julia accepted Walter's arm, as he assisted her into the back seat. "You are truly a bother of a brother."

They all laughed, but Walter's cheeks turned pink. Had she gone too far?

❀ ❀ ❀

No more than an hour passed before they pulled up in front of the shop again, with Lizzie perched in the front seat. When Julia alighted from the carriage, Kate waved from the doorway. As she raised her arms to assist Lizzie, Kate dashed down the steps and out to the street. She pulled the poor, exhausted girl right out of the carriage, and into a fierce embrace.

Anne came up beside Julia and watched with her, as their two young sisters hugged, pulled back, and then hugged again.

"She is so thin," Anne whispered in Julia's ear. "Do you think she is well?"

"Her smile is certainly healthy." Julia patted Anne's shoulder.

"Lizzie is a big girl." Anne's eyes glowed. No doubt about her joy.

"With her broad shoulders and long limbs, she towers over Kate." Julia moved closer.

Shockingly thin arms wrapped entirely around Kate. The outline of Lizzie's bones showed through the sleeve of her dress. She smiled and laughed, making a valiant effort to reassure Kate of her good health.

Still, exhaustion clouded her eyes and tiny creases surrounded them. Most startling of all, Lizzie's ghastly pale complexion covered her gaunt face. Where were the rosy cheeks from all those many years ago?

Lizzie's grand smile brightened her appearance, a remarkable contrast to her shabby frock, surely the ugliest shade of tan ever seen. It stirred memories of wartime days, when cloth of any kind had grown scarce and everyone in the city wore frayed and patched clothing. With her hem uneven and far too long, Lizzie's dress dragged on the ground.

Julia edged closer. Lizzie's bonnet, likely a dark shade of brown at one time, looked a disgrace. It had been mended in spots and the seams along the brim had pulled apart. Had Lizzie and her clothing been dragged along through a patch of mud?

She sighed. Could Mother not have made her a new hat, or at least hemmed her dress? When Kate found an opportunity for a close appraisal of Lizzie's traveling clothes, she would tend to her, for sure.

"Are you well?" She had to ask.

"I am fit, really." Lizzie embraced Julia, Anne, and Kate with both arms. "I am so thrilled to be here with you. Ah, 'tis wonderful." She straightened her shoulders and looked into each of their eyes. "I am weary, is all."

Pulling away, Julia escorted Lizzie to the bakery entrance. "You must meet our Mary. She has permitted us some time alone, but I see her waiting just inside the shop." She held the door wide and made room for Lizzie to pass through ahead of her.

"Welcome to Dempsey's, Lizzie." Mary stood at the counter, holding a plate of cinnamon biscuits, a wide smile spread across her face. "We are happy you have come, at last."

"Mary, how's yourself, then? I feel I know you already. I am Lizzie.

"My sisters have told me of the many kindnesses you and Walter showered over them." Lizzie patted Mary's cheek. "Now, I will live in this grand place with all of you. I cannot thank you enough."

A lovely pink covered Mary's face.

Lizzie took the tray from Mary and linked her arm with hers. "And I have carried a letter with me from your aunt and uncle. I already passed it along to Walter."

"Are they well?" A tear ran along Mary's cheek, and she attempted to brush it away with her sleeve.

"They are both grand." Lizzie nodded down at Mary.

"She comports herself with such ease and grace." Julia moved closer to Anne. "An introduction seemed unnecessary. And herself barely sixteen and just off the boat."

"Come closer and meet our Lizzie." Mary waved to the group of neighborhood women, gathered in the shop to extend her a proper welcome.

Julia eased Lizzie from Mary's embrace. Taking her elbow, she guided her around the room. 'Here is Mrs. McNulty." The woman shifted her shopping basket and accepted the biscuit on a tiny plate Lizzie offered. "She brought us the first word of your coming."

"Sure, and you are a fine girl, Lizzie." Mrs. McNulty, both arms occupied, could manage only an awkward hug. "News of your arrival caused a grand stir here at Dempsey's, and that's the truth."

Julia nudged Lizzie along. "Here is Mrs. Rice waiting to greet you. She is mother to Brendan, whom you met in Boston. And, you will soon come to know her daughter, Bridget, who works most days at our St. Vincent's mission." They stopped a moment to speak with Mrs. Rice, and then moved on.

"And here is Mrs. Kerry…and Mrs. Flynn…." The introductions continued, as Lizzie offered biscuits to each of the women.

"We are excited to meet our newest arrival from home." Mrs. Flynn took Lizzie's arm, handing the tray off to Julia. "You must tell us all the news."

"I am pleased to meet all of you." Lizzie's cheeks became flushed.

As she listened to Lizzie converse with each of the women, Julia's heart reached out to them. Here stood a poor soul from home, weary and disheveled. Another of Ireland's children had weathered the terrible crossing. With their own sisters, parents, and cousins back home waiting to come, Lizzie represented hope. They all must endure the hardships of the journey, but God willing, they would be here one day.

Displaying poise and maturity well beyond her years, Lizzie answered their questions. Julia placed her hand over her heart, as though it would burst with pride.

The room became hushed. The women inched closer to Lizzie. "This is why we've come. 'Tis what we've been waiting for." Mrs. Flynn set her plate and biscuit aside. "We wish to hear you speak. Your voice carries the sound of Ireland only you can bring us. Your manner of speech transports us back to the home we all long to see once more, but likely never will."

Lizzie would lose that special quality all too soon, but for now, Julia joined them in basking in the melody of her words.

Kate dragged a chair across the room for her, creating a space between Lizzie and the women.

With a sigh, Lizzie sat down. "As the ship pulled away from the harbor, my final look at our dear home was of an emerald seacoast, dotted with cottages and varied hues of deeper green hillsides off in the distance."

While Lizzie visited with the women, the other Dempsey girls made their way out to the shop. Grace Donahoo, also from Blackwater, greeted her first, her expression troubled. "Do you have news of my family, Lizzie?" She cast her eyes down to the floor.

"Yes, Grace. I brought along a letter from your brother William. He said they are all well and you are not to worry." Lizzie squeezed Grace's arm. "When we have a private moment, I will hand the letter over to you and tell you more of the tale."

When Grace raised up again, relief shone in her eyes.

Ellen threw her arms across Lizzie's shoulders with a grand flourish. "Ah, Lizzie, welcome to St. Louis. 'Tis happy I am to meet you at last. Your Kate has been telling me stories of your days back home. Sure, and we will become fast friends in no time."

"Such a warm welcome," Julia whispered to Anne. She glanced across the room, where Cara stared at the bakery floor. She moved to her side.

"Cara, you must meet our Lizzie." Julia tugged the slight, dark-haired young woman toward her sister.

"Cara, dear," Lizzie grasped Cara's hands in her own. "I'm pleased to meet you. Julia has been telling me what a wonderful friend you've been to all of my sisters." She embraced the timid girl. "I'm sure we will soon be close pals."

Julia allowed her proud smile to shine. And here, she had been thinking of Lizzie as her baby sister.

A woman from the rear of the crowded room made her way forward. "Lizzie, tell us about the condition of the crops."

Lizzie paused in her talk with Cara. Her warm smile faltered. "I must admit to the truth of the sad situation back home. Crops have failed all over Ireland. Many have been put out of their homes because they cannot pay their taxes. Wanderers roam the roads of our beloved land, homeless and hungry."

The shop bell jangled, and Walter slipped inside. Making his way through the crowd, he stationed himself in the archway at the rear of the room. Shaking his head, his thick wavy hair flying about, he faced Lizzie. "So, my dear, are you holding up under this scrutiny?"

"Come with me." Julia led Lizzie over to stand beside Walter. "Tell everyone the story of her arrival."

The room grew quiet.

"We found her and her trunk already at the pier." With a twinkle in his eyes, Walter nodded to Julia.

She relaxed. Either her foolish teasing had been forgotten, or perhaps, he had not been upset after all.

"In truth, she sat atop the trunk." Julia grinned, then stopped. "Oh sorry, Walter. Please continue."

The dear man smiled in her direction. "Well, Lizzie assured Julia and Anne she had not waited long and did indeed feel well. And then, before I knew it, those three laughed and swung each other about. It looked for the entire world as if it had been weeks rather than years since their separation."

Anne tugged at Julia's sleeve and twirled her around as freely as the crowded room would allow. "You see, we are still swinging and giggling." Anne bowed to Walter.

"It was a treat for my eyes, Anne." Walter shook his head again, sending his curls in all directions. "It was also grand to experience Lizzie's reaction to the bustling riverfront, the crowds of people, and the many tall buildings—"

"I want to know…" Kate stepped between them. "How are you really? Is this grand effort to appear well a performance?"

Julia pursed her lips. "Yes please, Lizzie, tell us." Kate had been fretting about her condition. She'd worried their little sister had been permanently impaired from working at Hogan's. Could it be true?

"I am fine. I am delighted to be here with all of you." Lizzie framed Kate's face with her hands. She grinned toward Julia and Anne then extended her smile to Walter, Mary, and each of the women in the shop.

"Four Carty girls here in America together, is it not wonderful?" Julia patted Lizzie's cheek. She swirled around and bowed to each of the women gathered around them. "We sisters thank you all for coming to share this happiness with us."

"And now, we've only Michael and Maggie to bring out." A thoughtful expression replaced Anne's smile for the first time since discovering Lizzie waiting at the riverfront.

"This day will be set aside for welcome." Julia grinned at her serious, worrywart Anne. "Plenty of time to return to our concerns about the rest of the family in Ireland. Let us give thanks to God for Lizzie's safe arrival and rejoice that she is well."

Walter abandoned his position in the archway. "Lizzie appeared exhausted when we first saw her. You see her jovial manner here. Well, when Julia introduced us, though I observed her weariness, she favored me with the most brilliant smile I have ever encountered. As I helped her into the carriage, she told me she felt more tired than anyone has surely ever been in the last hundred million years."

"I did say that." Dimples broke out in Lizzie's cheeks, when she nodded to Walter.

"Well, Miss Lizzie, take some time now to rest and recover your strength. You will be feeling your old self in no time." He moved along the hallway toward the back of the shop.

Lizzie returned to conversing with everyone, but with each movement of limb, or turn, or bow of her head her strength faded.

"It is time to settle you in our attic room." Julia touched Lizzie's elbow, steering her away from the crowd.

"We consider the cozy little place our own." They headed for the stairway. "Walter and Mary are kind enough to allow us to do so." After a last wave to the women gathered in the shop, Lizzie climbed the steps followed by Julia, Anne and Kate.

Walter's head appeared in the stairwell. "Four Carty sisters ascending to the attic is causing such a ruckus we hear the rumbling back in the oven room. Dempsey's may never be the same again."

Julia chuckled. Lizzie had come! After this grand and glorious day, none of them would ever be the same.

Chapter Six

"'Tis the grandest moment of all, Lizzie. We have dreamed of having you here, sitting with us in our bedroom." Julia grinned at her sister. "Look at Anne's pleased expression. And Kate's smile? Have you ever seen her face in such a state?"

"Sure, and my sisters have been resting here in fine style, and that's the truth. And I am thrilled a hundred times over to be resting here with you." Lizzie sat on the edge of the bed Julia had prepared for her, cradling a pillow in her arms and rubbing her chin across the soft covering.

The change from the crowded cottage in Blackwater must be remarkable for Lizzie. While furniture filled the small attic room, as it did in their home in Blackwater, the similarities ended there. The attic room held three sturdy beds with comfortable mattresses and soft feather pillows, in comparison to the straw pallets lined along the floor of the loft shared by all the sisters at home. It also held a substantial wardrobe large enough to store their clothing, a writing desk, and a wide row of shelves in the far corner, a sharp contrast with the few coat hooks and shelves used to store the family possessions in Blackwater.

Julia most enjoyed the pair of small windows, adorned with soft, white curtains that afforded a view of the city spread out below them, including the church steeple, and in the distance, the river. Her little sister would come to treasure this cozy place.

Lizzie interrupted her thoughts, waving her hand in front of Julia's face. "I only wish to touch my head to these soft feathers. You will allow me to have a go at it, will you not?" She stretched out on the bed, nestling her head on the pillow. Releasing only the barest of sighs, she drifted right off to sleep.

Anne removed Lizzie's shoes and covered her, but the poor, weary girl did not stir. "I understand her exhaustion," she spoke in a whisper, "but I cannot push back a small grain of disappointment. If only, Lizzie could have answered one or two questions about our dear ones."

"We may as well leave her be and return to work." Kate tilted her head to the side, her expression stoic, but she brushed away a tear as she placed Lizzie's valise and handbag on the desk. "Sure, we will have an opportunity for talk this evening." She headed for the stairway, and Anne followed.

"She must be refreshed in time for our supper." Julia lagged behind them. "I wish to hear the full story about everyone at home." Pulling her eyes away from her sleeping sister, she tiptoed out and followed the other girls downstairs.

❁ ❁ ❁

Later, when Julia delivered the day-old goods to St. Vincent's, she discovered the mission packed with immigrants. Since midday, tired hungry people, had been arriving at the door and finding places at the rows of long tables. Though the room held only two small windows, the warm, yellow walls and glowing gas lights made the place cheerful and welcoming. Several volunteers worked in the kitchen. Pots of soup simmered on top of the two huge stoves. The enticing aromas filled the room, making her insides ache. Oh how she wished to hurry back to Dempsey's for the wonderful meal awaiting her there.

Her eyes wandered the room, her blissful mood tempered by the uncertain faces gathered all around. Their eyes bore weariness, just like Lizzie. Kate had good reason to worry over Lizzie's fatigue.

And yet, joy filled her heart. Humming, Julia arranged the bread and rolls on trays. As soon as her help was no longer needed, she waved to the mission workers. "I must hurry home and see to Lizzie."

"Thank you for the bakery goods, Julia." Bridget placed her arm around her shoulder. "Lizzie will be fine. You know it takes some time to recover from the journey."

She patted Bridget's hand and stepped out the door. Walking briskly, she climbed the hill, her good cheer growing with each stride. Perhaps Lizzie would be awake when she arrived home.

What a charming young person Lizzie had grown to be. She displayed such warmth and poise, as she spoke to the women gathered in the shop. Her sincerity, as she expressed words of appreciation to Walter and Mary, were touching.

Julia skipped along a few paces. Sure, Lizzie would be filled with stories of home to share with them. Ah, and she held a story of her own to tell: Martin's declaration of love and their plans for the future. God had blessed her and her sisters, indeed.

Arriving back at Dempsey's, she paused in the entry and drew a deep breath. She attempted a serious expression. Impossible. Despite her strong effort, a silly smile stretched hopelessly across her face.

❀ ❀ ❀

She found a few of the Dempsey regulars already gathered in the dining room. Lizzie, changed now into a fresh but still shabby dress, looked a bit more restored. Erect and smiling, her cheeks displayed a bit more color. She stood with Anne, who beamed as she introduced their young sister to her tall, sandy-haired husband. James Duff's brother, Ned, joined them, and Lizzie waved to her childhood friend and former schoolmate.

After Lizzie and Ned renewed their acquaintance for a few minutes, Julia captured Lizzie's arm and promenaded her around the room, introducing her to those few she had not already met. Then, she escorted her to a chair beside Walter, who already presided at the head of the table.

James rushed over to hold the chair for Lizzie. "It is a pleasure to seat you in this place of honor, my dear sister-in-law. We are all happy you have come. Let me attempt to explain our customary Welcome celebration." He made a deep bow. "You see, the kind and gracious Dempseys gathered this little group together and made us a part of their own family. Now, each time one of our loved ones arrives, it represents a victory for us all. Sure, we would none of us be kept away from a party honoring a fine girl from our beloved home such as yourself."

"James is right about both things, little sister. Sitting at Walter's right is an honor reserved for very special guests." Julia extended her arm in a dramatic sweep. "And, we are all thrilled you are here."

Kate entered the dining room through the doorway that led to the back of the building. "You look grand, Lizzie." She hugged her sister. "It is wonderful to see some color in your face."

Kate's helper, Ellen came right behind her. She pulled Lizzie from her chair and folded her into a grand hug. "How are you faring?"

"I feel as if we are old friends, my girl." Lizzie pinched Ellen's cheek. "Sure as you're born, you remind me of a Blackwater lass."

Guests entered the dining room from three directions, milling around, their voices raised in greeting to one another. Martin came in with his brother, Patrick, just as Mary urged everyone to take a seat.

Julia could not hold back a smile, as he maneuvered toward her.

"Good evening, Julia. How are you?" Martin leaned her way then glanced around and straightened.

"I am grand." She giggled when he led her to a place at the table and sat down beside her.

"It has been a glorious day, Martin." She attempted a serious nod, but a smile bloomed across her face. "Sure, I am thrilled you were able to attend the party this evening and meet our Lizzie."

"She seems a fine girl," Martin's expression held more politeness than affection, still it caused a swift shiver to pass through her being.

"Will you be free to slip away for a walk after dinner?" Martin leaned close and spoke in a low voice.

"I will manage it." She lowered her head and allowed only a brief sideways glance his way. "You will be pleased to know I have had neither the time nor opportunity to spill our secret, even to my sisters." Was that a wink that crossed his face?

Grace reached between them to place a bowl of steaming vegetables on the table. Mary and Cara set platters of potatoes and roast beef at either end of the table, and Julia's mouth watered as she inhaled the wonderful aromas.

Mary arranged her platter on the table and hurried back toward the kitchen. "I will fetch the salad. If you will bring out the basket of bread, Grace, we will be ready."

A sharp rap at the door drew their attention. Walter stood and walked out through the shop. "Father Burns and Father Ryan have joined us."

Conversation ceased.

"God bless all here." The two priests called out in unison, as Walter ushered them into the dining room.

"God keep us all." Everyone responded.

Lizzie sighed.

Julia's attention flew to her little sister. She likely suffered from homesickness. Would this familiar prayerful greeting bring her comfort?

In moments they were seated. The room quieted while Father Burns offered a prayer of thanksgiving for the wonderful meal before them. Father Ryan added his own words of thanks for Lizzie's safe arrival.

After the prayer, the dining room became spirited once again. "Welcome to St. Louis and your first Dempsey dinner, Lizzie." Anne raised her water glass to her sister.

"Welcome, Lizzie," came from all around the table.

"Slante!" "Best wishes" and "long life" resounded from every corner of the room.

Lizzie, spoke right out, adding her own mark of warmth to the occasion. Not a bit of shyness from her, even in this crowded room.

"If you knew what I have endured to reach you," she gestured to everyone, a spoon resting in her hand, "you would understand how thrilled I am to be sitting here." Laughter rang out around the table. Lizzie joined in, but after a moment, she turned to Julia, her brows drawn in.

Julia reached across Anne and grasped Lizzie's folded hands. "The misery of the crossing is fresh in your mind, my dear little sister. We all see the hardships of the frightful journey etched across your face and the weariness marked in each turn of your head. We understand your exhaustion, but you must remember, we too lived through these painful experiences you have just endured."

Ned Duff, fresh from the voyage, echoed Julia's statement. "Each one of us here endured the long voyage, climbed aboard the jolting, screeching train from the east coast to the Mississippi, and crossed the mighty, smelly river to reach the banks of this great city. As time passes, the wretchedness of it will fade, but I do not believe any one of us will ever forget entirely. I know I never will."

"I am sure you all understand my feelings of relief to be here, among so many folks from home." Lizzie's expression reflected a whirl of thoughts. "The privilege of sitting down at this table with all of you fills me with great peace and contentment. I am well and truly grateful my sisters decided to stay in St. Louis and relieved beyond words I was not required to travel on out west to meet our Uncle James." She raised questioning eyes to Julia.

Julia nodded.

Lizzie inhaled a quick breath and then proceeded. "I am not sure how much longer a journey it is to reach Oregon, but I do not think I could continue another day. I understand now, you have all had these same experiences. I credit what you are saying. Still, I cannot envision traveling on the vast distance required to reach the West Coast. I cannot imagine the hardships such a journey would entail." She gazed around the table. "Do you all not agree with me on that much?"

Glancing to her left, Julia caught Anne's eye. Had her sister been as taken with Lizzie as she?

Anne nodded back. "I am thrilled with our delightful, poised, little sister. She speaks easily with each of the folks seated around the table. In spite of her obvious weariness, her humor and grace come through with every nod and gesture."

When Julia turned to Martin, he responded with a gentle touch on her chin. Color rose in her cheeks as Lizzie raised an eyebrow.

"I appreciate the kindness my wonderful hosts have extended toward me." Julia's tight shoulders relaxed. Lizzie's attention had already moved to a new topic.

"I am pleased to meet all of you." She acknowledged each one seated around the table. "Since Walter and Mary have offered me the opportunity to work for them, I will surely come to know each one of you."

"We are pleased to have you here, Lizzie." Ellen clapped, and everyone around the table joined in.

"I am overwhelmed by this grand supper you have prepared in my honor. Thank you so much, Mary and Grace and Cara. It has been a magnificent meal. Once I've had a rest, you'll find I will do full justice to your excellent cooking."

Had Lizzie's head fallen slightly forward? Julia frowned. Or had it? Perhaps she imagined things.

Lizzie's expression of gratitude had faded, and a mischievous grin now crossed her face.

"Father Burns and Father Ryan, I am most happy to make your acquaintance. My parents will be pleased, when they learn I've met you on my first evening. My sisters have sent countless letters home describing St. Louis and the fine people here. Still, the folks back home picture the city to be a wilderness, with church and priests a mountain and forest removed."

A murmur swelled up around the table.

"They worry this daughter, much more so than the others, will be in constant need of your spiritual guidance. I pray my letters will be eloquent enough to allay their concern."

Laughter erupted. Father Ryan pushed his chair back. "Ah, Lizzie, you appear to be a fine upstanding girl. I am sure your parents have no need to worry over you at all."

"My dear child," Mary shook her head at Lizzie, "you are a lovely girl, and that's the truth of it."

"I have observed nothing but genteel behavior since you arrived, my dear." Walter searched the table for agreement. "I must add, though, you possess the extraordinary humor we have come to appreciate in a Carty girl."

Laughter burst forth around the table again.

Lizzie joined the merriment for a moment, but then she quieted. Julia regarded her sister intently. Was the fatigue claiming her, or was Lizzie about to move on to still another new topic?

In an instant Lizzie's expression grew grave. "I suppose my sudden arrival surprised you."

Julia sighed. She'd expected sad tidings, since Lizzie arrived. When her sister raised her brow, Julia cast a slight nod her way. Lizzie would soon learn of the close ties held around this table. No subject need be held back from any dear friends in attendance this evening.

"Well, I believe it has been two years now, since our Aunt Mary promised to bring us all out." Lizzie drew in a deep slow breath.

After Julia sent an exaggerated smile in her direction, Lizzie turned to Kate, seated beside her. "You remember? Sure, Aunt Mary proposed the idea even before you left Blackwater."

"I remember." Kate folded her arms, scowling.

"A few weeks after Kate left, Aunt Mary fell ill, delaying her plans. Then, her sudden recovery and her even more surprising marriage cancelled the trip altogether." Lizzie shook her head, her brows knitted together. "She meant no harm, of course, but she never should have stirred our hopes with her stories and promises. In truth, it did not distress me as it did Michael. After my time at Hogan's, I rejoiced to be at home. Desperate as conditions are in our small cottage in Blackwater, I longed to stay there."

Julia glanced around. The room had grown still, no forks scraping, no chairs creaking. Everyone anticipated Lizzie's next words, just as she did.

"Well then, Aunt Mary's offer was set aside, and we all managed to put the disappointment to rest. And behold, she and her new husband, Mr. Walsh, came to us at Easter and offered passage money for me. I hesitated to believe it. Even when the money did materialize, I opposed the idea. But, Father and Michael insisted I must go."

"Can you tell us about Michael?" Julia drew her hands into fists. She, Anne, and Kate worried for many years over their brother.

Lizzie bowed her head and grew silent. When she looked up again, a more serious face than Julia had seen since her arrival settled over her. "I am not sure I can speak of him just now."

"Lizzie, please, what is wrong with Michael?" Julia shook her head in disbelief.

Kate pounded her fist on the table. "You must tell us, Lizzie."

Lizzie looked down, a slight shake of her head, the only answer.

Anne gasped.

Silence fell over the room.

"I believe it is time for cake." Mary rose and moved toward the kitchen. She returned in an instant holding a magnificent chocolate cake.

Thankful the slicing of cake and passing of plates and forks provided a distraction and change of subject, Julia studied Lizzie. She ate only small morsels. Her fork appeared heavy in her hand, and her head had dipped a little lower.

"Grace, you could take over cake baking." Walter saluted her with his fork.

"It tastes grand." Cara broke her silence. "Congratulations, Grace."

With everyone's attention focused on Grace and her fine creation, Julia tugged at Anne's sleeve. "Should we take Lizzie upstairs?"

Anne signaled Kate.

Julia turned her attention to James Duff. "Will you allow us to steal Anne away for a few moments? Many years have passed since we sisters have been together. It would be wonderful if we could all go up to the attic room to settle Lizzie in for a long rest."

"Ah, go on with you now." James stretched his long legs out under the table. "You may be amazed at how well we all survive around the table here without one Carty girl present."

"Mary, is that suitable?" Julia ran around the table to hug her dear friend. "We will return in time to help clean up." She made her way to James and Walter and hugged them.

"Come, Julia." Anne called out, waving her on as the sisters headed for the hallway.

"Hurry!" Kate's forceful pounce already bounded up the steps.

Julia sighed and extended only a nod to Martin. Did she read a look of relief in his eyes?

❀ ❀ ❀

"What a wonderful party." Lizzie's shoulders slumped against the arrangement of feather pillows placed at the head of her bed, her voice weak.

Julia fetched a nightgown from the wardrobe, and Kate helped remove Lizzie's worn shoes and thin, cotton dress.

"Now, you will be comfortable." Anne pulled back the quilt and guided Lizzie into bed.

Settled on the soft mattress, her head propped on the pillows again, Lizzie faced her sisters, a slight frown across her face.

Julia pushed her toes into the floor. Would Lizzie ever tell them news from their family back home?

Lizzie sat up suddenly, cradling a pillow in her arms. "Whatever Kate told you about Hogan's, it is all of that, plus two years of added deterioration. Filthy, unsanitary, and unsavory, have I said it strong enough, Kate?" She rubbed her chin across the soft pillow.

"Yes you have, and I have not forgotten one moment of it." Despair filled Kate's eyes.

Lizzie tossed the pillow aside and rubbed the back of her neck.

Julia waited. Did she share Kate's bitterness and resentment over being sent to work at the place?

"We worked the entire day without ceasing. We stocked food and other goods on the shelves, cleaned the place, and cared for the animals." Lizzie's words came slower, softer.

"We were allowed no opportunity for rest at all. Our meals consisted of crusts of bread and nothing more." Tears streamed along Lizzie's cheeks, as Kate sobbed.

"Though I tried to please, Mr. Hogan beat me if I just laughed out loud. I must say, little about the sorry place brought laughter."

"You poor dear." Anne patted Lizzie's shoulder.

"After I had been there a few months, the damp ground in the shack where we slept got the better of me. When I began to cough day and night without relief, Mr. Hogan brought me home and dumped me on the doorstep, offering no words of concern or regret. Indeed, I needed no further conversation with the likes of him. I crouched there, until I heard his rasping bark urge the horse on. Relief poured through me as he drove away. I pulled myself up and crept into the cottage."

"I rejoice that you fell ill and Mr. Hogan was forced to take you home." Kate's words came out in a harsh whisper.

"I am not so sure." Lizzie shook her head. "I was happy to be shed of Hogan's, and that's the truth. I do not believe I ever regained my former strength, though, even with the passage of many months. The cough I developed there remains, even now."

"You and Kate endured such dreadful times at that appalling place." Julia moved to Lizzie's bed and drew her up from the pillows. She held her in her arms. If only she could protect her from further harm. "This situation cannot continue. What must we do to stop this horror? Do the other children and their parents complain about the conditions at Hogan's?"

"Some tried, Julia." Lizzie looked to Kate.

"They only send them home and find other desperate children to replace them." Kate paced the floor. The bang of her footsteps grew more pronounced as she walked. "Did Father and Mother even read the demanding letter we sent them?" She turned and paced back the other way. Each small foot battered the floor with increasing force.

Julia grimaced. Hopefully, the stomping could not be heard in the dining room, two floors below.

"Ah, the distance between us is just too great." Anne's tears began again. "Our influence with Father and Mother is stretched out across the Atlantic Ocean, diluted by each rolling wave. I cannot bear it."

Julia's tears spilled freely.

"I did not see a letter that referred to Hogan's." Lizzie sat up straight in the bed. "I suppose Mother destroyed it, before Father or the rest of us could read it. Well, no matter. Maggie is too young to be sent away. I believe she will remain at home, at least for the present."

"Did you know of the money we sent for your passage?" Julia wrung her hands. She and Anne and Kate suspected what had happened to the fare money, but they all needed to hear the truth of it from Lizzie. "On two separate occasions, we sent passage for you and Michael. We expected you both would arrive here in time for Anne's wedding. Were you aware of this?"

"We knew you girls were working hard to acquire the funds to bring us out, but we knew nothing about any passage money already sent." Lizzie covered her face with her hands. "I am so sorry."

"We must set aside this matter of passage money for another time. I apologize for bringing it up." Julia rose from the bed and stood behind Kate, placing her hands on her sister's shoulders.

"It is time to give thanks and rejoice that our lovely little sister is with us at last." Julia took Anne's hand and drew her close.

"You, Lizzie, sitting here in the attic room with us, are surely a dream come true. You are the answer to our prayers. Let us offer our dear Father in heaven our gratitude and praise."

Anne grasped Lizzie's hand and the girls bowed their heads.

"Dear Lord, thank you for Lizzie's safe arrival. We also remember our precious brother and sister now lost to us. Please hold our poor, brave Jimmy and our beloved little Maura in your care."

Tears swelled up in Julia again. "L-lord…" Sobs overwhelmed her.

"Dear Lord…" Anne pressed her lips together, but she gave in to tears of her own.

Julia wiped her eyes with her sleeve, and spoke in unison with Anne. Together, they managed to finish their sorrowful prayer. "…May they rest in peace, amen."

"Only Father, Mother, Michael, and Maggie remain in Blackwater." Anne blew into a tiny, lacy square. "We will increase our efforts and save every penny for their passage. Surely, Father realizes that, with the home James made ready for them, they can no longer delay. They must sell the farm and separate themselves from our beloved homeland. They must make the sacrifice for the children."

"Ah Lizzie," Julia sat beside her on the bed, "I cannot wait until you see the lovely home James has given Anne. You will agree, our entire family will be comfortable there."

"Julia is right." Anne squeezed in between Julia and Lizzie on the bed. "Large, comfortable rooms are waiting for them."

The pleasure of sharing the cozy attic with her sisters calmed Julia's worries. Pain from the sorrowful memories weakened. Still, unease lurked at her consciousness. Something was amiss. Some anxiety or emotion pulled at her thoughts. In all of Lizzie's brave talk this evening, had she held something back? Why had she avoided speaking of Michael? Was there a secret so dark she was afraid to tell her sisters?

Julia stood with Anne and Kate, as Lizzie snuggled deeper into the pillow. Her heavy lids blinked open and shut. The truth would not be revealed tonight. Perhaps tomorrow she would be rested enough to share the story with them.

Before they returned to help tidy the kitchen, Anne slipped a sheet of paper under Lizzie's pillow, extending far enough for Lizzie to see. "A letter from home. The first one we received after Kate came. If she wakes while we are gone, the letter may ease her homesickness."

Kate stiffened.

Julia knelt beside the bed. She needed to ease her own homesickness. In spite of the dim light, Father's familiar handwriting jumped out from the page. She drew in a deep breath.

My dear children,

We received your kind and welcome letter on the 3rd. It gave us great pleasure to hear you were well as this leaves us here, thank God for it. Dear Kate, we were happy to hear you arrived safe in St. Louis. We were sorry to hear that John Doran did not go with you. There was a letter from him about a fortnight ago. He is with the Doyles of Ballynard in Laurence. His father and mother were sorry he did not go with you to St. Louis.

Dear Kate, all the boys have left this place and gone to Liverpool. Thomas Murphy is gone to sea with Captain Connors. John Dunne is gone to Gorey, so this is a lonesome place now. I hope it won't be long until we all will be together in St. Louis.

We are sorry to tell you Dr. Cartin died a week ago. My dear children, we are happy in having you three together so contented and I hope you will not think hard in sending a little in the next letter. The money you sent was hardly enough to fit her out, the passage was so high at that time. It is but 5 guineas now. Mr. Hogan—

Kate knelt down beside Julia and squeezed her arm so hard the letter dropped to the floor. Poor Kate, she could not bear to hear even a few words from home. If only, something could be done to help her.

Julia placed an arm around Kate. As they rose together and headed for the stairs, she searched Lizzie's face, one last time. Sweet and angelic. What dreadful secret lurked beneath that dear countenance?

Chapter Seven

I have taken a day off from my duties at St. Vincent's to visit my family at their farm, just outside of the city limits—

Julia placed Father Burns's note on her desk, as Father Ryan entered the office.

"Prepare yourself, Julia. I'm taking advantage of Father Burns's absence today." He sent a sly smile her way. "I hope you will forgive me."

Julia smiled at the younger of the two priests. "Nothing to forgive. We should all be thanking you instead, Father, the parishioners, the poor immigrants and war refugees and the Irish Benevolent Society."

"Well, I've concluded that if we wish to provide aid to the poor folks arriving at our mission in ever increasing numbers, we must be organized." He chuckled. "I developed a plan requiring a complete inventory of the goods available in the storage area." He aimed a pleading look directly at her. How could she say no?

"Your project will be just what I need." Julia retrieved her handbag. "The physical exertion will push all worried thoughts of Lizzie from my mind. And, an updated inventory of the storeroom supplies will be a great help to the workers and the Benevolent Society." She followed Father Ryan out of the office and paused to lock the door.

When they reached the small supply area, Julia inspected the place with a critical eye. Shelves lined three sides of the room. Two long tables placed in the middle of the floor occupied most of the remaining space. Beneath a layer of dust, supplies filled all surfaces. When had the place become so unkempt?

While Julia collected her inventory lists, Father Ryan placed sacks of beans on a corner of the table. "Twenty-two."

She noted the number on her list then lifted the scrub bucket.

Father Ryan took it from her. "The soapy water will smear your inventory." He cleaned the emptied shelves, and she dried.

"It is an impossible task to keep this area tidy. The place could never be described as anything other than a cellar." Julia brushed dirt from her sleeves.

After they refilled the shelves, she found a broom in the corner and swept the floor. Best not to identify most of this waste.

"I enjoyed the fine supper at Dempsey's last evening." Father Ryan took the heavy trash basket from her and headed out the door. He propped the door open with the empty basket. "Your young sister is a fine girl. I know you are happy she's come."

"We are all thrilled. Poor Lizzie, she was so weary. She could say but a few words last night before falling asleep. I look forward to having another talk with her this evening."

"And the Dempseys can use her help in the shop." Father Ryan rearranged the tables in the center of the room. "Lizzie's arrival is a grand thing for everyone."

While he cleaned, Julia straightened the shelves and reviewed her lists until she was satisfied the inventory was complete.

"I did not realize you were such a scrubber." Julia laughed, and he joined in with her. "You managed the hardest work while I've made lists and such. The task has taken longer than I imagined. You will be too late for lunch."

"Sure, I will find something in the mission kitchen." Father Ryan stored the mop, broom, and bucket in the corner. "I thank you, Julia. You've been a magnificent help. The kitchen workers will be thrilled with your supply lists. I hope I've not made you late for the bakery."

"When I describe our project to Mary, she will understand. She loves nothing more than a clean, organized room." Julia removed her apron and washed her hands. "Tomorrow, I'll help your kitchen workers draw up a supply order."

"That's grand." Father Ryan closed the door behind them. "For now, you must be off to Dempsey's."

"Good day, Father."

❈ ❈ ❈

Julia trudged up the hill toward the bakery, with slower steps than usual. Exhaustion nagged at her, though her small exertion in the storeroom paled in comparison to Lizzie's difficult weeks of travel. Would she be rested today? Would her recuperation—

"Wait, Julia. I'll walk with you."

"Ah, Grace, I'm happy to see you." Julia waved to her friend. "With my mind occupied with my sister, I did not notice you approaching. Come along. We will climb the hill together and have a nice talk."

"You are later than usual, Julia." Grace struggled with a small handbag, a huge shopping basket, and an ungainly cardboard carton.

Julia took the carton from her. "You are looking well, Miss Donahoo. Is that a new dress?"

"It is, and I have your Kate to thank for it. With yard goods still scarce in the shops, I cannot imagine how she found this nice cloth." Grace's cheeks glowed as she touched her sleeve with her free hand. "It is the most beautiful dress I've ever owned."

"It looks lovely on you." Julia gave Grace an appreciative nod. In the past few years, the girl had worn drab, ill-fitting clothing and allowed her hair to hang limp and lifeless. Now, dressed smartly in a Kate Carty creation, she had transformed from a drab shadow into brightness and color.

"Thank you." Grace smiled at Julia. A truly rare occurrence.

Julia examined the blonde waves spilling from Grace's cap. "Have you changed your hair?"

"Well, not me, exactly. Ellen considers herself an artist with hair styles. She taught me how to arrange it." Grace turned, showing Julia the side and back of her head. She had brushed it to a grand shine and looped the once limp strands at her ears and neck. Erect posture and a look of confidence replaced her former slouching walk and gloomy manner.

"You look marvelous." Julia dipped toward her in a slight curtsey. "With your grand new style and your success as Dempsey's cook, you have carved out an entire new life for yourself. I am pleased for you, Grace."

"It is more the help from everyone at Dempsey's." Grace's shoulders rose another inch. "When Will cast me off and married another, I thought I would never recover from the blow. But, it is difficult to remain sad at Dempsey's."

"How right you are. I always look forward to returning to the warm atmosphere at Dempsey's." Julia turned a raised eyebrow toward Grace. "So, Missy, what brings you to St. Vincent's on this glorious summer day?"

"An errand for Mary." Grace held her chin up, rather than ducking it, as in times past. "She baked a cake for Father Burns, in thanks for some favor or other. I volunteered to deliver it. Though it is a warm day, I could not resist stretching my legs and breathing the fresh air."

"And thus, the empty carton." Julia jiggled the box.

"Father Burns has gone away for the day—I suppose you knew that. So, the housekeeper promised to guard the cake carefully until he returns." A little grin crept along Grace's jaw.

Julia shook her head in wonder. Was this truly their Grace, smiling and chatting?

"Your Lizzie is a grand girl." Grace's expression became wistful. "I love hearing her laugh. She reminds me of the girls we left behind in Blackwater."

"The sound of home in her voice sends a thrill though me, too." Julia slowed as they approached Dempsey's. "Have you seen her today? She was fast asleep, when I left this morning."

Grace shook her head. "She came down just before I left the bakery. We managed time for a 'hello' and no more."

Once inside, Julia blinked. Lizzie stood at a table in the back of the shop, looking for the entire world as if she owned the place. Where was the bashful child she left behind in Ireland? And, who was this charming creature standing before her now?

"Ah, Julia and Grace, here you are." Lizzie gestured toward the table set for tea. "We were only waiting for you to come join us."

How wonderful to see her looking relaxed and cheerful. Julia drew closer. Ah dear, that awful dress. Kate must see to her right away.

Mary appeared through the back entryway balancing a tray that held a teapot and cups. "You are in good time."

Lizzie placed the cups out on the table. "You must sit with us, Grace. And why don't we inquire if Kate will join us?"

Julia could not suppress a giggle. Lizzie had, indeed, taken full charge.

"Ah, no, I cannot," Grace waved her hands in front of her. "I must rush to finish my dinner preparations."

"Please stay." Julia borrowed Father Ryan's pleading look.

"Yes, Grace, our teatime will not be the same without you," Lizzie held Grace's fluttering hands.

"Ah no." Grace shook her head. "I must tend to my work."

"Well then, take some tea along with you." Mary placed two cups on the tray. "And, here's cake for you and Cara."

Grace opened her mouth. "I—"

"Now, I'll not hear another word." Mary patted her cheek. Moments later, Grace headed toward the kitchen, the tray piled high with desserts.

While Lizzie placed slices of cake on their plates, Julia ran to fetch Kate from her shop. At last, they settled around the table.

"Last evening's supper would constitute a week's food back home, perhaps two." Lizzie shook her head, her braid bouncing. "It is impossible to obtain these little sweets, or the ingredients to bake them. Even folks who possess the means cannot obtain the goods. Last Christmas, our meal consisted of boiled potatoes. As a special treat, we shared a loaf of bread."

"Have the potatoes gone bad again this summer?" A scowl crept over Kate's face.

"There are none left. Turnips or cabbage have been the usual fare." Lizzie bowed, but not before revealing her bereft expression. "It seems wrong to sit here and enjoy this delicious fare."

"Ah, child." Mary leaned forward. "They are in a sad state. Don't we all worry and fret because they are hungry? We will bring them here to this land of plenty as soon as we can do it. Meanwhile, eat and regain your strength. You will do no good at all if you fall ill."

Julia frowned. What words could she add to this advice? "Listen to our Mary, Lizzie. She has guided us well these many years."

"I know you are right, but it's been heavy on me." Lizzie pulled out her handkerchief and dabbed at her tears. "Our dear ones are working hard in the cottage and the field, and they are hungry. Oh my! And I not there to help them." She shut her eyes tightly.

Julia reached across the table and squeezed Lizzie's hand.

Keeper of Trust

"Our parents' lone pleasure in this life is knowing their daughters are flourishing in America. If they could see your wonderful lives, it would give them even greater joy."

Lizzie rested her gaze on Kate. "If their actions now fall below our expectations, we must remember hunger has taken the strength of purpose they once possessed. They give a large share of their own food to our Michael to strengthen him for his hard work."

Julia rubbed her finger along Lizzie's pale cheek. "I will not stop, until you smile."

In a moment, Lizzie grinned up at Julia. "Our little Maggie is a good child—almost twelve now—quiet, serious, and eager to please."

Julia blew softly on the hot tea. Hearing Lizzie's glowing account of their baby sister was fine, but what their brother?

"Michael is a fine, unselfish person. He remains strong and patient in the face of hopelessness." At last, she has spoken of him. "His friends have all left the country, and he longs to come here. He labors over the crops. Father provides what help he can, but each year the blight and the weather conspire against them."

Julia turned to Mary. "Do you remember when Anne and I worried over whether Michael was old enough to come to America on his own? That was no more than two years ago."

Mary draped her arm around Julia's shoulders. "I do remember. From what Lizzie is saying, I would surmise he has matured nicely."

Julia nudged Kate. "It is amazing, is it not?"

When Kate favored them all with a smile, Julia hugged her. How wonderful. Lizzie's praise for Michael and Maggie brought joy to Kate. Had she still left something out? Something about Michael seemed enveloped in trouble and secrecy.

"Mother's hands have stiffened, and yet she sews every moment she can. Yard goods are scarce, though. The village shop closed, and everyone must travel to Enniscorthy or Hogan's, only to discover scant supplies on the shelves there. Shopkeepers hold little hope of receiving provisions from Dublin or Cork. I suppose Hogan's will need fewer children workers. That is a blessing perhaps, but a twisted one."

Two women entered the shop. Julia motioned to them to remain seated. "Go on with your talk. I'll be listening."

"Well, Aunt Mary did finally produce passage money." Lizzie lowered her voice. "I packed my trunk and stood ready to travel to Cork and board the ship." A frown appeared now. "The money only paid the fare from Cork to Boston. I did not wish to leave them with additional debt, but Father and Michael insisted I must go. With me already here, Michael reasoned he could follow that much sooner. In the end, Father borrowed the funds to send me on to St. Louis."

"Do not worry, Lizzie." Julia waved to her customers as they left the shop and returned to the table. Had additional fare money been the source of Lizzie's concerns? "We will send Father and Michael what they need to satisfy the debt. We sisters have practiced saving passage money. We will manage it again."

"They will, Lizzie." Mary picked up her napkin from the floor. "Your three sisters are the hardest working girls and the most successful at saving their coins I have ever known."

"Oh, I am relieved to hear it. Thank you so much." Lizzie's frown softened. She lifted the teapot and added warm tea to each cup.

"You remember, Julia, how we all gave Mother a hard way about her demands for cleanliness?" She handed the sugar bowl to Kate.

"I do." Julia rubbed the butter dish across the table in a scrubbing motion. "It was our life."

Lizzie shifted in her chair. "Poor though we were, Mary, Mother insisted we make sufficient soap to scrub ourselves, our clothing, and our home. She required us to be spotless under even the worst possible conditions. My disgraceful appearance when I arrived in St. Louis would have shamed her."

"It's because she has strong daughters to haul her water to the house." Kate jumped up and paced the floor. "If Mother hauled her own water buckets and did her own scrubbing, her standards would be less rigorous." She walked back to them, sat beside Lizzie, and tapped her spoon on the table in a steady beat.

Julia raised her cup to hide a grin. Kate's description of their mother was truer to the mark than she dared admit.

"She certainly relaxed those standards when she sent us to work at Hogan's, to sleep in the dirt and eat from bowls we cleaned without soap or warm water." Kate fidgeted, grinding her heel into the floor.

Lizzie stilled Kate's knee. "Mother has never been to Hogan's. She would not have allowed us to live there if she had seen the shop for herself. The only way she could justify persuading Father to send us to work at the filthy place is to pretend all is well. You know she seldom ventures from the house, except to walk the few yards to church."

Kate tapped her spoon again. Julia reached out to draw her close, but she pulled away.

"Sure, she would be pleased to live here at Dempsey's, would she not?" Lizzie's voice quivered as she looked toward Kate. "Mother would love the water pump back in the oven room. Imagine, water flowing right into the building."

Kate stiffened.

"The fine group seated around the table last evening surprised me." Lizzie circled her teacup along the tablecloth.

Julia allowed herself a long, slow sip of tea. At last, a more pleasant subject.

Lizzie focused her attention on Mary. "Sure, I know Ned Duff, and while we were schoolmates, he spoke of his brother James. Last evening, I observed James, carefully. What a fine husband he is for our Anne, and how happy they are together. 'Tis grand."

"We all love James." Mary took Lizzie's hand. "He is a wonderful man."

Lizzie slipped a generous portion of cake in her mouth. "Mmm, delicious. How do you stay so thin, Julia?" She reached for another bite.

Mary grinned. "She stays busy."

"I do not remember Grace Donahoo and Bridget Rice, and here they are both Blackwater girls. I will soon come to know all of your friends." A twinkle appeared in Lizzie's eyes. "With the matches all around us, last evening seemed patterned after a novel. The scene at the supper table unfolded as a stage play might proceed, though I never attended such a thing myself."

"Whatever do you mean, Lizzie?" Julia cut a second helping of cake for everyone. Kate nudged her slice away, but when Julia waved the wonderful cinnamon cake beneath her nose, she accepted the plate.

Lizzie placed her fork on the table. "You and Martin Tobin, of course, Julia. Are you courting or betrothed?" She chuckled. "He appears to be a fine man…I am so happy for you."

As Lizzie leaned across the table and planted a kiss right on her nose, Julia's cheeks warmed. While she had whispered a little of her secret to Kate last evening, she assumed Lizzie had been sleeping soundly.

"Oh, I—"

"Eddie and Grace make a fine match, too." Lizzie folded her hands on the table. Was she pretending not to notice her discomfiture? "Am I not correct in guessing a particular glance passed between those two?"

Julia and Mary exchanged looks. Kate frowned and shook her head, but Lizzie laughed out loud.

"Ellen is a beautiful girl, and did I not notice the special smile she bestowed upon Martin's brother, Patrick? Well I am sure of that one." Lizzie tugged at her chin and shrugged confidently. "I could see it at first glance."

"Eddie and Grace," Mary said. "How have we not seen it? Ellen and Patrick?"

"Could it be?" Julia reached under Lizzie's cap and tugged at her braid. "Or, my little sister, have you come here in search of romance?"

"Perhaps it takes fresh eyes to discover these things." She stood and curtsied to each of them.

Julia placed an arm across Lizzie's shoulders. "I have missed so much of your growing up time at home. I am only now learning what a tease you are."

"A mischief maker." Kate scrunched her lips at Lizzie.

"Well, now that I am here, Kate," Lizzie giggled, "we will move right to work on no less grand husbands for the two of us."

"Will I not be involved in your scheme as well?" Mary placed a hand on each hip, as she rose from the table.

Julia beamed. What a wonderful moment. Mary, who never stopped working, taking time to laugh with them. Lizzie, only one day in St. Louis, seemed ready to lead the entire show. Even poor, troubled Kate, if only for a while, forgot her sadness and laughed along with them. How God had blessed them.

❦ ❦ ❦

That evening, Julia found Lizzie sitting in a chair drawn up to the attic room desk. "Shall I help you unpack your trunk?"

"Sure, that would be grand." Lizzie pushed her pen and paper aside. "I do need some fresh clothing." She moved to the trunk and pulled out a handful of garments.

While she worked with enthusiasm, the dark circles around Lizzie's eyes and her pallid skin revealed her weariness. Julia sighed. Surely, the warm atmosphere and fine food at Dempsey's would restore her.

Julia sorted and folded the clothing and arranged them on the bed. The stacks grew until she had covered the entire quilt. "Where did these garments come from? And why did you arrive in St. Louis wearing a dress that could best be described as ragged?" She cringed. She should have held that comment back. "Could you not have chosen something from this array of fresh, new things?"

"The clothing came as a surprise, to be sure." Lizzie sat, her eyes steady as though lost in deep thought. "Imagine the scene back home. I packed my trunk, dressed, and waited for Aunt Mary and Mr. Walsh to transport me to Cork. The entire family gathered around to say goodbye. Suddenly, Aunt Mary burst into the cottage, her arms filled with garments. Without even a word of greeting, she shouted for me to load them into the trunk. In the next moment, she rushed back out the door and returned immediately, laden with another armload of clothing."

Julia gasped. "This trunk, filled with clothing, sat in the attic for two days, its treasures unknown to everyone but you?"

Lizzie shrugged. "Aunt Mary declared her husband was at the ready with his carriage and insisted we must not keep him waiting. I managed to slip a few dresses aside for Mother and Maggie. Then, while I bid a brief final farewell to everyone, Aunt Mary placed the rest in the trunk, and latched it." Lizzie ran her fingers along the lid. "When I boarded the ship at Cork, the trunk was sent on ahead of me. This is my first opportunity to examine the clothing."

Julia shook her head. "Where did Aunt Mary obtain this large supply? And, why did she send it to America with you, rather than share the goods with her poor neighbors? You know, charitable groups all over America are organizing drives to collect food and clothing for destitute folks in Ireland."

"I understand, but I hold no answers. You do remember Aunt Mary's skill at the loom. Her work keeps her in high demand. Merchants and villagers alike offer money, food, or whatever they possess in exchange for her hand-woven cloth. I suppose she read accounts of shortages of goods in America since the war. And have you forgotten her independent spirit? Somehow, she finds her own way."

Julia lifted a shirtwaist from the bed. She examined the cloth, expelling a quick breath then took up a skirt.

"As we rode along toward Cork, I pleaded with Aunt Mary to give Mother any superfluous garments or materials. I reminded her our mother could make over a frock of any size for Maggie or exchange it with a neighbor for food or other things our family needs so desperately." Lizzie shut the lid of the now-empty trunk. "Since I knew I'd not likely see her again, I admit I spoke boldly."

"I cannot imagine that." Julia twisted a curl from Lizzie's once-perfect braid. "You are the kindest, sweetest girl in the world."

"Well, thank you, but I was pretty stern with Aunt Mary. I said I knew our mother was not her favorite person and begged her to look past those feelings and consider Michael and Maggie." Lizzie shook her head. "I believe Aunt Mary took my words in the right spirit. She agreed to do what she could for the family. I only pray she does not forget her promise. She sometimes moves at a rapid pace and looks past the hardships of her family and friends."

"You have done your best, Lizzie." Julia held a serviceable brown dress in front of her. "We will keep good thoughts about Aunt Mary."

"What will we do with all of these things?" Lizzie waved her arm across the array of garments on the bed.

"One of these fine, sensible dresses will do well for each of the girls at Dempsey's. And we could donate some of the clothing to the mission, if you agree."

"Let's stack mission garments on the chair in front of the window." Lizzie moved another assortment of dresses to the top of the trunk. "We'll set these aside for the other Dempsey girls to choose from. I'll place the few that would be suitable for us on an empty shelf in the wardrobe."

"Kate has cloth at her disposal, and with her sewing ability, she will have little need for these things. Still, I am sure she would enjoy a garment woven by Aunt Mary's hand." Julia handed Lizzie an elegant gown. "What do you think of this deep, green? Shall I set it aside for her?"

"That is a fine choice for Kate," Lizzie positioned herself in front of the small mirror. "You are right. It is likely all she will want. You and I and Anne, though, would be happy to have a change of blouse or skirt to wear. And, the thought of a new set of undergarments sets my heart to humming." She took up a handful of lacy cloth and waltzed around the room.

"You must select a suitable dress or two for work in the shop, Lizzie." Julia smiled at her little sister. "I will find my scissors. We'll have a go at cutting that dreadful garment you have been wearing into squares for Cara's rag bin." She rummaged through the desk drawer.

Lizzie crossed her arms in front of her. "Wait, I'll change to my nightgown, before you cut my dress away."

Julia rejoiced at Lizzie's laughter. They could use lighter moments here in the attic room.

"I first considered Aunt Mary's gift a foolish gesture, but it was a thoughtful one after all." Julia avoided Lizzie's gaze as her laugh dissolved into a cough.

A pretty, blue nightgown lay among the clothing still on the bed. Julia handed it to her sister. Once Lizzie changed and settled into the pillows, the cough eased and turned to yawns.

What could she say to keep her awake until Kate arrived? She wished to tell her sisters the details of Martin's proposal while they were together.

"I'll brush your hair for you." She unwound Lizzie's long braid, and taking great care, worked out the tangles. "You look weary. I pray a few nights of rest will restore you and ease that cough."

Lizzie only nodded.

What was keeping Kate? If only she would hurry. Julia eyed the pillow where she and Anne had tucked the letter.

"Since word from home seems to cause Kate pain, I've hidden the letters away. Let us read through one, or at least a part of it, before she comes. She pulled the stack from beneath the bed. "Here is one from last winter."

My dear children,

We received your kind letter yesterday and we were happy to hear you were well as this leaves us at present. Thanks be to God.

Dear Anne, we are in great trouble about Kate and I want to know the reason neither you nor Julia spoke of her in your letter. We were expecting Kate would send us a little help this hard summer. I hope she will not forget her father and mother. Nell Carty

"The next part is in Michael's hand." Julia passed the sheet to Lizzie. "These firm, bold strokes are his, are they not?"

Lizzie examined the page and smiled.

Dear sister, I expect to see you and Anne and her husband in St. Louis in short, the passage is very low now. It is only about #5 from Queenstown to New York. Lizzie is eager to come out with me. She says if you three would join and bring her out with me in the fall, it is the best time to go, so we would be in for the winter. We could go in the spring and be in for the summer but would be in danger of sickness and also the passage is so low in the fall and

> *then so many will be going in the spring which also makes it high. That is all at present. Michael Carty*

"And now, I believe this is mother's hand." Julia held out another page for Lizzie. "Sometimes it is impossible to tell who is writing."

> *Dear Anne, I am sorry to inform you that your Aunt Margaret Read is dead since the 2nd of this month, and Joseph is in jail. I need say no more about the Reads. Until I go to America, you need not mention one of them in your letter. Dear Anne tell Kate that Mr. and Mrs. Hogan and family wish to be remembered to her. Bridget Malone is at Hogan's. Lizzie got sick and she was not able to stay in it. We never can forget Mrs. Hogan.*

Kate walked through the doorway, as Julia folded the letter and inserted it into the envelope.

Julia held her breath. This moment could not be blemished by Kate's ill humor. She held her own precious tale in her heart for nearly three days. Only a few whispered words slipped out to Kate. But now, together, in the privacy of their attic room, she would allow neither distraction nor weariness to delay the telling of the wonderful, beautiful story of her engagement.

Chapter Eight

September, 1866

The sun gentled and the days melted away, each more delightful than the last. On an evening two weeks after Martin left the army and began his new job, Julia sat with him on Dempsey's porch enjoying the pleasant night air.

"We are fortunate to have this time alone, on such a fine, cool evening." Julia pushed back the curls the breeze had freed from their pins. "And to think you'll not be required to rush back to the Army base."

"Where is everyone tonight?" Martin stretched his legs along the cobblestone steps. "I would have suggested a walk, but we have privacy right here."

"They will be along shortly. For now, we can enjoy the clear night air and the scent of the few remaining flowers on our own." The porch spanned the passage connecting the two buildings that made up Dempsey's bakery. Mary's small flower garden separated it from the road running along side of the buildings. Two small boys played out front, kicking a tin can back and forth. No one else was in sight.

Martin cleared his throat. "I wished to say..." He coughed. "I feel confident...I will be able to handle the Omnibus job."

Her spirits soared. If he felt secure in his job, it could be their new beginning. "The horses are behaving themselves, are they? I suppose the cooler temperature is better for them."

"I've had no problems at all. My training at school has served me well." Martin rose from the steps and stood before her.

A few seconds passed. She glanced at her shiny new shoes then raised up and smiled.

"And, the huge, heavy bus, holding so many passengers, is it difficult to maneuver? I cannot imagine how you control the entire business all at once." She searched his face. Was he harboring any concern at all? It didn't seem so.

"After a few days, I adjusted to the rhythm of the horses and the weight of the wagon." Martin knelt beside her on the porch and steadied himself against her arm. "The bosses tell me I am a suitable driver. The other fellows assure me this is grand praise. They say the bosses never compliment anyone."

"Ah, Martin, I am so proud of you." The touch of his warm skin sent a shiver through her. Why had she ever held reservations about his ability with the horses? She leaned close and rested her cheek against his.

"I promise you, I will continue to seek employment more suited to my training." Martin lifted her hand and brushed her fingertips across his lips. "Until that perfect situation comes my way, I will be satisfied with the Omnibus position. I've figured the costs of housing, food, and our other needs. My salary, along with the funds I saved over the war years, will be ample to care for you." He placed his arm across her shoulder and sat, drawing her closer than before. "Let us set the date for our wedding."

"Oh, my dear." She blinked, but her cheeks still grew damp. "You have planned for our every possible need and expense. I am pleased and proud to be betrothed to such a thoughtful, considerate man."

"Thank you for your faith in me, Julia." Martin ran a finger along her cheek and wiped away the last of her tears.

"No obstacle rests in our path. We should not wait any longer." She shifted away from Martin a few inches. "If Father

Burns' schedule allows it, we could speak with him tomorrow evening."

❊ ❊ ❊

After Martin left, Julia rushed up to the attic, skipping a step and nearly toppling. "Kate! Lizzie!" She ran through the doorway and tossed her shawl on the bed.

"What is it, Julia?" Lizzie pulled pins from Kate's hair and lined them in a long row across the top of the writing table.

"Is something wrong?" Kate turned, the sudden movement causing her dark hair to spill free.

"I am so happy you are here, Kate. I wished to tell you and Lizzie together." Julia took in a deep breath. "Martin's Omnibus job is going well. We plan to meet with Father Burns tomorrow and set the date for our wedding."

Lizzie rushed to sit beside Julia. "And to think I only guessed at a romance between you and Martin. I never expected a wedding so soon after my arrival. Oh my! I am thrilled for you." She beamed at Julia. "'Tis wonderful, indeed."

"Well, I'm not at all surprised. You have shared stories of the progression of your courtship all along. I extend best wishes to you and Martin. I know you will have a happy life together." Kate patted Julia's shoulder.

"Tell me what it was like when you planned Anne's wedding. Did you discuss the details right here in the attic room?" Lizzie moved to the wardrobe and searched the lower shelves.

"We talked of little else but the wedding for over a year." Kate pulled a nightgown from beneath her pillow. "What are you looking for, Lizzie?"

"I discovered a length of white cloth…oh, here it is." Lizzie took the folded material from the bottom shelf and moved toward Julia. "I thought we could talk about a wedding dress." She held the silky fabric in front of her. "Oh Kate, I did not think… you will likely create a gown for our lovely bride."

"I do wish Anne was here this evening. I am a little worried about her." Julia held out her arms and allowed Lizzie to drape the long cloth around her shoulders. "She does not seem her usual, unruffled self. You know, Lizzie, before her marriage, Anne spent evenings in this little room, dreaming along with Kate and I of what our future lives would hold. Now, grand developments are happening in my life, and I have been unable to talk any of it over with her."

"I noticed nothing amiss," Kate said. "Perhaps a new bonnet would cheer her. Or, I could make a small handbag similar to the one I made for you, Julia."

"I intended to visit her today, but I was still too weary for even a short walk." Lizzie jumped up from the bed. "I will go tomorrow. A nice chat will lift her spirits."

Julia nodded. "Fine suggestions, but...." She closed her eyes for a moment. How had Anne looked at Lizzie's party? Even with the excitement, she'd appeared quieter than usual. "We must do something to change this situation. We would never wish to cause our dear Anne a moment's unhappiness."

❃ ❃ ❃

The numbers of immigrants arriving at the mission had grown each week since the end of the war. Julia's work at St. Vincent's increased as well. Several busy days passed, before she felt confident she had brought her workload under control. Surely, the priests would not miss her for an hour or two, while she visited Anne.

"Julia, how are you keeping today?" Anne greeted her with a grand smile and all but pulled her into her kitchen. She rushed to place the teapot on the stove.

Julia removed her shawl and draped it across the back of a chair. "I'm sure you already know Martin secured a position."

"I did hear that from James." Anne brushed back her already-perfect hair and smoothed her skirt. "What are you and Martin planning?"

Julia set out cups, silverware, and napkins. "We have arranged the date for our wedding. It will be on June 29."

A grand smile beamed across Anne's face. She opened her arms, and Julia rushed to receive her hug.

"While Martin trains for his position, his salary will not be substantial." She sat at one end of Anne's long kitchen table and watched her sister prepare tea. "We will rent a small apartment, and save toward a place of our own."

A low, insistent whistle erupted from the stove, and Anne rushed toward it, towel in hand.

"Since arriving in St. Louis, we have certainly become practiced at saving, have we not? Well, of course, you and Kate are much better than I." Julia held up her right hand, palm extended toward Anne. "Rest assured, I will continue to contribute to our immigration fund."

"I know you will, Julia." Anne placed the kettle on the stove and reached out for another hug. "I am so happy for you, dear." She returned to pouring their tea.

"Remember when we sat together in the attic room and dreamed of our weddings? At times, we doubted it would happen for either of us. Now..." A flick of a frown crossed her face. "Tell me what you and Kate and Lizzie have been talking about. Are you planning the wedding already?"

Rather than sit beside Julia, Anne moved to a shelf across from the table and pulled out a paper and pencil. "Now...about your betrothal celebration."

"At Dempsey's?" A tremor passed through Julia to see Anne's clenched jaw. Had she further upset her sister?

"Oh, Julia. Please do not tell me Mary made plans already."

"We have not yet discussed the wedding with Walter and Mary," Julia said. "You know how our Mary is, though. She talked of a menu as soon as Martin secured a position."

"I understand a Dempsey betrothal supper is a custom. I only hoped for the privilege this time." Anne tapped the pencil on the table, slowly, quietly. "I prayed Mary would relinquish the honor. Since we moved into this house, I have dreamed of hosting a celebration for you and Martin."

"That is kind of you. Perhaps, if you talk it over with Mary?"

"I am not at all kind." The usually calm, composed Anne's lip quivered. "Oh dear! I have become apprehensive and silly. Since I relented and agreed Lizzie could live with Walter and Mary, I am forever imagining your grand conversations. It feels I miss out on everything. I wish you were all here with me. You see. I am selfish."

Julia dragged her chair along the table, right beside Anne. "Of course, you are not selfish. The girl who cast her own life aside to save every dollar for passage money for our family? The sister who delayed her wedding and placed her own happiness in jeopardy to bring our family to America? Hah! I refuse to even listen to such talk."

Anne pulled a handkerchief from her pocket. She blew her nose, sniffled, and blew again.

"I would be thrilled to hold our celebration here." Julia rose and took Anne's hand. "We could talk to Mary together? Perhaps you could join forces to work on the meal. Our dear Mary will happily follow your wishes in this."

Julia linked her arm with Anne's and pulled her through the hallway toward the front of the house, stopping beneath the archway leading to the dining room. "Just see your magnificent green walls and matching draperies, and imagine the gas lights flickering and candles glowing everywhere. Would it not be a grand setting for the occasion? This long dinner table will hold the entire group from Dempsey's."

"It is one of my favorite rooms." Anne brushed her fingers across the drapes. "And, you are right. Mary is most understanding. She may have foreseen I would wish to host your betrothal supper. Please, forgive my foolishness." She rubbed a few remaining tears away. "I will discuss it with her tomorrow."

"That is best. But I must ask why, besides my engagement party, is my strong, brave sister at the point of tears?"

Anne lowered her head for a moment, raising it again to reveal brilliant pink cheeks. "I suspect…I am carrying a child, but I am not yet certain." She waved her hand in front of her face. "Ah, that is not so. Of course, I am sure."

"Oh, Anne, what thrilling news." A rapid patting commenced in Julia's heart and progressed to a steady thump. She had only meant to tease. "Are we not allowed to celebrate, to sing and dance and cheer?" Her brows drew together. "Are you well?"

"I am fit. Nothing more than a few mornings of upset. And now, in the last few weeks, I have endured this foolish weepiness." Anne twirled her handkerchief in the air. "I am sure a baby is the cause."

"A baby!" Julia rose from her chair and twirled Anne about in a circle. "A baby!"

"It is our secret, Julia. I have not even told James."

"I will keep your counsel. Will it not be a wonderful thing, though?" Julia hugged Anne. "I will pray for you and James. But please, tell him right away. He will be proud and happy. And you know I cannot keep a secret for long."

"I intend to tell him tonight." Anne dabbed her forehead with the handkerchief.

"Why, Anne, dear, you are pink." Julia cupped her sister's chin. "Surely you are not embarrassed to tell James? He is your husband."

"No, not embarrassed. I should have…I have already waited too long." A tear escaped and rolled down Anne's cheek.

Julia brushed it away. "Do not upset yourself one more day. Tell James tonight. He will be relieved it is not him making you weepy. Tell him. You will feel much better."

Anne nodded.

"I have an idea." Julia took up her shawl and wrapped it around her shoulders. "Tonight, I will speak with Mary. Perhaps, we can all discuss the betrothal supper tomorrow. And if you speak with James, both of your concerns will be resolved by morning."

"I will do it." Anne blotted her eyes with her napkin.

"Now, do not worry for even a moment. You and Mary will work this out. You will see. It will be grand. Are there any other earth rattling problems your big sister can solve for you?" Julia inclined her head toward Anne. "If not, I must rush home to help close the shop."

❀ ❀ ❀

Back at Dempsey's, Julia helped Mary ready the bakery for closing and fill the baskets with baked goods for the mission. She held the lid for the long bread basket while Mary latched it.

"I do appreciate your offer to hold a betrothal celebration for Martin and me, but Anne wishes to have it in her home. You know, I have been concerned about her. She imagines we have a constant party here and she is missing out. I hope planning our party will lift her spirits."

"Ah, Julia, I agree." Mary untied Julia's apron and folded it for her. "I love Anne as my own sister. If she wishes to hold the celebration, she should do it. I will assist her, if she will allow it."

"Oh, Mary, thank you. Your kindness has resolved the entire crisis. This is a grand relief for me, and Anne will be thrilled."

If only she and Mary could solve all problems with a quiet talk between them.

❀ ❀ ❀

The next morning, Julia and Mary consulted with Anne, and they settled on the following Saturday evening for the betrothal supper. The week flew by, and before she could blink, Martin had arrived at Dempsey's to escort her to the Duffs' house.

A composed, glowing Anne welcomed them. Displaying not a sign of her earlier weepiness, she ushered them inside. "I have already expressed my happiness to Julia, Martin." Anne slipped her hand in Julia's and then whirled around to take Martin's arm. "I congratulate you, as well. I am pleased to have you for a brother."

"Thank you, Anne. Julia and I appreciate this party." Martin smiled down at Anne, as she led them through the entry hall. "Your home is beautiful and the dining room looks very nice."

"James and I are thrilled for you both. We agree a more deserving couple could not be found in the city—"

A sharp knock interrupted her well wishes. "Oh, excuse me." Anne walked out to the hallway.

Martin closed the space between them. He bent and whispered in her ear. "I love you."

"I love you, too."

Her words were scarcely out before Anne returned with James and the entire group from Dempsey's: Walter, Mary, Kate, Lizzie, Grace, Ellen, Cara, George, and Eddie. A murmur of voices circulated about the room.

"Congratulations, Julia!" Grace moved to her side and whirled her around. "Your dress is lovely."

"Thank you, Grace."

"I am so happy for you," Ellen wrapped Julia in a great hug.

"Martin, Julia, congratulations!" Walter's booming voice filled the room, quieting everyone.

Julia placed her hand over her heart. Could it burst from the joy? She and Martin had waited so long, and now at last, their dream was beginning to unfold.

"Tell us about your wedding plans, Julia." Ellen said.

"We met with Father Burns, and he entered our wedding date, June 29, on the parish calendar."

"How wonderful, that sounds. June 29." Anne glanced at James and they shared a knowing look. "Back home in Blackwater, the posting of a wedding date has always been a serious, solemn act." Laughter and nods of agreement circulated around the table.

Lizzie shook her head. "Could you not schedule it sooner? How will I wait so long? Perhaps a Christmas wedding?"

"Be patient." Julia patted her arm. "Since coming to America, we have all learned to bide our time. We wait for savings to grow and families to join us. And, for wars to come to an end."

"And we survive." Martin's Army uniform had been replaced by a new grey suit. He stood erect, looking confident, as he reinforced Julia's words. "See now what the Duffs' waiting has accomplished. Here they are, after years of striving, settled together in this beautiful home and hosting a celebration in our honor."

Another knock came from the front door. James left and returned with Father Burns and Father Ryan. Bridget Rice and her brother came close behind them, Brendan having received a special invitation from Anne. The room stirred.

Julia covered her face to hide her grin. Brendan would receive a thorough interrogation, just as all the other Irish immigrants had on their arrival. A fresh source of information, and a happy reprieve for poor Lizzie.

In the midst of a shower of questions for Brendan, James answered the door once more. "Welcome, Ned! Patrick!" He led the two men into the room. "Martin, the brothers are here." He laughed. "And here they are, opposites in every way but their Irish heritage and the best of friends."

Martin grinned. "It is true. Who would have imagined your mild-mannered accountant brother and my lively carpenter could have forged such a friendship? Thank you both for coming."

"You and James are daft." Patrick punched his brother's shoulder. "Ned and I walk home the same way, is all."

Finally, they gathered around the Duffs' dinner table. From the gleaming chandelier high above them, tall, flickering candles cast a lovely glow over everyone. Julia's breath caught, as she took her place on James' right. The smiles of the dear faces all around the table filled her with warmth. How could she not shout out with joy? She pressed her lips together and sat quietly.

Father Burns offered a prayer of thanksgiving: "Dear Lord, we thank you for gathering us together this evening. We ask for your blessings upon Julia and Martin."

"Amen!" came from everyone around the table.

Father Ryan followed with his own brief prayer. Julia bowed her head and prayed along silently. How blessed she was to receive their kind intercessions.

Though Walter had taken "the pledge" and never touched a drop himself, he had donated wine for this special occasion. When he and James had filled the goblets all around, their host moved to the head of the table and raised his glass.

"Health and happiness to Martin and Julia!"

Calls of *"Slainte!"* resounded around the table. Best wishes and long life. Julia could ask for nothing more.

In the midst of the excitement and commotion, another guest slipped quietly into the room. James seated him in an empty spot next to Kate. "This is Francis Reilly, our neighbor, who lives in the corner house across the way."

"Good evening, sir." Kate welcomed him with a bow.

"Good evening." Mr. Reilly leaned forward and extended his hand to Martin then nodded to Julia. "Congratulations to you both."

"Thank you." Julia smiled at him. Dressed neatly in a dark suit and tie, with his hair and beard trimmed, he conducted himself in a gentlemanly manner.

"Tell us about yourself, Mr. Reilly." Lizzie sat back in her chair. Julia observed a look passing between her sister and

Brendan. Were they passing along a share of the questioning to the newcomer?

"I've operated a pub four blocks south of here for a few years. And then, after my military service, I invested my earnings with some business partners in the purchase of a downtown hotel." Mr. Reilly nodded to Lizzie, and then fastened his attention on his plate.

Julia opened her mouth to address him, but he and Kate had begun to converse. As the evening progressed, the two spent the greater part of the time engaged in conversation.

She exchanged a grin with Martin. "Our party is magnificent!" She surveyed the entire scene around the table. Kate speaking seriously with Mr. Reilly, Lizzie's cheeks glowing with excitement, and Anne maintaining a calm demeanor as their guests tasted her wonderful dinner and engaged in conversation.

Anne moved up behind her and placed a basket of bread on the table. "Are you enjoying your betrothal supper?" The smile spread across her sister's face could only be described as joyful.

"I have just pronounced your meal a resounding success. You prepared all of my favorite dishes," Julia spread her arm out to include the entire table.

"Mary worked with me most of the day, helping with the preparations." Anne waved across the table to Mary. "Julia is enjoying our meal."

"Indeed, there was little for me to do." Mary leaned toward them. "Our Anne has become a superb cook."

"It is a grand feast." Walter clapped, and the entire group burst into applause.

"Thank you. It is wonderful to have you all here to honor Julia and Martin." Julia followed Anne's gaze as she turned to her husband. How thrilling to see the look of pride James bestowed on his wife.

Anne bent and whispered in Julia's ear. "I have shared our wonderful secret with James." With a little grin, she moved away. They made no announcement, and Julia had not expected one. Such things were not discussed. It was not done. She sighed. *Lizzie's arrival, her betrothal, a baby…what wonderful blessings the Carty sisters have received.*

Grace entered the room, bearing a magnificent white cake with pink roses strewn across the top. A hush fell across the table. *How confident she looks, holding the platter high for all to admire.*

"Ah Grace," Julia rose, "it is beautiful. I cannot wait to taste your grand dessert."

"Eddie helped me." Grace looked down the table and rested her gaze on the stocky, bushy-haired young man.

"I only stood by." He raised his arm in salute. "The entire creation is Grace's doing. It is a marvelous thing, is it not?" Eddie's face turned red.

"You have done a grand job, my girl," Mary said.

Grace's face glowed.

"I'll help serve." Julia slid back, but Anne pushed her down in the chair.

"You are our guest of honor. Sit right here and enjoy every minute of your celebration."

Julia looked at Martin, and they shared a laugh. "It has been a perfect evening, has it not?"

Martin took her hand. "We owe our friends a world of gratitude. The wonderful food, the wine, the dessert, and our dear ones all gathered to wish us well. Surely, our days will be filled with many such happy moments."

"We will be together, Martin. It will be wonderful."

❀ ❀ ❀

Later, in the attic room, Julia, Kate, and Lizzie sat together on Lizzie's bed. Julia bounced a little. "I know I will not sleep a wink. It was all so delightful."

Lizzie sat with pillows propped around her. "Which was your favorite dish, Julia?"

"Dessert." Julia laughed. "I will never forget Grace holding up that grand cake. Her new self-assurance is wonderful." She held out her hair brush. "Are you too tired to do my hair?"

"Lizzie reached out for the brush. "Of course not. I love helping you."

"I have some news of my own." Kate edged closer to Lizzie. "During the meal, Mr. Reilly and I shared our business experiences. Francis described his expanding enterprises, and I told him of the customers Ellen and I have already acquired. By the end of the party, he hired us to create curtains for the inn's guest rooms and public areas. With an abundance of work ahead, Ellen and I will no longer worry over obtaining enough trade to support two seamstresses."

"Your hard work is reaping rewards," Julia said. "Ellen can put her worry to rest. She will not be forced to return to the garment factory. I am thrilled for you both."

What a magnificent evening. Hopefully, it marked the beginning of a successful business venture for Kate and Ellen, as well as a grand new life for Martin and her.

Chapter Nine

November 20, 1866

On a chilly afternoon, a few weeks after the betrothal supper, Julia arrived back at the shop to find Mary, Cara, and Grace finishing up their planned cleaning. "I'm disappointed." She hung her cloak away. "I rushed through my work this morning, so I could help."

"Ah but, you have not escaped entirely." Mary handed Julia a tray stacked high with bread. "We will accept your help with putting the place back in order and thank you for it. If you will hold this tray for me, I'll return bread to the bins." She climbed the step ladder and moved the loaves from the tray to the top shelf.

"We've not talked of the wedding since breakfast." Mary dropped a napkin over Julia's head. "Have you made any new plans?"

Julia extended her hand to Mary, as she stepped down from the ladder. "I've been thinking about the dress we made together for Anne." She retrieved a second tray and held it while Mary filled the lower shelf. "I believe I could alter it to fit me. I do not think she would mind my wearing it, do you?"

"She will be thrilled to have you wear her lovely dress. I'm sure of it." Mary's expression turned thoughtful. "And, Anne is still in agreement with our plan for the wedding supper?"

"Anne has not changed her mind." Julia wiped the emptied tray with a damp cloth. "Since the betrothal celebration was held at her home, she has given her blessing to the wedding party being here at Dempsey's."

"I consider it an honor that Walter and I will be the hosts for your grand celebration." A twinkle appeared in Mary's eyes. "I must admit I have been regaling everyone who comes in the shop with my plans and preparations for the wedding supper." After she gave the bakery counter a brisk rub, they made a new arrangement of biscuits and rolls along the glass top.

"Things are back in fair order now." Mary tucked the empty trays under her arm and headed for the hallway. "Lizzie will be out here to care for the shop in a few minutes. Why don't you visit Anne and talk the matter of the dress over with her?"

"I thought I would speak to her at church on Sunday." Julia reached under the counter for a bakery apron. "It is only a few days off."

"Aw, go on and see her now. Anne will love the company."

Julia kissed Mary on the cheek. "Thank you. I will only stay a few minutes." A mischievous little grin had spread across Mary's face. Perhaps, she had misjudged her clever friend. Had she guessed the reason Anne had given in to holding the wedding supper at Dempsey's? Did she already suspect her sister would be caring for a newborn infant at the time of the wedding? Though it consumed all the patience she possessed, she had not divulged a word of the secret.

❀ ❀ ❀

In only a few minutes, Julia sat in Anne's kitchen. "Are you well? You look radiant." With the sun shining brightly through the kitchen window, the strong rays beamed down on her sister.

"I am fine, a little sleepy in the evenings, is all." Anne's happy smile spilled forth.

"I have observed one difference in your appearance, you know." Julia reached out to pat Anne's neat bun. "Your hair has turned a bit red."

"James also noticed that." Anne pulled a strand from what had been a perfect hairdo and attempted to pull it across her eyes. "I cannot see it myself, but if you both detect it, I suppose our lovely secret will be out soon."

Julia reached across the table and nudged Anne's arm. "I have been bursting with impatience, but I have not told a soul."

"I am sorry, but you remain the only other person to know our joyous news."

"Could you not tell Kate, Lizzie, and Mary?" Julia pinched Anne's arm. Could the information be squeezed from her? "It is so hard to keep the secret from them."

"I will tell them soon, I promise you."

"My coming here was Mary's idea, you know. And, as I left the bakery, a roguish little smile crept across her face. I must warn you, Mary may suspect something." Julia poured another cup of tea for her sister, watching for her reaction.

"I have taken this responsibility for keeping the secret seriously, Anne, but you do not seem all that concerned that Mary may have guessed it?"

"I am so happy you are here, Julia, nothing could upset me. We do not have opportunities to sit and chat like we did when I lived with you in the attic room at Dempsey's." The petite Anne, dressed in a fitted green dress, made for her by Kate, showed no sign of an expanding waistline. "Let us have our tea and talk of the wedding. I wish to hear every word of it."

"The wedding is the reason I've come." Julia slipped a speck of sugar into her cup. "While Mary and I worked together in the shop this afternoon, we discussed the wedding supper she is planning for us. Then, I mentioned an idea I had recently. I thought perhaps I could wear your wedding dress, if you—"

Julia jumped at the sound of sharp thudding on the front door.

"Mrs. Duff!" A voice boomed. "Mrs. Duff!"

The two girls rushed out to the foyer. "Yes?" Anne opened the door a few inches. A police officer and two older workmen stood on the porch. "What is it, please?" The men grew quiet, as she pulled the door wide, and cast their eyes down at the floor.

"God be praised, but there has been an accident, Missus." The policeman cleared his throat and shuffled his feet, as if waiting for a wave of courage to overtake him. He raised his head. "A gentleman, known to you, a Mr. Tobin, has been hurt."

"Ah no..." Julia clapped a hand across her mouth, but the cry had already escaped.

Anne placed an arm around her shoulder.

"Another gentleman, a Mr. Dempsey, remains with him, kneeling on the ground at his side." The policeman, inhaled sharply and continued. "He asked me to come to you. He said you were friends of the poor fellow."

"Oh Martin! Oh my." Julia's knees grew weak. "Is he badly hurt?"

She ignored the numbness, giving thanks for the burst of strength that filled her. Snatching their wraps from the hall tree, she passed one to her sister. Anne ran to the closet and pulled out two heavy blankets then handed them to the policeman. They rushed out the door, still tugging on their coats, with the men following behind them.

The officer took the lead, holding the blankets in one arm. Julia, Anne and the workmen followed behind him.

"How far is it?" Her voice strengthened, as she walked.

"Just two short blocks." Crossing the second intersection, they encountered a crowd gathered in the square patch marked off for passengers waiting to board an Omnibus.

"Martin!" He lay stretched out in the dirt, unmoving. Julia pressed closer. Walter knelt beside him, talking quietly.

"He is so still. Is he breathing?" A spell of shivering took hold of Julia, making her teeth chatter. She pulled her cloak close around her, but the added warmth had no effect at all.

"He is alive, but his pulse is weak." Walter rose from his kneeling position. "I spoke to him and assured him I would stay right beside him. He appeared to recognize me, but a few minutes later, he lost consciousness." Walter shook his head. "I am surprised to see you, Julia. I had no notion you would be with Anne. I see the hand of God in it."

"They will transport Mr. Tobin along to the hospital as soon as the ambulance arrives." The policeman spoke directly to Julia now. He had stationed himself with his feet planted on either side of Martin's head, attempting to protect him. She drew in a breath. *Please, God, let it not be too late.*

Walter searched the road. "Surely, the wagon will be along soon. We will follow behind them."

"Thank you, Walter." Julia took a blanket from the policeman and knelt beside Martin. Another, thinner sheet covered him, hiding his injury. Placing the heavier blanket over him now, she watched the wool cloth rise and fall with his breaths.

"Aside from the breathing, his body remains motionless." She raised her head and spoke quietly to Anne. "Ah, look now, spots of blood are seeping through the two layers of coverings along the outline of his left arm." Julia pulled the top blanket up to Martin's chin. She restrained herself from crying out, but another great chill seized her already shaking body.

Anne took her hand and held it fast. "I must run back home and leave a note for James." She turned to leave.

"Wait. Stay with Julia. I'll ask someone in the crowd here to direct James to the hospital." Walter moved over to one of the bystanders to make the request.

Julia willed herself to remain calm. She would be no help to Martin if she crumbled to pieces. She longed to gather him in her arms and sooth him. No…he would not wish her to make a public display. She grasped the edge of the blanket and held on tight.

A wagon rolled up and halted a few feet from where Julia knelt. "Step aside, folks. Let us in, please." Two attendants lowered a stretcher to the ground, and several men gathered on either side of Martin. A groan escaped, when they lifted him.

With slow measured steps, the men approached the vehicle. "Careful now. Steady." The ambulance driver directed the men, as they settled Martin in the wagon. Julia felt the warmth from Walter and Anne, hovering close on either side of her.

While the driver fastened the pallet in the wagon bed, Walter climbed inside and knelt beside the handle of the stretcher near Martin's head. Julia's breath caught as he bent and brushed away dust and grime from his face and hair.

"Anne! The blood!" She pointed to the spots seeping through the blankets that had formed into a pool on the floorboards. "Oh my!" Deep red liquid now ran along the floor of the wagon and dripped down into the road.

"Mmgnx." An unintelligible moan escaped from inside the wagon. Was he attempting to call out to her? Leaning in, drawing as close as she could come to him, Julia searched Martin's eyes. She found no spark of recognition. Surely, he had slipped into unconsciousness.

"What is his condition?" She directed her question to the ambulance driver, but occupied with securing the stretcher, he shook his head and gave no answer.

Walter eased from the wagon and stood with the girls, while they watched the men minister to Martin.

"Do you know what happened?" Anne voiced the question that had been whirling through Julia's mind.

"I came upon the scene only a few minutes before you girls arrived," Walter said. "Some bystanders told me Martin had been struck by an Omnibus. No one around seems to hold any additional information. I'm sure we'll learn more, once we arrive at the hospital."

"He is so still. If only, he will be all right." Julia concentrated her thoughts on Martin, pushing back the panic creeping around her. She commanded herself to be calm, but she could not will the shaking away. Walter removed his jacket, and Anne helped him wrap the fine wool over Julia's own coat. The shivering slowed.

❊ ❊ ❊

At the hospital, a short time later, Walter arranged chairs in front of a window in the waiting room. "We will be comfortable right here. Perhaps the brilliant rays of the sun shining through the windows will warm you, Julia." He settled the girls in the chairs and started for the door. "I must find someone to dispatch a message to the bakery and inform Mary. She will wish to know what happened."

"Oh my, yes. I promised her I would be gone only a short while. I am sure she is worried about what has become of me." Where Julia had taken no notice before, the white walls appeared all around them and the dark wooden floors, jumped toward her, polished to a gleaming finish.

Trapped in the throes of a dark, thunderous mental cloud, a few blinks cleared her senses long enough to remember Martin's brother. God was guiding her. "Ask Mary, please, to send word to Martin's brother at the rail yard. Patrick will wish to come and sit out this vigil with us."

Anne leaned toward her, until their heads touched. "He will be all right, Julia."

"Martin's injury is serious, I know." She spoke to Anne quietly. What would she have done without her comforting presence? "The ambulance driver would not have transported him to this hospital otherwise."

Julia straightened her legs in front of her, and then pulled back. Remain calm. But how could she, after seeing those growing crimson stains? "I cannot push aside the image of Martin's blood dripping from the wagon into the street." She wrapped her arms around her body. Though her thoughts cleared, she could not stop the shivering.

"Do not think of it." Anne scooted over in her chair and positioned her right shoulder against Julia's. "Concentrate your thoughts on your future with Martin. You must remain calm. He will need your strength."

"Your words are wise and true, Anne. Let's watch the happenings in the hallway. I see people passing the door. I hear their voices, but I cannot distinguish their words." She settled back in her chair. It was a hopeless thing. Nothing would distract her thoughts from the sight of Martin, prostrate on a stretcher, helpless and bleeding.

Julia glanced up to see a policeman standing in the doorway, as a sentry. "It is the same kind man who came to your door to tell us of Martin's accident."

He entered the room with Walter, and they approached the girls. "My name is Daniel Quinn, miss." He stood erect and still. "I was there. Oh, aye, I saw it happen. Mr. Tobin's a hero, he is."

The policeman's earnest, sorrowful look touched Julia so deeply that, for a few moments, her shaking subsided. Perhaps this good man held the answers she waited for.

"Well now, while he stood beside his bus and collected fares, a crowd waited in line to board." Officer Quinn shuffled his feet, as if fortifying himself. Then, he settled into a firm stance. "Suddenly, a woman cried out. Her child had slipped from her arms and landed in the street right in the path of an oncoming bus. Mr. Tobin jumped forward, caught the boy, and pulled him from the vehicle's path. He saved the child's life, that's sure."

Officer Quinn stopped a moment and rolled his hat around in his large hands. He glanced at Walter.

"Please, go on." Walter nodded to him. "We must hear it all."

"Aye, begorra, it all happened in a flick of a moment. Mr. Tobin lost his balance and fell beneath the wheel of the bus himself. Some men rushed to pull him to safety, but their help came too late. The damage to his arm appears severe."

"Have you seen the doctor, Officer Quinn? Have you had any word from him?" Julia rose from the chair. "Does the doctor know we are here?"

"A nurse in the surgery promised to bring the doctor to us as soon as he is able to leave Martin, Meanwhile, I will stand guard at the door here, until we learn something of his condition. I will not allow anyone…no matter how well-meaning… to disturb you. If you are in need at all, just call me."

"Thank you, Officer Quinn." Walter guided Julia back in the chair, and the two men headed for the hallway. "We will rest easy here, knowing you have taken things in hand."

With Officer Quinn back at his station in the hallway, Walter pulled up a chair and sat beside Julia and Anne. "When I came upon the terrible scene, I spoke to Martin and he opened his eyes. A few moments later, he lost awareness. Surely, he remained unconscious along the way to the hospital. I doubt he will retain any memory of the harsh pain."

"I am sure you are right, Walter." Anne placed her hand on Julia's arm. "He speaks the truth, you know. Martin will remember none of this."

"So many people standing at the sight wished to help him. They insisted on telling me what a fine man Martin is and how they admire him." Walter's dark brows were drawn together. His eyes reflected his anguish.

A heavy mist once again threatened to control Julia's thoughts, but she willed herself to concentrate on Walter's encouraging words. It must be important to him that she grasp his meaning.

"Martin will recover. He must. A wonderful future awaits you both. I know God is watching over you." Walter looked as bereft as she felt. She reached out and touched his hand.

Likely an hour passed, she could not be sure. No sound or message came from the surgery. An attendant brought a tray filled with a steaming coffee pot, cups and sugar, and spoons and napkins. The kindness of the young girl touched Julia. Even though her body warmed with each sip, her shaking continued.

The smell of the coffee, the conversation in the hallway, and the constant motion of people passing the door now pulled at her nerves. The attendant left for a moment and returned with an additional blanket. When she placed it across Julia's knees, the shaking slowed."Thank you," she whispered.

The afternoon faded to dusk when Mary walked through the door with Kate and Grace behind her. "I am soothed just to have you standing beside me." She attempted a smile as she hugged each of them, but the effort brought tears.

"How are you, Julia?" Kate pulled a chair so close their knees touched. "What have you heard of Martin's condition?"

She opened her mouth, but no words came.

"Come and sit with us." Walter pulled up additional chairs. "Sure, and our Martin's had a terrible accident. We are waiting to hear from the doctor."

Mary handed her a fresh cup of coffee. When she took a sip of the hot liquid, it burned her tongue. She set it aside.

Why had the doctor not come to speak with them? How could she bear the waiting? She rose from the chair, forcing Kate to move back. She must go to Martin.

Officer Quinn entered the room, blocking her path. "Another doctor has arrived, Julia. The Omnibus Company sent him. When I conducted him to the door of the surgery, Dr. Gallagher came out of the room." The kind policeman took hold of Julia's shoulders and positioned her before him. "He said he will come and talk with you as soon as possible."

"Thank you." She sat back again to wait.

Mary and Grace pulled on their coats.

"I will return after we tend to the bakery and supper," Mary said. "Is there anything I can do to help you my dear? Is there anything at all that will ease your pain?"

"There is nothing to do, but pray for Martin."

"I will be praying." In a flurry of hugs and well wishes, Mary left the waiting room with Grace at her side.

The sun disappeared and darkness settled around them. Still, they waited. Martin's brother rushed in from work. Julia's heart reached out to him. Patrick and Martin, reunited in America after a separation of many years, facing another hurdle. They now lived in the same rooming house, and though they found the place barely livable, they rejoiced in each other's company. Patrick would be heartbroken.

"We are all praying." She placed her hand on his bowed head. "I know he will recover." After sitting with them long enough to hear the story of the accident, Patrick paced in the hallway, passing back and forth in front of Officer Quinn.

Julia listened for any sound from the surgery room.

"Such a long hallway separates us from that place, it would be impossible to hear anything." Kate spoke with confidence.

She was likely right. Julia settled back in her chair again. The minutes plodded on. No footsteps approached. She closed her eyes, attempting to summon Martin's face before her, then willed her thoughts to intercept with his and her strength to support him.

Father Burns arrived and joined the vigil. "Let us gather around and pray for Martin.

Julia poured her soul into her prayer. "Father in heaven, please watch over Martin..."

When the prayer ended, she found Father Burns beside her. "Will you be all right here, Julia? It could be a long night of waiting."

"I am well." Julia held his hand for a moment. "You know, Father, the sound of your voice and your calming presence remind me of my own father back home in Ireland—"

"Mr. Tobin?" Dr. Gallagher entered the room, and all conversation ceased. Patrick walked in right behind him. Walter pulled up chairs so they could all sit down together. Officer Quinn stood just inside the room.

"He is alive, but weak after the great loss of blood. He called for Julia?" The doctor lifted his brow at Patrick.

A sob escaped Julia, but she pressed her lips together and held her breath. If only she could settle herself and calm the shaking. She would not collapse. She would control her emotions long enough to hear the doctor's words.

When Walter placed a hand on her shoulder, the doctor spoke directly to her. "The news is not all good, Julia. Martin sustained grave damage to his left arm. There was no possibility of saving it." A gasp reverberated through the room. Was her own cry a part of the sound? She could not be sure.

"The bone had been severed just below the elbow by the wheel of the bus. It has taken all this while to stop the bleeding and close the wound."

Julia felt Anne's comforting arms wrap around her. She recalled that, after the war, James refused to return to St. Louis until he was confident he would not lose his injured leg. Martin would possess that same measure of stubborn pride over his arm.

"The danger has not passed. We will watch him closely throughout the night." The doctor patted her arm. "We will do our best, my dear."

"Thank you." She reached out to him, but he'd already moved away. "I appreciate all you have done for Martin."

The numbness in her legs now crept over her entire being. Helpless to prevent it, her body slid toward the floor. Walter and Patrick moved quickly, raising her up and guiding her back into the chair.

Julia filled her lungs then exhaled a long breath. "The doctor did say Martin lost part of his arm, did he not?" Had her mind betrayed her? The stubborn mist now seemed lodged in her brain. "Did Doctor Gallagher say Martin could still die?"

He walked back to her and faced her directly. "Yes, Julia, he has lost his left forearm, and he is still in danger. It is a hard thing to accept I know. I promise you, my dear, I will do all I can for him."

After stopping briefly to speak to Walter and Patrick, the doctor moved away. In another moment, he headed back toward the surgery room.

James and Ned arrived as the doctor took his leave. The men stood around in a group, reviewing the story of the accident and retelling the accounts of Martin's bravery.

She tried not to listen, but it was no use. "Martin lost part of his arm. His life hung in grave danger."

Each of Walter's words battered her heart, as if a blow had been struck.

Father Burns spoke softly to her. "I must return to St. Vincent's for a time. Let us pray for Martin again before I leave." He knelt on the waiting room floor. "Please dear God, hear the prayers of your faithful followers gathered here and place a curing hand on our dear friend, Martin."

A moment of peace settled over Julia.

As Father Burns left, Mary and Cara returned, laden with baskets of food. Julia managed a smile. Had she appreciated the love and friendship of these dear people?

The doctor came again. "Martin has regained consciousness." He sat beside Julia. "Before I left his room, he had slipped off again. He will sleep now for hours." Removing his glasses, he pulled a handkerchief from his pocket and polished the lenses. He looked at each one gathered there. "I cannot say for certain he will live, but I do believe if he survives until morning he could make it."

He placed an arm across Julia's shoulders. "You should go home and sleep now. He will need all of you in the coming days. I will check on him throughout the night."

"Thank you for the encouraging words," Julia said. Of course, she could not leave until she was sure Martin would live. She rose and escorted the doctor out. "I appreciate the wonderful care you are giving Martin."

As she turned back into the room, Walter took command. "Will you take everyone home, James? My wagon is out front. I will stay with Julia and Patrick."

"Of course. I will see the girls home, and return later to collect you." The set of James' shoulders as he glanced at his wife proclaimed he would hear no argument.

Julia threw up her arms. "Oh my word, I have been selfish, Anne. I wished to have you with me, giving no thought to your needs. You must go home and rest."

Amid a flurry of hugs and promises of prayers, they gathered their things and said goodbye. Kate did not move with them. She took a firm hold of Julia's arm and led her to a chair. "It may be a long vigil, but we will wait this out together."

The night wore on. The hallway emptied and the hospital quieted. Julia settled in with Kate and Walter beside her. Patrick and Officer Quinn continued their vigil in the doorway. What would the morning bring?

Chapter Ten

Hurrying along toward the hospital the next morning, Julia thought only of reaching Martin.

"Are you feeling well?" Lizzie hovered at her side, searching her face, making it difficult to keep up her brisk pace. "You returned home so late last night you had little opportunity for rest."

"I am weary." Julia rubbed her eyes, finding no relief. "It is more than tiredness, though. My head is filled with worries about Martin, our future, what will happen now? My legs will not carry me along quickly enough. One good word from the doctor and my exhaustion will disappear."

"My poor Julia. Could you go home and sleep, once you've seen Martin?"

"It's possible. Each time I began to drift off last night, yesterday's happenings rushed before my eyes. I could not forget Martin's lost his arm and his unbearable pain."

"Walter offered us a ride," Lizzie said.

"I know he did. I thought the exertion would clear my head, and all."

Lizzie struggled to match her steps. When she coughed, Julia slowed her pace. "I suppose I should have accepted the ride."

"What time did you return home?"

"We left the hospital at four o'clock. Officer Quinn pledged he would not leave until he had to report for duty.

When Patrick insisted he would stay with Martin, I relented and rode home with Kate and Walter."

"I yearned to sit with you last night. I only stayed back at Dempsey's, because Walter asked." Poor Lizzie practically skipped along, trying to match her steps. Julia slowed again.

"He told me you wished to come." Julia patted her sister's cheek. "Actually, Walter's idea proved a sound one. You are well rested and able to accompany me this morning. Walter insists someone accompany me to the hospital. Like you, I wish to do his bidding."

"Do you mind if I ask how you came to find Martin in the street?" Lizzie held Julia's arm. "Is it too painful to speak about?"

"Well, let me recall. Officer Quinn, a kind policeman you will likely meet today, came to Anne's door and led us to the accident." Julia grimaced. Oh, if she could push the entire memory from her mind.

She passed quickly over the moment she and Anne found Martin stretched out in the road, hurt and bleeding. "We rode to the hospital in Walter's wagon, following behind the ambulance. In the waiting room, Officer Quinn related the story of Martin's saving the young boy's life."

"He is a brave man." Lizzie held fast to Julia's bonnet when it threatened to blow off.

"Late in the evening, officials from the Omnibus Company arrived at the hospital." Julia lowered her head. A less painful subject than Martin's injuries. "They spoke with Martin's brother, assuring him they would pay for his medical needs. They failed to mention his wages. Patrick surmised that Martin will not be paid while he is incapacitated."

"They should have been ashamed for their company." Lizzie's sweet expression disappeared. Anger at the Omnibus Company shone on her face.

"Mr. Collins, the father of the boy Martin saved, called in. Patrick offered to bring him to the waiting room, but he refused.

He did not wish to disturb me." While they walked, Julia lifted her head high. She swung her arms ahead of her, then back. Would nothing distract her from her worry?

"I will never forget the kindness of the good people in the hospital. Someday, in some way, I will show each of them my appreciation."

Within two blocks of the hospital, the massive three-story building loomed ahead of them. Was the cold, forbidding image forewarning tragedy just inside its doors? She shook her head vigorously.

"Do you think the policeman still holds his vigil?" Lizzie examined the building, a look of uncertainty in her eyes.

"I am not sure. He will be required to report for duty today. His shift ended yesterday afternoon, and he watched over us last night out of his own goodness. Surely, he needs sleep." Julia paused. It was dark last night. Had she been aware of the enormous windows, the heavy wooden doors? "Well, we are here. We will know soon." Julia took Lizzie's hand, and they climbed the steep front stairway to the main hospital entrance.

❀ ❀ ❀

They walked toward the waiting room, Lizzie holding fast to Julia's arm. Halfway along, she looked up to see Dr. Gallagher approaching.

"The news is magnificent, Julia." A tired, but pleased smile crossed across his face. "Your Martin improves as each hour passes. He is a strong fellow."

"Ah, that is wonderful." A heavy mantle of worry slipped from her shoulders. "I long to see him. Is he awake? Has he spoken?"

"He will likely stir when you walk into his room, but he will not remain alert for long. He'll sleep throughout most of the day. Are you able to stay for a time?"

"I will be here. Father Burns insisted I spend the day with Martin." She remembered her manners. "This is my sister, Elizabeth. The kind Dempseys requested she attend me this morning."

"Pleased to meet you, Elizabeth." With a short bow, the doctor started to walk away. He turned back. "I leave Martin in good hands. With you beside him, my dear, he will pull through." And then, he was gone.

"We must find Martin's room." The doctor's confident words pushed Julia forward. "I am so happy he is improving." She took Lizzie's arm. "His convalescence will be long and difficult, I am sure, but I will be by his side every possible moment." She pulled her shawl from her shoulders, slowly. "Ah, that is impossible. I must return to work tomorrow morning."

❦ ❦ ❦

For the next week, Martin drifted between semi-consciousness and a drugged sleep. Father Burns urged Julia to leave the church office early each afternoon and visit Martin. The Dempseys encouraged this as well.

On an afternoon in the second week after the accident, Julia arrived at Martin's doorway with Ceil Brown and found him in a deep sleep.

Ceil winced with each gasp from Martin. "Does he always hurt so?"

"The pain appears too great for a person to bear. Once I begged only for his life, but I now add a prayer that it will subside." Julia shook her head. "The nurses promise me he will not remember this agony when he awakens."

"I pray that is true." Ceil placed chairs beside the bed.

"Now that I am settled, will you cross to the post office and mail our letters?"

"Of course." Ceil accepted Julia's envelope. "I'll hurry back."

Keeper of Trust

Julia found herself alone, beside the sleeping Martin. She glanced at the lump beneath the sheets where his damaged arm lay. The truth struck with the force of a physical blow.

Oh my word. His hand is gone. The fingers that entwined with mine, causing my heart to skip, are no more.

Great, gulping sobs rushed forth. Covering her face, Julia fled Martin's room, rushed down the long hallway, and entered the waiting area.

The head nurse, a tall, imposing woman, stopped in the doorway. "We must have quiet in here, miss." With a "tsk-tsk," she marched off down the hall.

Julia rose from the chair and gazed out the window at the tall elm trees, their stark limbs now bereft of even a fluttering of leaves. She blew her nose forcefully. How could she halt these foolish tears?

A young, curly-haired nurse appeared in the doorway. "Settle in your chair. Take deep breaths. I will be right back." The girl returned immediately and placed a warm, moist cloth over Julia's eyes. Sitting down beside her, she rested an arm across her shoulders.

"Now, have not a worry over Miss Sharon. We have all been in a dreadful rush this morning, and she received some distressing news herself. When she recovers from her own sorrow, she will regret her stern words."

Julia brushed back the wisps of hair that escaped from beneath her hat. "Please assure her I have regained my composure. I will not allow myself any further tearful displays."

"We all know of the tragedy." The nurse spoke to Julia in a soothing voice. "Your outburst is understandable. And, you were not disturbing anyone. I did not hear a peep, until I came right up to the door. The empty waiting room will not suffer over a few tears."

Julia took several deep, cleansing breaths. "For a moment, I allowed my sorrow to gain hold of me. The tears washed out like a giant wave crashing around my head. I am capable of taking up the vigil in Martin's room now." She lifted her gaze and offered the girl a smile. "Thank you for your kindness."

Ceil entered the waiting room. "Oh, dear. You needed me. Please accept my apology." She turned to the nurse. "Have not a care, I will tend to Julia."

She and Ceil followed the girl down the hall. With each step, Julia clenched her fists. Her foolish tears should be set aside. She must remain in control. Martin had another hand to hold and another arm to draw her close.

❁ ❁ ❁

A week before Christmas, Julia helped in the oven room. The Dempsey group had worked long hours, preparing bakery goods to fill everyone's holiday requests. Her arms and shoulders ached. Surely Walter and his helpers felt similar exhaustion.

"I am learning what a favorite Martin is with everyone here," Lizzie said, as they entered the attic room. "No one will wish to celebrate Christmas without him."

"I agree." Kate waited on the bed. "We will observe Christmas day in a quiet fashion this year."

"You must go on with the usual festivities." Julia shook her head vigorously. "Celebrate in Martin's honor. He would not wish to cause a sad holiday for everyone. Please, proceed with the planned events."

"I suppose you know best, Julia." Lizzie slipped out of her shoes.

Julia lowered herself to her bed, still clothed. "After spending so many evenings at the hospital in the past few weeks, I have missed the Dempsey suppers. I am surely looking forward to the feast the girls will prepare for Christmas."

When the great day arrived, Julia sat at the table between Kate and Lizzie, surrounded by her Dempsey friends.

"You must set aside your worries, if only for a short time." Mary patted her on the top of the head. "We all miss you in the bakery and at supper, you know."

"I have no gifts for anyone." Julia lowered her head. "I am so sorry."

"You must not give a thought to presents." Tears welled in Lizzie's eyes. "Having you here is gift enough."

"Thank you all." She forced her shoulders to relax. "What a wonderful meal. Everything is delicious." The lively talk and warm laughter circled around Julia. Had she already forgotten what fun Dempsey meals could be? She nudged herself to participate, even managing a slice of Grace's chocolate cake. "I have missed being here with everyone."

When the grand meal ended, she gathered her cloak and shawl.

"I will go with you, Julia," Kate said. "No protests now. I have my coat already."

Lizzie waited by the door. "Here is a gift for Martin." She handed Julia a tiny wrapped package.

"And another from me." Ellen handed Kate a plain paper sack.

"What could that be?" Kate winked as she pulled the door open. "Well we will soon see."

"Wait," called Mary.

By the time they started off, they each held an armful of small packages.

❧ ❧ ❧

Martin's eyelids fluttered, when they entered his room. Only a short time later, he drifted off again.

"You must go on home, Kate. You work so hard, and I wish you to enjoy this rare day free of chores." She kept her voice low. "Ellen has been telling me of a game she created with different colors of ribbon and painted stones. You must not miss the girls' holiday plans."

"I cannot leave you here alone, Julia. Not on Christmas day." Kate folded her arms.

"Please, humor me, Kate." She stilled, attempting a stern look. "I am assigning you two special tasks. Since this is our Lizzie's first Christmas in America, you must see to it that she enjoys every minute of the celebration. Also, Anne and James will be coming by for dessert this evening. You must observe her carefully and report her well-being back to me."

"No, Julia, I cannot—"

Julia sat up straight in her chair. "Once begun, I will not pause in my pleading. Give in and return to Dempsey's. I'm sure you agree that is true."

"Very well, Julia, I will go, but when Walter comes to collect you later, I will accompany him." With a hug, Kate left the hospital room.

Sitting beside the sleeping Martin, Julia's heart ached. She missed him so, his gentle words, his warm touch. Her shoulders slumping, she reached in her pocket and withdrew a stack of letters. Perhaps, a message from home, even an old letter, would help.

12 Aug. 1861

To Miss Anne and Miss Julia Carty,
My dearly beloved children, I received your kind but heart-rending letter. I wish I had you both at home rather than near to danger or difficulty.

We are well, thank God, but it caused us a great deal of anxiety to think you are poorly situated in a strange country. My beloved children your Mother and I would sacrifice everything to get you right but what can we do the wide Atlantic roles between us. If you could come home, oh how contented would we be to have you both home under our auspices and within the grasp of our embraces. Alas, it is not the will of Divine Providence.

Let us know about the war and state of the country as we will be uneasy in our minds until we hear from you. I hope you will have better news for us the next time.

We conclude by all sending you our love. God go with you and protect you,
John and Nell Carty

Julia folded the letter. Even reading her father's words, written five years ago, just after the start of the Civil War, made her teary. So few letters from him now. Months sometimes passed before they heard a thing.

She gritted her teeth. This situation could not continue. Why had there been no word at all since Lizzie came? And what of Michael? Martin's accident had distracted her from her quest for the truth. She would insist Lizzie tell them what had happened back home.

❈ ❈ ❈

Julia continued her vigil into the early weeks of January, sitting at Martin's bedside each afternoon. She consoled him when he cried out in pain. While he slept, she prayed for him. Each time he awoke, he did not remember the accident and he discovered the loss of his arm all over again. He appeared disoriented and spoke few words. She treasured each "hello" and rejoiced each time she heard "Julia."

On one particularly sunny day, she found him sitting in a chair beside the bed. "Oh, Martin! Good afternoon. It is grand to see you awake." She pulled over a chair for herself and placed it beside him.

"I feel I've been lost for awhile." His raspy speech, barely audible at first, gradually gained strength. "Though I search my memory over and over, I cannot recover the details. Each time I awaken and realize my arm has been severed, a shower of terrible blows rains down over me."

"You remember me." Julia shoulders lifted. "Nothing could be more important, I would say."

Martin answered with a weak smile. "I have not absorbed the truth completely. I am stunned with the horror of it." He placed his good hand across his eyes. "Deep in my heart, I imagine it is only a dream. Still, I am alive. Doc Gallagher tells me I am lucky to be so."

He turned back to her, his expression more peaceful now. "I owe you my life, Julia. With you beside me, I recovered my desire to live. I am determined to grow strong enough to care for myself."

Julia brought him a glass of water. "You will reclaim your former vigor. You will always be perfect to me, you know." She crossed her hands over heart. She had been saving so many things to tell him. Would he be ready to share them?

"Since you are awake and alert, there are some matters I must discuss with you. I am sure you have heard the constant bang of the door here." She spoke quickly. "Our neighbors have inquired after you, offering prayers and good wishes. Each kind Dempsey friend, has shared the vigil with me."

"We are fortunate to have such good friends." Martin sipped his water.

Closing her eyes, she filled her lungs. She had only begun. "Walter and Mary allow me to visit each afternoon. Father Burns encourages me to devote myself to sitting beside you. At his insistence, Ceil Brown accompanies me from St. Vincent's."

"Ah, they are fine people, good friends." Martin's eyes shone clear, as she had not seen them in weeks.

"Walter and James, in turn with Patrick, sat at your bedside throughout each night until you were out of danger."

"I had no idea they were here every night." Martin drank from the glass again. He seemed parched. Should she save the

Keeper of Trust

more difficult conversations for another time? "I appreciate your telling me, Julia. I will thank them for it."

She gestured to the chair she used for her visits and the table beside it. "I will enjoy our hours together even more, now that you remain awake."

"I have grown fond of having you by my side." Martin grinned at her again. "I will miss you when I return to work."

A chill rushed through Julia. She hesitated to disturb his positive spirits, but there was more. "An entire world of generosity has been extended to you. The parishioners at St. Vincent's sent a draft and another arrived from your fellow workers at the Omnibus Company."

Martin remained stoic.

She squirmed in her chair. Lord, please give me courage. "I hesitated to accept any of it on your behalf. Patrick and I discussed it." She cleared her throat. "When Father Burns visited the following evening, we sought his advice. Father said it comforted your friends to express their sorrow over your injury. He recommended that Patrick hold the checks for you—"

A knock interrupted their conversation.

"Excuse me, folks." Officer Quinn came through the door. "Mr. Collins, the father of the child you saved, has come to see you. He has visited several times. Julia invited him in, but he refused while you remained so ill."

"Hello, Mr. Collins." Julia made room for the two men. "Is it not grand to see Martin sitting in a chair?"

"I thank you with all my heart, Mr. Tobin, for your brave act." Mr. Collins wiped his handkerchief across his brow. "My son, Joseph, escaped the accident with naught but a few bruises, while saving his life cost you such terrible injuries. I am deeply sorry."

"A pleasure to meet you, Mr. Collins," Martin said. "Please sit with us for awhile?"

Mr. Collins shook his head. "It is wonderful to see you have begun to recover, but I do not wish to tire you. With your permission, I would like to visit again. Perhaps I could bring my wife and son along one day."

"It would be grand to see them." Martin chuckled. "I've no memory of our first meeting."

Mr. Collins bowed to Martin, and in a moment, he disappeared through the doorway.

Julia stood. "Officer Quinn, please stay a moment."

The policeman stepped back into the room.

"Do you remember Officer Quinn at all, Martin? He was with us at the scene of your accident. Since then, he has stationed himself outside your room every possible moment. With your grand recovery, he may be able to take a day of rest." She turned to the policeman. "We are thankful for your kindness."

Martin looked directly into the officer's eyes. "Thank you. I particularly appreciate your watching over Julia. I stand forever in your debt."

"Ah, 'twas nothing." Officer Quinn tipped his cap and headed for the door. "I will be around for a time. If you need anything, call for me."

❋ ❋ ❋

"Hello, Mr. Collins. What a pleasant surprise." Julia moved from the frosted window.

"May I see Mr. Tobin?" He shifted from one foot to another. "January slipped by since my last visit."

"Of course. Please come in." Julia pulled up a chair. Was Mr. Collins nervous?

"Good afternoon. It is good to see you again." Martin covered his injured arm with a blanket stretching from his shoulders down to the floor. His good arm remained free, and he extended it to Mr. Collins. "Call me Martin, please."

Mr. Collins pulled an envelope from his pocket. "I brought a check for you, Martin. I trust this will keep you until you are able to return to work." He handed him an official looking packet.

Martin held the envelope toward Mr. Collins. "A fine gesture, but I do not want your money. I did not pull Joseph from danger to earn a reward."

"Nonsense." Mr. Collins brushed the envelope aside. "I will continue to call on you, if I may, but—"

"You are most generous, but I cannot accept such a gift." Martin pushed the paper back to Mr. Collins.

Julia sat back and watched the exchange: Martin more alert than he had been since the accident, and Mr. Collins' usual mild countenance now displaying forcefulness and determination.

"Mr. Tobin. Martin, please. My wife and I..." He stepped forward, his eyes growing moist. "You see, Joseph is all we have. When you saved him...you restored our family. Please allow us this small gesture to help you."

He lifted his brow to Julia, as if seeking her help. "Besides, the money has been deposited in the bank in your name. This voucher represents a mere formality." With a wink, Mr. Collins tipped his hat to them and disappeared from the room.

Julia and Martin grinned at one another and shook their heads.

"Imagine." With a little difficulty, Martin pulled the voucher from the envelope. He turned it over in his hand. "A thousand dollars? I cannot believe it. What generous people they are."

❀ ❀ ❀

Later that night, in her bed at Dempsey's, Julia tossed and turned. Another, more persistent worry haunting her.

Kate came and sat beside her. With Lizzie fast asleep, she spoke quietly. "You look troubled. What is it?"

"Martin grows more alert each day." She sighed. "It is difficult to speak of...to explain. His manner has changed toward me. Though I kiss him often, on the forehead or cheek, and he smiles in return when I do, he makes no overtures toward me. No kisses. No hugs." She drew her lips together. "I should be grateful he is recovering and not worrying about such frivolous things. I cannot help it."

"Roll over on your side." Kate massaged Julia's shoulders. "You know how reserved Martin is. You once told me that from the early years of your courtship, his manner was polite but reticent when others were present. Since I arrived in America, though, I have witnessed his steady devotion to you."

"You are right." Julia's muscles relaxed under Kate's firm hands. Tears trickled down her cheeks.

"Martin is a private person. I understand it, because I am a little like him." Kate put her head down and giggled. "Though I would like to be more like you, or James Duff, we are not all made that way."

"Of course." Sniffling, Julia wiped her tears on her pillowcase. "On many occasions, I've fought to banish my jealousy when James hugged and kissed Anne for the world to see. I suppose Martin's reserve has been ingrained in him by his years of military training."

"Maybe so." Kate reached out to help her sit up.

"Still, since becoming betrothed, Martin relaxed somewhat toward me." Her tears slowed. "While not openly demonstrative, he touched my arm or gazed into my eyes as we talked. Those tiny signs of affection thrilled me."

"Blow your nose." Kate passed her a handkerchief.

Julia blew, grimacing as Lizzie stirred. "Now, Martin offers only politeness and restraint. He remains distant, even when we are alone in the hospital room. No declarations of love or mention of our wedding, only a few months away."

"Ah, more tears." Kate chuckled. "Go on and cry. You are always so calm at the hospital." She pulled another handkerchief from her pocket.

"I attempt to show concern for his injury and his pain, and be grateful he will live." Kate's kindness drew the bold words from her. "Dare I wish for more? At times, I can think only of the wedding. Does Martin intend to fulfill our plans? Could I even pray for this one more blessing?"

Kate tucked a loose curl behind Julia's ear. How fortunate she was to have an understanding, caring sister. Her eyelids fluttered, as sleep clouded her senses.

❀ ❀ ❀

A few evenings later, Walter brought Julia home in his carriage.

"How was he today?" Concern showed in his dear face.

"Physically, he grows stronger each day." Julia squirmed.

Walter raised his bushy brows toward her. This talk proved more difficult than she expected. "I am worried about the short time that remains until the wedding."

"You must have patience, and allow Martin to heal." Walter kept his eyes on the road. "Imagine waking up and discovering your hand and part of your arm have vanished forever. I cannot comprehend it myself. This must surely be the most tragic shock of his life. And he could have died."

"I am sorry, Walter. I've made you uncomfortable."

"I'm not uncomfortable, Julia, just searching for the right words." Walter gazed directly at her now. "With Martin's strength returning, his emotions will settle down. You will see. He will not be able to live without you. His lost limb will hold little consequence for either of you."

Walter's advice rang true. Martin's life had been returned to him. If only he would remember they planned to share that life.

Chapter Eleven

February, 1867

Julia returned from work at St. Vincent's, on a blustery winter afternoon to find Lizzie presiding in the shop. "If you don't need help from me, I'll head to the dining room and set the table for Mary."

Lizzie waved from behind the counter. "That is a grand idea, Julia. Mary's all in a flutter. Mr. Reilly, himself, will dine with us tonight."

"And, if it is not our Miss Julia." Mary patted her cheeks, when she passed through the archway into the candlelit dining room. "Brr. Your skin is chilled. It must have been a cold walk. But it is a grand thing to have you here with us. I've missed you, you know."

"I've missed you, too, Mary, but I will be enjoying supper with you for the next two days. Dr. Gallagher said I cannot see Martin until Thursday. A visiting doctor from Philadelphia has developed a method of treating amputee patients. He will be working with Martin to help relieve him of pain." Julia took Mary's warm towel and pressed it against her face. "If his pain can be lessened, I will gladly stand aside for a time. And here I am now, home for supper and about to be treated to a visit with Mr. Reilly."

"Kate has worked with him at the inn, and they appear to be building a friendship. I have invited him several times." Mary placed a stack of dinner plates on the snowy white tablecloth. "Until now, he always offered an excuse. Wouldn't I soon be thinking it was my potatoes?"

"Of course, that is not the case." Julia held up knives and forks. "Have I seen these before? They are beautiful."

"It's called Sheffield Silver, made in England in the early 1800s. My father purchased it in Liverpool."

"Well, Mr. Reilly will be impressed." Julia giggled. "Kate claims he spends days working at the new hotel and evenings at his pub. It seems he has no time for social events. Likely, he has learned of your marvelous cooking skills and is unable to resist your fine fare any longer.

"I, too, wondered about Mr. Reilly." Julia paused, tapping her finger against her lower lip. "On the evening of our betrothal party, he appeared quiet and rather stern in his manner. Apart from the few minutes while James introduced him to everyone, he focused his attention on Kate and rarely spoke to anyone else."

"Perhaps, with fewer people tonight, he will converse more." Mary pulled chairs from against the wall and placed them at the table. "We will come to know him a little better."

"The evening did bring about an important turn of events for Kate," Julia said. "She and Mr. Reilly agreed right then she would make the draperies and bedspreads for the hotel."

"Our Ellen is so pleased about the opportunity. She no longer worries about being forced to return to the garment factory. She is a dear person, and I am delighted for her. Both girls are so talented with the needle. Their fine work amazes me."

Julia held a soup bowl to the light. "These dishes compliment the silver."

"Nothing fancy." Mary straightened a place setting and moved on to the next. "Just pottery. But it was my mothers and it was made in County Wexford, not far from our home. I've always treasured this set." She moved to the buffet and arranged coffee cups, spoons, and dessert plates on an empty corner.

"And, the hotel work has increased Kate's drapery business. The girls received orders from all parts of the city. They have worked hard these past weeks, sitting in their shop, day after day, buried beneath heavy material. On many nights, they return to their shop after supper and remain long into the night. They do seem to enjoy the work. Neither girl has offered a word of complaint." Mary's curls bounced as she spoke.

"Kate tells me they hired on Mrs. Flynn's daughter Janey for a few hours each week, for hemming and such." Julia hummed as she placed miniature candles at intervals along the table. "I do hope she will lessen their heavy workload."

"The shop is closed tight." Lizzie came through the doorway and circled the table. "It is lovely. What can I do to help?"

Mary inspected the table. "Our preparations are complete. Please fetch Kate and Ellen, Julia. Lizzie and I will help bring the dishes from the kitchen."

Julia walked the long hallway to the seamstress shop. "Your supper awaits, my dears...Oh..." She clapped a hand to either side of her face. The curtains had been drawn, the lamps turned down and Kate and Ellen approached the doorway. "You girls are seldom able to follow me right to the dining room."

❁ ❁ ❁

Francis Reilly, their only guest for the evening, arrived promptly. Walter led him into the dining room and directed him to the high-backed chair beside Kate. "You met everyone at the betrothal supper, but I'll refresh your memory. Here's Eddie and George, my bakery workers...now our fine cooks, my sister Mary, Grace, Lizzie, and Cara...and here comes Julia, Ellen, and of course, Kate." Walter directed him to a chair on Mary's right.

"Pleased to see you." Francis bowed to each one. "Thank you for having me." He nodded to Mary.

As Grace and Cara placed platter after platter of steaming delicacies on the table, Julia's gaze rested on Lizzie, who brushed away a tear. "Are you remembering the meager meals we were accustomed to back home?"

"Yes, cabbage or turnip soup. Bread, only if we could obtain the ingredients to make it."

"After all these years at Dempsey's, I have never become accustomed to the plentiful array set out for our supper." Julia gestured to the platters before her. "Two vegetables, a salad, meat." She shook her head. "No matter how long I live in America, I will never forget the constant state of hunger we endured. I suspect no one seated around the table will ever allow the sad state of our homeland to slip from their minds."

Walter pushed back his chair. "Let us offer our thanksgiving." Julia lowered her head.

"We thank you Father for this bountiful meal. We ask for your healing touch upon our dear friend, Martin. Amen."

"Your meal is excellent." Francis nodded in Mary's direction as soon as Walter's prayer of thanksgiving ended. A slight, balding man with a thin mustache and short beard, he turned to address Julia. "How is Mr. Tobin? Kate tells me he is making some progress in his recovery."

"He is making remarkable progress. He is undergoing some special treatments designed to reduce the pain he has been experiencing." Julia swept her arm over the others around the table. "You will all tire of me. I will not be able to see him for the next few days."

"We are all pleased to have you with us, Julia." Walter dropped his fork, but caught it when it bounced off his knee. "We will hold good thoughts for Martin. The pain he endures is more than anyone should bear."

A hum of agreement rose in the air. "A terrible thing, the fiercest pain ever," and "poor fellow" came from all around the table.

"It has been a long time since I've been home for supper." Julia nodded to her friends. "I thank you all for the prayers and concern, including you, Francis."

"You will be amazed at the wonderful work Kate is doing at the hotel." Francis smiled at Kate. "I have come to seek her advice, not only on draperies and bedspreads, but on furniture, carpeting, kitchen equipment, and the appointments for the public rooms."

"Sure, I possess little knowledge of refurbishing and renovations." Kate's confident air betrayed her words.

"I must disagree with you." Francis sat forward, his shoulders erect. "Your opinions have been helpful, and to this point, your instincts have proven correct."

"You'll hear no arguments from us, Mr. Reilly. We've always known Kate possesses excellent sewing skills." Lizzie turned to Mary, a brow raised.

"I agree." Mary extended the platter of beef to Francis, but he shook his head. "Kate and Ellen are both excellent seamstresses, and we all admire their hard work."

"With the help of Kate and Ellen my inn will be the most stylish in the city." Francis lowered his gaze to his plate, his expression sobering. Conversation gave way to clinking knives and forks.

Julia glanced his way from time to time. Had he finished speaking for the night?

Toward the end of the meal, Francis sat forward in his chair and cleared his throat. "I have been following the construction work along the riverfront, Walter. Additional space for the barges will be a good thing for business."

"The improvements to the levee are welcome as well." Walter turned to Julia. "Do the immigrants at the mission appreciate the changes?"

Julia placed her fork on the table. "I generally hear how much more convenient it is here than at the port in New York. Father Ryan—"

"That's a fine thing." Francis inclined his head toward Julia.

"I do think, Walter, building up the shipping area will contribute more to the city's growth and prosperity." He gazed at his plate.

Julia leaned toward Lizzie, and when she felt a kick at her ankle, she stifled her giggle. How little weight her words must hold with Mr. Reilly.

"I suppose you are right." Walter turned to Eddie, who sat beside him. "Will our flour supply hold until next week's shipment?"

Francis grew silent once again.

❀ ❀ ❀

When they retired to the attic room, Kate untied her apron, straightened her sleeves, and smoothed her hair.

Julia stood beside her, pulling pins from her hair, waiting. Would she ask for their opinion of Francis? Would it be possible to give a favorable response and still be truthful? On her brief opportunity for observation, the man appeared absorbed in his wide-ranging ventures to the exclusion of all other matters.

"I have something to share with you." Kate held her folded hands in her lap. "Francis has proposed marriage."

"Marriage...Oh, Kate..." Julia held up her handkerchief to hide what must be a frightful expression.

"Julia, I am so sorry. With Martin's condition...is this subject distressing?"

"Of course not, Kate." Julia mustered a half-smile. "Your news surprised me, is all." A few deep breaths and she would gain control of her senses.

Mr. Reilly's sudden appreciation for Mary's cooking made perfect sense. And yet...such an abrupt proposal...and Francis so much older than Kate. Well, in fairness, he treated her with kindness and respect.

She glanced at Kate, squared her shoulders and lifted her chin. No intent to ask her or Lizzie to give their blessing.

"You will make your own way, Kate. Lizzie and I will support whatever path you choose." Julia reached for Lizzie's hand.

"Will you write to our parents for permission?" Lizzie moved to Kate's side. "Will you apply to Father Burns?"

"Francis is able to support a family, and I am of age." Kate crossed her arms and straightened. "I obtained my baptismal certificate before I left home and brought it along with me. I have not agreed to the marriage, as yet. If I do, we will arrange a wedding date with Father Burns." Her words grew forceful, her tone, bitter. "No further permissions will be needed."

Lizzie stumbled back, her hands covering her face.

Julia stepped between Kate and Lizzie. Had she been mistaken about the deep bond existing between Kate and their little sister? It must be so.

Lizzie lowered her head, and tears filled her eyes.

"Kate, please. Calm yourself. You are frightening Lizzie." With an eyebrow raised, she fixed Kate with a stern stare.

Silence filled the little room. Julia closed her eyes. Minutes passed. She dropped her arms to her sides.

"Well now, my Kate, if not for permission, you will write to Father and Mother, will you not?" Julia took a few breaths and lightened her tone. "You will surely share your plans with them and assure them of your love for Francis?"

"When I find a spare moment." Kate moved to the desk, her head averted, not meeting her eyes or Lizzie's.

Julia rubbed her fingers along Lizzie's arm. Could she find the right words to soothe Kate and ease Lizzie's distress?

Kate's love for their little sister seemed to win out over her poor temper. She moved back to Lizzie, her look contrite. "You see, Francis and I are of a like mind in almost every area. He wishes to establish a home, raise a family, and work toward a secure future. We hold these considerations to be more important than romantic love."

"But, Kate, no courting?" Lizzie took a small step toward Kate.

Kate clasped Lizzie to her with great force, continuing the embrace until she squirmed from her grasp. She offered another apologetic smile to them both.

Julia stared at the hand Martin once held in his pocket. How she longed to experience those exquisite loving gestures once more. Did Kate hold such disdain for true affection and devotion? "Surely, you love Francis?"

"He is a good, sensible man. I hold him in high regard. I will come to love him in time." Kate held her head high. "Do not fret, Julia. I am only now beginning to experience some success with my dressmaking shop, and I have Ellen to think of." A flicker of defiance crossed her face. "I will consider the matter of marriage for some time, before I give my consent. Do not worry, I will be fine."

"I pray you will, Kate." Lizzie edged closer and touched Kate's hand.

When her sisters had gone off to sleep, Julia tossed and rolled in her bed. Would Kate agree to marry Francis Reilly, a dour man, twice her age? Would she agree to a union with a man she barely knew, a man for whom she admitted she held no real feelings of affection?

Julia sighed. She needed a man…ah…like Martin. Her dear Martin, if only the new treatment would lessen his pain. She closed her eyes. *Please dear Lord, allow the treatment to help him.*

Her eyes flew open. Anne…oh my. *And, please watch over Anne.* She pictured Anne holding a baby before she drifted off.

Chapter Twelve

Julia and Lizzie worked together the next afternoon, packing up the day-olds goods.

"Did Kate's announcement last evening really surprise you?" Julia covered a tray of currant rolls with a cloth.

"'Twas a shock, and that's the truth." Lizzie's eyebrows lifted. "What are your thoughts about Francis Reilly, Julia?"

"I scarcely know what to think." Julia shrugged her shoulders. She couldn't hide her own concern. Sharp-eyed Lizzie would notice her twisting and shifting. "I suppose we must trust Kate. She does display good sense when it comes to business. All we can do is pray she possesses equally good judgment in this matter with Mr. Reilly. This talk of marriage just seems to have come about so suddenly."

"It is time you begin making plans for your own wedding." Lizzie giggled. "I admit to an ulterior motive. When you leave Dempsey's to marry Martin, I will be left to take over the shop girl position on my own. I look forward to the opportunity to prove myself capable of handling the work. Do you understand?"

"Of course, I do. And you have already done a grand job of taking over while I'm at the hospital." Julia clasped Lizzie's hands and swung their arms back and forth. "I am proud of you. Your sisters are all proud of you."

"'Tis not only the shop, Julia. I cannot wait for your wedding. Will there be dancing?" Her shoulders slumped. "If only Father and Mother could be here."

"I hesitate to make too many plans for the wedding with Martin still so ill," Julia said. "I also do not wish to make any major decisions without Anne."

Lizzie slipped a handkerchief from her pocket and attempted to smother a cough. "We must speak to her soon. Could we go for a visit?"

Julia cast a questioning eye to Lizzie. "Are you coming down with a cold?"

Lizzie waved her hand in front of her face. "Not to worry. A catch in my throat is all."

Julia gazed at Lizzie for a long moment. "Well, since I must not go to the hospital for the next two evenings, perhaps, I could ask Mary to invite Anne and James for supper tomorrow, and we'll have a grand talk. I know Mary will not mind."

"Mary will be happy to have them. I will run back and discuss the idea with her right now." Lizzie disappeared along the back hallway.

Alone in the shop for the moment, Julia smiled. Her little sister had all but taken over running the bakery shop, embracing the position with delight. She made the bakery workers and customers feel her joy. Her cheerfulness certainly helped ease worries of Martin.

Mary entered the shop quietly, holding a stack of empty bank pouches tucked under her arm. "I understand we're to have Mr. and Mrs. Duff for dinner tomorrow."

"I did not think you would object." Julia winked at Mary. "We all know Anne is your favorite."

"Ah go on with you. You are nothing but a tease, Julia Carty." Mary's jolly expression quickly dissolved, turning to a look of concern.

"What is it, Mary?"

"I am sorry to be the bearer of this distressing news." Mary dipped her head a moment. "It is a story I cannot keep from you. Jack Conan waylaid Walter, while he was out on his delivery rounds. A fellow newly arrived from Blackwater told him your brother hired on with a farmer outside of the village. He said Michael signed a three year contract."

"I suspected something," Julia's shoulders drooped. "Months have passed without a letter from anyone at home. And, since Lizzie arrived in St. Louis, I have been unable to dispel the idea that she has been holding something back. I never even considered this." Could the story be accurate? She folded her arms, but could not block the truth from pounding at her heart. "Michael indentured. Ah my, it cannot be." Her words slipped out as more of a groan than intelligent speech.

Mary placed an arm around Julia. "I am so sorry." Mary's brown eyes darkened with concern.

"I am fine, really I am." Julia straightened. "Somehow my sisters and I must absorb the shock of this dreadful news. First, we must talk to Lizzie and find out what caused Father to send Michael into indenture."

"Yes, you must. As soon as possible. And Anne and Kate too." Mary brushed Julia's curls back from her eyes. "You and your sisters will find a way to help him."

"Poor Michael, no possibility exists of his coming any time soon. Three years! Oh, my word. What has Father done?" Julia eased away from Mary and paced the floor. "Michael, of all of us children, most wanted to come to America."

She shivered. "The idea of telling Kate worries me. She will not accept this latest development without an explosion of anger."

"What can I do to help?" Mary walked to the fireplace and tossed in a few crumbs.

"I must talk this over with Anne." Julia stepped away from the counter. "May I leave early for the mission with the day-old goods and stop and visit her on the way?"

Keeper of Trust

❀ ❀ ❀

In only a few minutes, Julia sat in a small upholstered chair in Anne's parlor. With her sister settled beside her at the end of a large overstuffed sofa, she explained about Martin's treatments. "I will not visit him for the next two days."

"I will pray these treatments help Martin with the pain." Anne searched Julia's eyes. "Something else troubles you. What is it?"

Julia pulled her chair close and reached out to take Anne's hands in her own. "I would rather perform most any chore in the world than come here with this tale." She shuffled her feet, and took a deep breath before she lost courage.

"It will be nearly three years before we can think of Michael coming to us. With the silence from Blackwater, we must also suppose additional passage money will be required." She studied Anne's eyes. With her sister's wavering emotions, how would she react?

Anne threw herself down on the arm of the chair and sobbed. Her tight bun loosened, sending wisps of hair flying all about. When she lifted her head, tears covered her face, rolling down to her collar.

Terribly, of course. Julia flew into action, passing Anne a handkerchief, and then rushing to the kitchen to fetch a cup of water. After waiting for her to take a long drink, she patted her shoulder.

Anne met Julia's gaze "How much longer can we do this?" As soon as the words were out, Anne shook her head.

"I am so sorry for this outburst. I should never have spoken such harsh words." Anne wiped the tears that poured out. "I should not even think of the money. Those poor, dear people. Michael indentured for two years—"

"The indenture is for three years," Julia said.

"Three years! Oh no. A lifetime. And Father ill—it must be so." Anne rose from her chair and began to move around the room. "We have not received a letter in Father's hand in many months. Mother and Maggie are surely doing the hard labor." She returned to her chair. "And they are all hungry, while we are well and contented here."

"Anne, please. You must calm yourself." Julia moved to the seat besides her. "We will help Michael, somehow."

"No more crying, I promise. Let us keep ourselves busy. I must finish my supper preparations, and I will put you to work, as well." Anne moved toward the kitchen, and Julia followed. "While we work there will be less opportunity for tears."

Julia found a sharp knife and scraped the carrots clean. "We have joined forces before, and we will stand together again…and again…until they are all here." She turned to her sister. "How big?" When Anne held her fingers an inch apart, she chopped. "Do not fret. You must be calm and not upset yourself. With God's help, we will not be deterred." She paused. "Will I also peel these potatoes for you?"

Anne handed her the potato knife. "My foolish weeping is no cause for worry at all. It is only the baby, I am sure." Anne's expression, just beginning to brighten, turned solemn once more. "Our concern now is, how will Kate bear this latest news?"

Julia's gripped the potato tighter. "That is exactly why I have come to you. I need your advice and strength to support me. You know Kate will be furious when I tell her. And to think, Lizzie has known all along. Why has she not told us?"

"I do have a plan we may consider." Anne said.

"A plan? What are you saying?" Julia tossed a potato onto the counter. How could she ever follow Anne's sudden and uncharacteristic changes in mood and demeanor?

"I should have told you this right off, before I gave in to tears. It may help us all bear the disappointment. In truth, it is James's idea." Anne placed a bright blue cloth on the kitchen table. "What an amazing coincidence. He came up with the proposal without even knowing about Michael's indenture."

"Dear James. What would we do without him? Julia retrieved the potato and continued to peel. "What is his plan?"

"He and Ned are putting money aside for passage for their father and brother, Dan. You know, James always sees the positive side of things. Well...he feels we could save enough in the next year or so to bring them all here together." Anne removed dinner plates from the cupboard. "He suggested we send the money to his father to purchase the fares. Then, as he said, 'we will have them all here and the matter will be put to rest.'"

"And Father and Mother will not be able to spend the money." Julia's lips turned up slightly. "What a fine idea. And James is a good soul. Even he must grow tired of sending money to our family and neglecting his own."

"A little, perhaps." Pride crossed Anne's face. "He never complains."

"It is a grand scheme." Julia placed the peeled potatoes in a pan of water. With Anne's words of support and James' excellent plan, she could face Kate.

"Do you wish me to accompany you, to stand beside you when you tell her of this new trouble?" Anne washed her hands, passing the soap to Julia.

"You stay here in your lovely home and finish your supper preparations." Julia headed into the hall and slipped her arms into her coat. "Just brace yourself. Kate will have ample opportunity to share her thoughts over Michael's indenture with you tomorrow." She followed Anne to the back door.

"Ah, I have forgotten my other mission. Mary sent me to invite you and James for supper tomorrow. I am afraid you will be hearing plenty of Kate's opinions on the matter when you see her then. Well...perhaps even she can approve of James's plan."

"Of course we will come tomorrow evening." Anne opened the door wide. "By then, Kate will have time to think over James's plan."

"Could you even imagine?" Julia crossed the porch, with confidence in her steps. "Do we dare to dream, all of them here with us? This scheme should also serve to ease the pain for Lizzie. Surely, she has been suffering over keeping back this secret." With a wave, Julia took up the bakery baskets and started for the mission.

❀ ❀ ❀

When she entered the bakery, she found Lizzie working alone in the shop. She approached her with a firm stride contradicting the turmoil raging within her. "Lizzie dear, I learned about Michael's indenture from Mary, who heard it from Walter, who—"

"Oh Julia, I am so sorry." Lizzie stepped away, and Julia could barely hear her next words. "I just did not wish to make you all unhappy." Her face reddened. She sobbed with great, gulping heaves. "I must stop this…I cannot behave so…in the shop."

Julia placed a wet cloth over Lizzie's forehead. "It is all right, dear. Take deep breaths…I'll get another cloth." There had been more than enough tears for one day.

"Listen to the plan James and Ned developed. It is marvelous and will make you feel much better." Julia related the story quickly. She breathed a long sigh to see Lizzie's eyes brighten.

"I believe we should run back and tell Kate right now, before I lose my courage."

"I agree." Lizzie sniffled. "Her anger is another reason I did not tell anyone about Michael's indenture. Her outbursts frighten me."

Julia took Lizzie's hand and they walked to the dressmaking shop in the back of the building.

"Will you be ready for supper soon, Kate?" Her sister sat alone in the room, slipping a needle quickly and expertly through silky red cloth. "Lizzie and I…"

Kate lifted the curious, rather gaudy material she held.

"We…Ah…came back here…" Julia picked up one end of the long panel. "What possible use could anyone have for this ugly cloth, Kate?"

"It is meant to be a covering for a table in one of the hotel's parlors. It is much too shiny and red for my taste, but I did not choose the material." A suspicious frown grew across Kate's face, as she shifted her gaze between Julia and Lizzie.

"Unless you two are here to order dresses for yourselves, I presume you have something to tell me. What is it?"

"James and Ned have a plan to bring the whole family out at one time. When they have saved enough, they will send it to their father to purchase the fares." She spoke rapidly, her voice rising. "Now we learn that Michael has been indentured to a farmer for three years."

"I knew it. I suspected they were up to something." Kate bent forward as if she had been pummeled to her midsection with a heavy stick. As Julia stepped back, she bounded up, holding the red cloth in one hand and shaking her other fist. "The conditions back home…The British…Those poor, dear children." The new plan had done nothing to soften this blow for her.

"Please, try not to be upset." Lizzie reached for Kate's arm, but she pulled away.

"Father and Mother had no right to send poor Michael into indenture. It's no more than slavery. Well, that is the end of it. I'll not hear another word from them, or read anything they have written. I am finished." Kate turned her chair around and sat down, placing her back to them.

Julia lifted the ugly red material from Kate's hands, and moved away.

"Oh." Lizzie gasped. "Julia!"

Kate advanced toward Julia. "Hand that back! The cloth cannot be soiled. I must finish the hem tonight." She picked up a long wooden ruler with a stand attached that she used for hemming dresses. Lunging closer, she caught a corner of the cloth with one hand, grasping the ruler like a sword with the other.

Spinning in the opposite direction, Julia ran, the length of red silk fluttering high above her head.

"Julia!" Kate followed her, lifting up her end of the cloth, holding the material taut between them. They ran through the passageway leading to the back door

Reaching it first, Julia skidded to a stop. She stretched her right arm high over her head to keep the long cloth off of the floor then jiggled the latch and attempted to pry it open.

She glanced to the side. Her sister was closing in on her. Kate clutched her end of the material with one hand, still waving the measuring stick in the air with the other.

Julia wrestled with the door latch. At last, it flew open. She pushed through the entryway on to the street, with Kate at her heels.

"What is this?" Walter's voice boomed from the open doorway.

Julia turned long enough to see her little sister standing beside him, her hands on her hips.

"I'm sure I don't know." Lizzie's voice carried to the street. "Julia has taken leave of her senses, and Kate is after her."

She gritted her teeth and pushed ahead, running in earnest now, sprinting the length of the deserted street.

"Right behind you." Kate's footsteps quickened.

Reaching the end of the road, Julia turned the corner. With Kate on her heels, they headed toward the farthest end of the bakery building.

They hurried along the back wall of Dempsey's, a way Julia had never ventured before. Scraggly bushes, weeds, and low tree limbs darkened the area and impeded their progress. Hindered by the brush and the uneven dirt path, Julia slowed her steps. What a gloomy, spooky place? So dark and chilly. She shivered. How had this silly run ever begun? If only they were both back in the warm bakery.

"I am coming." Kate's voice brought comfort. Her hand touched Julia's.

"Only because I'm pushing aside the brush for you." Julia lengthened her strides.

"You are captured!" Kate grasped a firm hold of her arm.

Occupied with keeping the material high off the ground, Julia could not wriggle away.

"Surrender my cloth, you knave." Kate laughed.

Julia's groan faded to a chuckle. "Ah, I will be happy to hand it over to you."

"It is dark back here." Her voice dropped to a whisper. She pushed a low branch out of Julia's path. "And scary. Double scary for you. If this cover touches the filthy ground, you are in a world of trouble."

They turned the far corner at last and headed back toward the entrance at the other side of the building.

"Wait." Kate spoke with authority. "Reach out straight."

Julia obeyed, and Kate wrapped the material loosely around her arms.

They moved on, Julia's arms aching to be released from the long, billowing bundle.

Kate hovered close. "I caught a flicker of light coming from Mary's parlor."

Julia sighed. "Thank goodness."

"I am sorry I yelled about Michael. It is certainly not your doing." Kate faced her and offered a slight smile.

"I'm sorry I ran off with your ugly tablecloth." Julia pressed her lips tight and drew in a deep breath. "You must promise to write to Michael and our parents, and not hate them."

They ascended the steps slowly. "Allow me to help you." Kate supported Julia's elbow.

"Please." Julia giggled.

The door opened as soon as their feet touched the porch. "Are you two all right?" Lizzie stood in the entrance, her eyes guarded.

Julia shook her head sharply from side to side. "Yes...Ah, I'm not sure?" She looked to Kate, a challenge in her eyes. "I must have an answer."

"Well..." Kate tapped her shoulder with the measuring stick. "I'll write to Michael."

"And our parents?"

"I will consider it."

Julia shifted her weight between her feet, as Kate unwound the cloth. "Take this corner for me, Lizzie. Hold it high, please." She rubbed her arms as they moved through the doorway together. Ah, relief.

The three girls sailed past the entire Dempsey group, who had gathered in the hallway. Lizzie led the way, followed by Julia, Kate, and the ridiculous red material. They giggled as they headed for the dressmaking shop, Kate still thrusting the yardstick high in the air.

As they passed Walter, he led the group in applause.

Julia scooted closer to Kate. She eased the measuring stick away and handed it to Lizzie. Bowing to the Dempsey folks, they disappeared into Kate's shop.

Julia sighed. Had her unthinking outburst brought about any resolutions? Had her foolish run eased the blow of Michael's indenture for Kate? If only it could.

Chapter Thirteen

A blizzard blanketed the city, interrupting an unusually mild February. Thick flakes poured down like heavy, white raindrops. In spite of the abundance of snow, Julia trudged along the streets from her work at the church to the hospital, the brightness all around her lifting her spirits and spurring her on.

On the first day after the heavy snowfall, Julia walked into Martin's room to find him in a sound sleep. At a quiet knock, she raised her eyes to see Martin's nurse beckoning to her out into the hall.

"Is everything proceeding as expected, Miss Cohan?" Julia pushed wisps of hair up into her bonnet. "Is Martin well?"

"Yes, he is more than all right. The visiting doctor's treatment worked wonders for him. I only wished to inform you of the grand progress he is making." The nurse sat on a bench, her back and shoulders straight and her hands folded. Her warm eyes revealed the kindness hovering beneath her prim appearance.

"Ah, that is grand to hear." Julia sat beside the nurse, stretching her legs out in front of her.

"You know the doctor challenged Martin to walk thirty paces around the room, three times each day?" At Julia's nod, Miss Cohan pulled out a notepad. "I must say, I did not believe he should try such a thing without help, but his response to the challenge has been remarkable. In no time at all, he moved the short distance from the chair to the bed with no difficulty."

"Am I right in believing this is good news?" Julia leaned closer.

"The doctor has now urged him further. He proposed a wager of a fine cigar, if Martin could walk a few steps out in the hallway, unescorted." She shook her head slowly. "This morning, he took his usual paces around the room, and then after a short respite, he proceeded along the hallway two times with no rest between rounds. He has already succeeded at winning the cigar. The effort left him so exhausted, he returned to his bed immediately and he has been asleep for hours."

"Ah, that is wonderful." Julia jumped up and paced in front of Miss Cohan. "Do you think this activity will strengthen him?"

Miss Cohan nodded. "I doubted Dr. Gallagher at first. The long walk concerned me. Martin experiences such dreadful pain and he is still so weak. The doctor proved right. With the added exertion, Martin is eating with enthusiasm and sleeping soundly. He is already growing stronger."

"'Tis wonderful." Julia grasped Miss Cohan's hands, almost toppling her notepad. "Thank you for telling me."

"Dr. Gallagher is a remarkable man. Martin is fortunate to have him supervising his care." The nurse rose to leave. "This is a beginning only. I see a wonderful recovery ahead for him."

"Thank you, again…" Miss Cohan had already hurried off down the hall.

Back in the hospital room, Julia restrained her excitement over this wonderful new development and sat quietly while Martin slept. When he awakened, he smiled at her. "How was your day at St. Vincent's?" His voice grew stronger. "Was it a cold trip to the hospital?"

"My day was busy, but otherwise fine. And no, it is not too cold." Why was he making no mention of his walk? "Since the great snowstorm passed, it has warmed considerably.

"But, tell me about you. I understand from Miss Cohan you've done some walking." She rose and approached him.

"Ah, I planned to meet you out in the hallway as you arrived, and then I fell asleep." He frowned. "I wished to surprise you. Well, tomorrow, I will do it."

"Oh dear, I have spoiled your plan. Do not worry. To see you in the hallway waiting for me will, indeed, be a grand surprise." She twirled around. Coming to a stop before him, she took his face in her hands. "I look forward to it. I am so proud of you."

"Thank you, Julia." Martin sat up straight, shoulders squared. "Your good opinion means the world to me."

"Does the walking provoke even greater pain?" She smoothed his pillow. "I cannot bear for you to suffer."

"Actually, it helps. Sends me right off to sleep." He yawned. "Do not be offended if I drift away in the middle of a sentence."

While they sat talking, he did fall asleep, and Julia rejoiced silently over his success. Still, worry tugged at her thoughts. Martin's manner toward her remained polite and friendly. She must be patient, she knew. She would not give in to fretfulness.

But, the year 1867 had dawned, the year they planned to be married. Since the accident, he had not said he loved her. He never mentioned the looming wedding, that great calamity rushing toward her.

❊ ❊ ❊

"I have received reports of Martin's grand progress." Father Burns set aside his appointment book as they worked in the office at St. Vincent's a few days later.

"He is making great strides physically, but I must confess my worry." She pulled at her chin. "Martin never mentions a word of our wedding. It is possible we will be required to postpone the ceremony."

"Give it time, Julia." Father Burns removed his glasses and placed them on his desk. "Martin experienced a terrible shock. I'm sure his tremendous pain alters his thinking. His strength amazes me. While I once wondered if he would ever recover, he has already begun to walk about the hospital. Have faith. He will rise above this terrible injury."

"When Martin sits in his chair, he always manages to cover his left side with a blanket." Julia attempted to explore her own feelings. Could she make Father understand? "I know what a tragic loss lurks beneath the covering. His arm is missing. Nothing will bring it back. I have difficulty grasping the truth of it, myself. While I grieve for his loss, I cannot know what Martin is thinking, how he is feeling. I am whole. He is not. There is naught I can do to change that fact."

"Do you suppose he worries you will no longer love him, since he is without an arm?" Father Burns spoke softly.

"I know he does." She raised herself up in her chair. "I cannot seem to convince him otherwise."

"Have your feelings changed at all?" Father Burns looked directly into her eyes.

Julia gasped. "Do you believe my love for Martin has lessened? Is that how I appear?"

"Of course not, my dear. I have observed you sitting at his bedside day after day, hour upon hour. Your devotion to Martin radiates from your every step and motion. I never doubted your constancy. I only wished to make you aware of how Martin may be thinking."

"The injury makes no difference in my feelings." Julia lifted her shoulders. "If anything, his bravery and strength have made me love him more than ever."

"You have convinced me." Father Burns patted her arm. "Continue to reassure Martin with that same forcefulness. As the pain recedes and his recovery progresses, your strong declarations of love will reach beyond his wall of resistance."

Julia brushed away a tear and nodded.

"And if we must postpone the wedding, we will make the change in the book." He held the calendar in the air. "It is only a day in the year, Julia. There will be many more ahead for you and Martin."

Julia picked up her pen, a smile pushing through. "Thank you for listening, Father. Putting my concerns into words is a grand relief. Your good counsel makes me feel better already." She turned back to her work, entering sums in a large ungainly ledger. Her fears had lessened, if only a little.

❀ ❀ ❀

Julia and Walter stood in the doorway of Martin's room the next evening, as his brother Patrick and Dr. Gallagher walked toward them. "Come to my office." The doctor gestured toward the end of the hall. "We must discuss Martin's discharge from the hospital."

"I intend to care for him." Patrick ran his hands through his thick hair.

"I, too, will devote myself to his care." Julia folded her hands in her lap.

"Well meaning as you both are, neither option will serve entirely." Walter sat on the edge of the doctor's desk, facing them. "Your position, Patrick, consumes a great portion of your days, and you have already taken on the handling of Martin's personal arrangements, paying his rent at the boarding house, and keeping records of his other expenses for him."

"He's my brother." Patrick shifted in his chair. "He would do the same for me."

"Martin will not be capable of caring for himself. He will need additional help, once he leaves the hospital. And, Julia's nursing of him would be impossible. It would not be considered proper. If you had been married before the accident happened, no such problems would exist." Walter reached out and patted her shoulder. "Sadly, that is not the case."

Julia planted her feet firmly beneath her chair. If only they had not waited...but useless musing changed nothing.

"It will be a few weeks before Martin's discharge." The doctor came around the desk to stand beside Walter. "A decision is not necessary tonight. I only wish you to plan for the day."

❁ ❁ ❁

Julia arrived at the hospital from St. Vincent's, a few days later, to find Mrs. Flynn visiting with Martin.

"I've come to steal Martin away." When Julia raised an eyebrow, she laughed. "I have a nice, comfortable room in my home for you, Martin, if you would consider it?"

"You are kind, Mrs. Flynn." Martin adjusted his chair until he faced her.

"That is such a generous offer." Julia closed her eyes for a minute then opened them. "Is there a first floor bedroom?" The Flynn's home had been designed around a maze of stairways and long hallways, with the bedrooms all on the second and third floors. She knew Martin shared her appreciation, but the arrangement would not work at all.

"We will consider it, Mrs. Flynn," Martin said. "Thank you."

A few hours later, Mary arrived with a basket of fresh biscuits and a grin for Martin. "We could transform one of the empty spaces at the back of the Dempsey's building into a bedroom for you." She sat in the chair beside Martin and took his hand.

Julia studied the bare branches of a tree brushing against their window. Mary meant well, but several factors stood in the way. The location of the room would place Martin a long way from anyone if he needed help during the night. Though, Patrick could move in with him. But, wasn't Mary worried over the propriety of her living in the same building? What would everyone think?

On a Sunday in late February, Julia arrived at the hospital to find Martin sitting up in a chair, in good spirits. "How are you? Have you experienced much pain today?" His smile came easier each time she came. But…each small progression took forever.

"I've been waiting for you," Martin said, "I wished—"

Anne and James entered the room, both wearing the same purposeful expression.

"What is it?" Julia looked from one to the other. "Is something wrong?"

"Nothing is wrong." Anne grinned, as James helped her out of her coat. He pulled up a chair for her beside Martin.

"We have something to discuss with you." Anne gripped the chair handles, lowering herself to the seat. She directed her words to him. "We wish you to stay with us when you leave the hospital. Would you consider it?"

"It is a kind offer." Martin glanced at Julia and hesitated. "Patrick and I have already talked about letting your upstairs rooms. But, I cannot impose myself on you."

Frowning, Julia patted her sister's shoulder. When Anne removed her coat and sat close to Martin, he surely noticed her condition. He must hold her same concern. His care would be too much for Anne.

James stood behind Anne. "We did take some liberty on that score, Martin. Anne learned of a nurse who has earned grand praise for her skill and compassion."

"I hope you will bear with my pushiness." Anne removed her hat and placed it on the bed. "I have already spoken with her on your behalf. I believe she is a fine woman. If you agree, she would come to the house each day until you no longer need her assistance."

Martin's brother appeared in the doorway, and Julia waved him in. "Ah, Patrick, you are just in time. The Duffs offered Martin a place to stay."

As James went over the plan again, Julia glanced toward Patrick. His eyes had softened. She turned in time to see Martin's grin. How many months had passed since the two brothers smiled together?

"It is a grand idea." Patrick removed his hat and coat and draped them over the end of the bed. "Have you completed the rooms to let? I could move in now, if you are ready to take me on as a boarder. I will care for Martin, when I'm not at work. And, he and I would both be thrilled to abandon our present unsavory rooming house." Patrick fixed his gaze on his brother. "Do you not agree?"

"I promise I will leave the extra care to the nurse and to Patrick." Anne offered the brothers a salute. "Will you come to us, Martin?"

Julia sat quietly, but her heart pounded.

"Yes. I think it is a find idea. I promise you, Anne, I will cause as little work as possible. I will work hard to become independent." Martin's blanket slipped from his shoulder a little, and he allowed it.

"It is a wonderful thing, Anne and James." Julia jumped up and stood beside her sister. Here, she'd worried Martin would be moved to a place where she would not be allowed to see him. She could imagine no impropriety in visiting him at her sister's home. And the burst of joy shining in Martin's eyes brought such pleasure. "Thank you both."

※ ※ ※

On the evening after the Martin left the hospital, Julia joined the group at the Duffs' for supper. He had finally given up on the blankets he draped around himself in the hospital, but now wore a bulky shirt to disguise his lack of an arm.

When the talk around the table centered on his progress, Julia held her breath. Would the attention upset him?

"I worried the move from the hospital would take a severe toll on you," James said, "but you seem to have made a remarkable recovery."

"I am feeling well," Martin nodded to James and Anne. "Your bright, cheerful home has helped to raise my spirits. Thank you both for allowing Patrick and me to move in here."

"And for finding Martin's nurse." Patrick passed a platter of chicken to Ned, on his right. "I admire her nursing skill, and I believe she and Martin have already formed a strong bond. She reminds me of our grandmother."

"Patrick is right." Martin raised his water glass to them all. "With Nurse Patty's coaching, I have begun to walk about the first floor. As a result, no one must carry a tray to me."

"And you passed that platter without spilling a drop of gravy on me," James grinned at him. "That Patty is a jewel."

Laughter spread around the table, including Martin. Julia beamed. How wonderful to see him happy.

❁ ❁ ❁

After supper, Julia and Martin moved to the parlor and spent a few moments alone for the first time since his move. When Martin settled into a chair, Julia placed a small pillow behind his slumping shoulders. Had the supper been too strenuous for him? Or, was she the cause of his blanched skin and sad eyes?

She blinked back tears. "Does my presence here make you uncomfortable?"

"Of course not." Surprise shone in Martin's eyes. "This is your sister's home. She wishes you to come for supper." He adjusted his collar. "And, I...look forward to your visits."

"If that is truly the case, you must accustom yourself to having me close by your side, sharing your every upward stride." Julia stood before the fireplace, gripping the box Kate sent with her. Why could he not offer further encouragement? Had his feelings changed?

Lifting her chin, she placed the carton in his lap. "This gift comes from my sister Kate."

"Thank you." He opened the box with his good hand, balancing it against his chest. A slight wince flickered across his face. He pulled out two shirts, brown and blue, and held them up, inspecting them thoroughly. A stiff cloth lined the inside of the left sleeve. A loop sewed into the cuff would attach to a button at the waist, making the missing arm appear less noticeable.

A slow grin crossed Martin's face. "I believe these shirts will work out well for me. Kate is a thoughtful girl, and her design is ingenious. Tell her I will try one of the shirts tomorrow and provide her with a full report." He spread the blue shirt across his body. "What do you think?"

"It brings out the blue of your eyes." Julia smiled at him.

"Please give her my thanks, and I will add my own appreciation when I see her." He reached out and squeezed her hand.

❋ ❋ ❋

"Sorry to inconvenience you, Julia, truly I am," Anne scrubbed a thick cloth across the dinner plates, "but you must no longer enter Martin's bedroom."

"I…"

Julia stared at her sister. She shook her head.

Anne waved away Julia's indignant surprise. "You must admit to the right in this. You and Martin are engaged to be married. Now that he is regaining his former vigor, we must keep our home and you in particular above any hint of reproach." Her lip quivered.

"I would never balk at anything you asked of me. You and James have shown Martin a world of kindness." Julia pushed back her distress and grinned at her sister. "Martin and I will spend our time in the parlor or in the dining room."

"It is for the best." Anne pumped water into the teakettle and placed it on the stove. "Do not worry, Julia. This arrangement will work out."

"The truth is, you have no need to worry at all." She touched Anne's sleeve. "While Martin acts genuinely pleased to see me, he treats me as an old school chum. No words of endearment or expressions of love. The subject of our marriage never arises." She lowered her head. The tears came, even as she struggled to push them back.

"If only you two were married already." Anne sighed.

"I have wished the same thing over and over since the accident, but my yearnings have changed nothing. It proves difficult to step back and watch as others help him." Julia rubbed the top of the sink, pressing until her knuckles turned white. "As his betrothed, if indeed I remain his betrothed, I must take no part in his care. It is not my place."

Julia averted Anne's gaze, attacking a stubborn spot on the counter. Would the time ever come, when she would take her place beside Martin? Or, would this new limitation widen the distance already developing between them?

❃ ❃ ❃

"I believe I will walk to the corner," A lightweight cloak thrown across his shoulders, Martin met Julia at Anne's front door, on a windy Saturday afternoon.

"Are you strong enough? It has only been two weeks since you left the hospital." Julia drew her brows together. "Shall I accompany you?"

"I must attempt this for myself, but have no care, I will return before you even miss me." He crossed the front porch and moved tentatively down the sturdy wooden steps.

Julia watched, inhaling deeply as he walked away. Exercise would be good for him. His desire for independence signaled a move toward recovery. She must not yield to her worry.

❃ ❃ ❃

The next Saturday, Julia waved him off as he left to conquer a two-block excursion. Another day, Martin reported he had walked to the park. "I may have pushed myself a little too far."

A beaming smile lighted his face. Julia's heart warmed to near bursting. It had been a long while.

"Along my way," he lowered himself into a chair, "I met Walter's baker friend Gus Mueller. Gus brought me to his turnverein."

Julia's eyes widened. "Is that the gymnastics club? I assumed the place was for the benefit of German men only."

"Well, I suppose that may be true." Martin's breathing remained heavy. "I had the impression Gus had already discussed my injury with the men. He must wield some influence among them, because everyone made me welcome and offered to help me."

"Gus is a nice man." Julia nodded.

"I met some fine fellows there, all working to improve the strength and agility of their bodies. The activities exhilarated me." Martin smiled up at her.

Julia could not hold back her own grin. Though Martin looked weary, he appeared relaxed and animated. "Is the exercise too strenuous for you? Is it painful?"

"Ah, there is some pain. It is ever with me. Still, in the hour I spent at Gus' turnverein, I felt alive as I have not been in a long time. I plan to go there each day." Uneasiness returned to his eyes.

"I do not mean to fret." She touched his face. "I only wish what's good for you."

"Do not worry. The doctor approves of the exercises. I stopped at his office on the way home and talked it over with him. He challenged me to push myself to whatever limits I can endure, until I've regained my strength." Martin's jaw firmed. "As I improve, I will need little assistance. Nurse Patty has been wonderful, but I do not believe I will need her help or my brother's much longer."

He stood beside her, his erect, confident stance a joy to behold. "I am sure Patrick will soon have a few free evenings."

Keeper of Trust

❀ ❀ ❀

Two weeks later, Julia hurried from the mission to Anne's. She rushed to the parlor, frowning at the empty chair.

"He has not returned from his daily visit to the gymnasium." Anne joined her. "Sit here and wait. I'm sure it will not be long."

Julia stood at the window, listening, until she heard the footsteps signaling his safe arrival.

"I found a job for myself." Martin bounded into the room.

Julia couldn't help but beam. What a joy to hear confidence in Martin's voice. "That is wonderful."

"I know my time as a driver is done. Ah sure, the managers all visited me at the hospital. They brayed over my courage and praised me for upholding the honor of the Omnibus Company." Martin circled the chair before he sat. "Their words proved nothing more than posturing. They have not dismissed me officially, but I know they doubt I could control the horses and passenger wagon. In truth, I felt a bit uncertain of it myself."

She had watched with pride as the activities he performed at the gymnasium returned Martin to near his former strength. Listening to him talk and seeing this new confidence was grand, but still...? Had he regained the balance and dexterity needed to handle this new job? She could not bear if he suffered further pain or disappointment.

"Today, I made the acquaintance of a fine German fellow, a friend of Gus and Tilda Mueller. Karl is starting up a shoe factory. While we worked at balance exercises, he talked about his construction plans." Martin tapped the fingers of his right hand along the arm of his chair. "Karl spoke of his attempts and difficulties at drawing up lists of supplies and equipment."

Julia inhaled sharply. "Just the work you are trained to do."

"When I told him of my Army experience, he proclaimed me the perfect man to take over the purchasing job. Of course,

173

he could see I had lost my left arm. Before he even asked, I explained what had happened. It did not seem to matter." Martin rose from the chair and paced again.

"He had made up his mind. Said the missing limb should not hinder me. Apparently, my work at the turnverein demonstrated that I have regained enough of my stamina to handle his position. He declared that, as long as my writing hand is sound, I will have no problem." Martin placed his hand over his heart. "He offered me a job right there and then. What a grand opportunity this is."

Julia threw her arms about his neck and kissed him on each cheek. "The position sounds wonderful. I am so proud of you." Heat crossed her cheeks as she drew back. Anne would restrict her from the parlor next.

Martin held her for a moment then he released her. "What a fool I am." In a flash, his fine smile vanished. "Ah no, my lovely lass, this will not do." He stepped back, placing a space between them. "Here I come in, bursting with pride over a new position…" Martin walked to the fireplace and held his hand before the flames. "Ah, my…I cannot even hold my girl in a proper manner."

"No." His optimistic mood could not slip away, even for a moment. She could not bear it. "Now my dear, I believe that embrace was fine and proper. To be certain, let us try once again."

Martin hesitated then gathered her close to him. "Oh, Julia."

She relaxed against his strong shoulders. "This feels more than good, perhaps magnificent. We must practice until our hugs attain their former grand status." She raised herself up on her toes and whispered into his ear. "One day, after our wedding, we will try them in a great warm bed." Her words sounded wanton, but this desperate situation necessitated drastic measures. May God forgive her boldness.

As quickly as it had come, Martin's smile disappeared. "I cannot consider loving you, Julia. I must be capable of supporting a wife, before I can allow myself to dream of marriage and a home."

"But, your new position?" Warmth radiated through her body. She clenched her fists. Would he not consider the life they planned together?

"You are a wonderful girl. I would not have survived after the accident without you by my side. I owe my life to you. I know it. If not for your encouragement..." A mask of sorrow covered Martin's face.

"And our arrangements?" Julia pressed her fists against her thighs. How could he go back on his word?

"Please try to understand. You deserve a fine home and a husband who will provide for you. Until I am able, I am honor bound to step back." He stood rigid, unmoving, ever the soldier. "Be patient with me, Julia. Allow me the time to become a full man again, a person deserving of your love."

"All right." Pain seared every ounce of her person. Her body numb, her command over her tongue unsure, she stumbled from Anne's parlor, and crept to the foyer. Martin followed behind her, watching silently as she slipped into her coat.

"Will I see you tomorrow?" Martin's eyes looked as sad as she felt.

"At St. Vincent's? Of course." She stepped out to the porch. "Please, tell Anne I cannot stay. I will speak with her in the morning."

"Will you walk with me after church?" Martin asked.

"Do you want me to walk with you?" Julia lifted her right brow. Did he? What had he been saying? Had he called off their engagement? Had he allowed his principles of honor to destroy their lives? And, did he now wish her to spend Sunday afternoon with him in the park?

Yet, how could she say no? He'd suffered such unbearable pain these past months. She could not cause him any more hurt.

"I will see you tomorrow."

❈ ❈ ❈

Later that evening, as she stretched out in her bed, Kate drew nearer and leaned in to meet her eyes. "What's happened, Julia? What is it?"

She scooted up, as Lizzie approached and eased down beside her. "Martin found a job...I hugged him...He stepped away." Surely her words made no sense. Her tears poured out. She could not go on.

"That cannot be. Martin is devoted to you." Lizzie removed her handkerchief from her pocket and handed it to Julia. "Anyone who observes him knows the love he holds for you."

Kate rubbed her shoulder. "Be strong, Julia. Things will work out. Once Martin experiences success in his new position and gains some confidence, he will change his mind. In the end, it will all be fine."

"Well, if Martin does toss me aside, I may make the journey to Oregon after all." Julia's laugh sounded flat. She bowed her head. Once she would have thrilled at talking of such a trip, but the thought of experiencing any adventure without Martin at her side, no longer brought her joy.

"I may just go along with you," Kate said.

"Oh no." Lizzie groaned. "I am only now recovering from my long journey. Please, please do not speak of going anywhere." She gazed at them with a pitiful look.

Julia and Kate both laughed.

"You have your sisters to help you. Everything will be fine. I know it will." Kate gathered strands of Julia's hair and twisted them into a braid.

"How can I help you?" Lizzie asked. "Do you wish to read a letter? Or, shall we pray?"

"A prayer, please."

They joined hands and Lizzie cleared her throat. "We thank you God for our many blessings. Please shower the Carty sisters with wisdom and understanding. And, please, please bless Julia and Martin with happiness once again."

Keeper of Trust

A measure of comfort and peace settled around Julia. How she longed for that prayer to be answered.

Chapter Fourteen

March, 1867

Julia raised her fist to the door, paused, and drew back her hand. Should she even visit? After Martin's grand declaration of honor before love, was there any reason? She let her arm fall to her side. Heart heavy, she trudged back to Dempsey's. How could she face him now?

The following day, she did the same. However, when she arrived back home, Mary awaited with a note from Anne. She scanned it, exhaling a sharp breath. "She's invited me to supper tomorrow evening."

"Aw, that's a fine thing. Anne is so thoughtful." Mary waved toward the counter. "If you will watch the shop, I must run to the oven room for a moment."

Julia held up the note...read it again. Oh, she wished to decline...she should. But Anne and James had done so much. She'd not upset them for the world. And, Martin...she missed him so.

She started off for her sister's home the next night, willing her unsteady thoughts to settle. What would she say to Martin? How would he respond? And, what explanation could she offer Anne and James for her absence?

She slowed her pace. Time to calm herself. She mustn't worry so. With each stride, her breathing became more labored. A heavy weight impeded each lift of her foot. The three-block walk took an eternity.

Martin waited in the doorway as she approached the Duff's home.

"Good evening, Julia." He offered no hug or kiss. "How are you faring?"

"I am well, thank you." She gave him a brief, curt nod. A twinge of guilt struck her, as hurt dulled his eyes. After an awkward pause, she followed him to the kitchen. What was he thinking? Were they to proceed as if everything remained unchanged between them? Had she imagined the devastating exchange of a few days before?

Anne stood at the sink, peeling potatoes and watching out the window. "Ah hello, Julia." After a quick hug, she went back to her preparations for their meal. "You and Martin may as well sit in the parlor for a while. I am concerned our supper will be delayed. I cannot imagine where James has gotten to."

Of course, Martin had not mentioned anything of the change in their situation. He kept everything to himself. But Anne...had she not noticed her absence?

Julia glanced sideways at Martin. Seeing his air of unconcern, she frowned. She stepped to the sink and seized a potato.

"Allow me to assist you, Anne. I'll take that knife and you can tend to your salad."

"Thank you, dear." Anne placed a cup and saucer on the table. "Martin, pour yourself some coffee."

As she attacked the mound of potatoes before her, Julia observed her sister's interaction with Martin. Anne sensed when he needed help. She allowed him to do what he could for himself, such as pour coffee into his cup. She went about things calmly, without fussing. Julia pursed her lips. There was her problem. She hovered and fussed too much.

Anne's smile toward Martin, one that would help soothe his hurts and fears, shamed her. While Julia had become so annoyed with him, her sister had not forgotten the gravity of his injury. How prideful to think only of herself. Poor Martin was far from restored.

In the next moment, James burst through the back door. Tension and agitation poured from his flushed face, punctuating his grim expression.

"My dear..."

"Oh, hello, Julia, Martin. I apologize for interrupting your conversation. I must tell you this incredible story and apologize at the same time." He paced around the kitchen table as he talked. "I do not know if I am madder or sorrier."

"Whatever is it?" Anne remained serene amid James's distress, with no trace of the upset from the early months of her expecting.

Julia face warmed, in spite of her attempt to maintain the same composure. She tapped her foot as she chopped the now peeled and cleaned potatoes into small chunks. What on earth had displeased him so? She placed her knife on the sink and leaned closer.

"Bill O'Brien asked if I heard of our neighbor's newest business venture. Francis Reilly purchased an additional hotel with some business partners in Chicago."

While he talked, James pulled out a cup and saucer and placed it on the table next to Martin's. When he attempted to pour the coffee, his hand shook the pot so mightily Martin took it and poured for him

James added cream to the cup. "O'Brien claimed one of the investors is Dermot Fortune. I could not believe it!"

"Do you think Francis knows about our history with Fortune?" Julia waved her hand in the air. "Oh, I'm sorry for interrupting, James. Please go on."

"I wished to give him every possible credit, and on my way home, I stopped at the pub to talk to him." James paced around the kitchen table. "Can you imagine my shock, when I learned he knows the full story and seems not to care at all?"

"It cannot be possible." Julia placed the potatoes in the large container she had pulled from Anne's cupboard. Pressing down hard on the handle of the water pump, she filled it and moved the pot to the top of the stove. Then, she walked over to stand beside James as he took a gulp of his coffee.

"'Do you know the man is a thief?' I asked him. 'Do you know of the money Fortune stole from Anne and Julia? Funds set aside for Kate's passage. Money that could have saved her from at least one year of work at that shameful Hogan's place? How could you do business with such a man?'"

James fell into the chair beside Martin, his face a blend of anger and sadness. "I am sorry to say I lost my temper. I shouted at him."

Julia could not suppress a gasp.

"The man must be a fool." Martin's cup clattered to the table.

James rubbed the back of his neck. "Francis tried to convince me, in a somewhat condescending manner, that this was business. He said Fortune's theft happened long ago. He insisted the new partnership would be a legitimate transaction among a reliable group of men. Could I ever believe one favorable thing about that dirty scoundrel?"

Anne walked to the table and placed an arm on his shoulder. "James, I—"

"I called him a d--- fool. Then, I left the place before I could pull my fists from my pockets. James put down his cup, rose from the table, and paced the floor again. "I am sorry."

James faced Anne then turned his sad gaze toward Julia. "I know you girls worry about Kate. My quarrel with Francis may cause a rift between you and your sister. Sure, and I'm the one who introduced her to the man. The shame's on me for it."

"I would have reacted the same way. Well, not the swearing, I'm sure." Anne put her arms around her husband and hugged him hard.

"I agree with Anne." Julia addressed James. "I am shocked to hear Francis would have dealings with Mr. Fortune. Can Kate be aware of this?"

She turned to Anne. "She must know, but how could she condone this? She is so angry with our parents for spending the fare money we sent them. Surely she has not forgiven Mr. Fortune for absconding with our savings?"

Anne's face grew pink. "I don't know what to think. I—"

James rushed to Anne. "Stay calm, my dear. What will I do for you?"

"I'm fine. Do not fret, James." Anne adjusted the strings of her apron.

"James, take Anne to the dining room. I'll handle supper." Julia checked the pots simmering on the stove.

"Do not concern yourself, Anne. I will have everything on the table in a few minutes."Julia shook her head. Had Anne's unsteadiness returned?

When Julia carried the last platter to the dining room, she found Martin's brother, Patrick and James' brother, Ned, regular boarders at Duffs', seated at the table.

James bowed his head. "Bless us Oh Lord and these thy gifts…"

Julia prayed the familiar words along with him. At his "Amen," she cleared her throat. "Dermot Fortune is from our home village. You likely know of his family, Ned. Our father trusted him to look out for us and guard our finances. He abused that faith and disappeared with our savings, a considerable sum." Anger rose within her, but she attempted a feeble smile for Ned then met Anne's troubled gaze across the table.

"Did you recover the money? And, where is Fortune now?" Patrick held the platter for Martin, while he served meat for himself.

"Well, James met him during the war," Julia grinned at her brother-in-law, "and in some mysterious way, recovered part of the money."

"I know my brother's ways well." Ned glanced at Anne and Julia, shaking his head. "Did the recovered money help bring your family out?"

"It was not all recovered." James banged his fork on the table. "These poor girls worked so hard to save the passage money, and that fool Fortune likely gambled it away."

"He disappeared without another trace." Julia bowed her head.

"Until now." James's face still glowed. "Francis Reilly entered into a partnership to build a new hotel, and here is Fortune himself a part of it."

"An unbelievable story." Patrick drummed his knuckles along the tablecloth.

When she returned to Dempsey's, Julia trudged to her room, climbing the steps slowly. The Francis Reilly and Mr. Fortune matter concerned her, but her own situation troubled her even more. Why had she allowed James's story to push aside her purpose this evening? Even during the walk home, Martin steered their conversation to the Mr. Fortune affair and gave her no pause for their own serious discussion. The time of their wedding drew near, and still, nothing had been resolved between them.

❈ ❈ ❈

The following afternoon, Julia prepared to leave for home, when Anne appeared at the church office. "We must tell Kate what we learned about Francis Reilly. We cannot delay. How should we approach her?"

"Let's set out for Dempsey's." Julia threw her shawl around her shoulders. "We can talk the matter over on the way."

"I only pray we can resolve it without upsetting Kate." Anne pulled her coat close, as they climbed the hill to the bakery. "I worry about her. One day her anger and bitterness will prove more than she can manage."

"I know what you are saying, Anne." Julia held fast to her hat, as a gust of wind threatened to send it skyward. "I will attempt to be kind and diplomatic."

"But, firm." Anne sighed. "We cannot brush aside what is right, in order to keep Kate happy."

When they arrived at the bakery, Lizzie waved from behind the counter. "Hello, Anne, Julia." She turned back to helping her customer.

Julia took Anne's arm and they walked toward the dressmaking shop.

They stopped in the kitchen and prepared tea then Julia carried the tray to a sparse room at the back of the bakery building.

"I'll fetch Kate," Anne said.

Kate appeared, a few moments later, her posture erect, a severe, pained expression spread across her face. She moved to the nearest chair, and sat without a sound. Julia offered her tea.

"No thank you." Kate's voice held no emotion.

Something had already gone terribly wrong. What could have happened? More bad news could send Kate into a seizure. Still, Julia could not avoid this conversation. She drew in a deep breath. "We must talk, Kate. There is something you must know. Franc—"

"I regret that James and Francis argued." Anne bumped her chair against Kate's knee. "I must say at the start, I cannot believe Francis would enter into business with Mr. Fortune." Anne's words poured forth. "Julia and I have already agreed James is in the right. Though we wish to avoid hurting you, we will not apologize for his harsh words."

"I only heard the whole of it last evening." Kate pressed her lips into a straight line and curled her fingers into fists. Passion burned in her eyes. "I am sure Francis knows this partnership is wrong. I believe the advantageous business prospects blinded him."

"But, Kate—" Julia jumped up. She knew!

Kate held up her hand, interrupting Julia. "I asked him to end the partnership. I told him how we had all been wronged by Mr. Fortune. I emphasized how strongly I felt about his deceit. I further explained to Francis about the pain and hardship I suffered at his hands, being forced to spend an extra year at Hogan's because he had stolen my passage money. He refused to consider my feelings."

"I am so sorry, Kate." Anne examined a fistful of the material from Kate's wide sleeve. "Lovely."

"I gained the impression Francis' business was his business alone." Kate sat back now, her body motionless. "He seems to hold the opinion that I, a mere woman, would not be capable of rendering intelligent advice or suggestions. In the beginning of our friendship, he listened to my ideas. I suppose he was pretending interest to gain my favor."

"I'm shocked he would treat you so shabbily." Julia placed her cup on the table, her lips puckering from the bitter tea.

"From then on, few words passed between us. In the end, I told him I could not marry him. We agreed I would complete the order for the draperies and such for his hotel. We will have little contact in the future."

"Is this matter serious enough to cause a permanent rift between you and Francis?" Julia's knees shook. She expected Kate would be upset. She was prepared for her sister's anger to be directed toward Anne and her. But, she never imagined she would hear that Kate had ended her association with Francis Reilly.

"My dear, I am so sorry for your pain." Anne pulled Kate into her arms.

"The partnership with Mr. Fortune is only one of many differences between us." Kate pulled back from Anne, and after offering a slight grin, she continued. "I've watched you with James."

She glanced at Julia. "I've observed the care evident between you and Martin—"

"Well, perhaps not so caring." Julia sat again and folded her arms.

"A serious barrier exists between Francis and me. I have been mistaken in supposing I could live without love such as you both have been blessed to experience." She turned toward Julia again. "Even with Martin's terrible injury, the devotion between you remains strong. The sad fact is, though I did try to garner feelings of affection for him, I do not love Francis."

"But perhaps, in time?" Anne approached Kate, arms outstretched, but again she backed away.

"Could either of you imagine me married to a man who considered my ideas good for draperies and bedspreads alone? Could you picture me living with someone who rejects my opinions on business matters as unimportant and who scarcely wishes to hear my thoughts on any subject?" Kate's laugh held a touch of pain. "Would it not be a bitter thing?"

Julia chuckled at Kate's words, but she sobered quickly. Though wise to break off things with Francis, she must be grieving over the disappointment.

"He asked me to bring you this money." Kate pulled an envelope from her pocket and handed it to Anne. "It is the sum Mr. Fortune took from you and Julia. I know it is the principle of the thing that angered James. I agree with him, but I thought you might at least appreciate Francis's desire to make reparation."

"You are right. It is not the money. This will not make up for Fortune's betrayal or Francis's poor judgment." Anne handed the envelope back. "You must take it, Kate. James will not accept it, nor will Julia and I. And besides, James already recovered a portion of the money. I suppose we did not tell you of their encounter during the war and James's rather forceful retrieval of the money he carried in his pockets."

Keeper of Trust

Kate looked to Julia then Anne, a question in her eyes. "You could put it toward the fund to send for our family and the Duffs, when Michael is free to come. I would send it to James's father, as he suggested, but I would not send it now. Mr. Duff might give Father his portion, and he will just spend it."

"I know he will, Kate," Julia said.

Later, as she undressed for bed, Julia found the envelope in her apron pocket. She would return it to her sister the next morning. Her family would not accept money from Francis Reilly, however well intended.

❀ ❀ ❀

Julia stood at the attic window. Little to see, with the skies darkening rapidly. "He is going off to work tomorrow. I cannot fathom it. When I saw him at church this morning, he appeared so weak and pale."

"Surely the owner would wait a few weeks for him to grow stronger. The man must have no compassion at all." After Hogan's, employers were all cruel tyrants to Kate. Julia did not bring up the fact that Kate had become one herself.

"It is not the fault of the owner, I am sure. Martin is so thrilled about this opportunity. I feel certain he volunteered to begin work immediately. He is determined to prove he is capable of handling the work. I pray he will be able to do it."

"Is he still in pain?" A worried look washed over Lizzie's face. "I do not believe I ever witnessed anyone enduring such agony as Martin suffered. He is a brave man, indeed. Well, I will pray for him as he begins his work tomorrow morning."

"Yes, Martin bears constant pain, even after many months." Julia hugged herself, squeezing her arms tightly.

Lizzie focused her attention on Kate. "And, I pray for you each day, as well. Are you lonely or unhappy without Mr. Reilly?"

187

Julia gasped. When Kate shrugged, she breathed out softly. "How are you bearing up, dear? You have done a brave thing, breaking it off."

Lizzie wedged herself behind Kate on the bed. She unpinned her braid then brushed out the thick silky strands.

"Have the days been difficult for you? Do you see him at all?" Tickling Kate's ear, Lizzie began braiding

"I have seen him a few times. Ellen and I visited the hotel last week to supervise the hanging of draperies, and he walked over to admire our work. His manner was cordial, but he spoke of business alone." Kate's manner softened. "He looked sad, and I felt a little sorry for him."

She had never divulged much about Francis or what they spoke of when they spent time together. In truth, she rarely mentioned his name unless Julia questioned her. "Are you having second thoughts?" She first suspected Kate felt relief to be shed of Mr. Reilly. Now? Perhaps not.

Kate frowned, causing Julia to grimace. Hopefully, she had not pushed too far.

"No, not at all." Kate punctuated her words by pounding her fist on her pillow. "In fact, each time I meet him now, my decision is reinforced. I do not love Francis. In truth, I do not miss him at all. We will finish up the work at the hotel in about a month. I suppose that will be the end of it. I will not see much of him after that. I am experiencing some guilt for hurting him." Kate's shoulders slumped. "I feel a little sorry for myself, too. I do not wish to always be alone."

"You have me. Do not forget your little sister who loves you." Lizzie finished Kate's braid, allowing it to hang along her back. She rose and knelt before her. "You are not alone. You have three sisters here in St. Louis with you."

"We could still consider going on to Oregon." Julia wrinkled her nose at Lizzie and grinned.

"Please, tell me you would not do such a thing." Lizzie placed her hand across Julia's mouth and giggled. "And then,

Mary, Grace, Cara, and Ellen all care about you and stand ready to offer you their love."

Julia slipped free of Lizzie's grasp. "I agree. You have many caring friends here at Dempsey's, and you are a beautiful girl, running a successful dressmaking business." She reached out to squeeze Kate's shoulder. "Once the word spreads that Francis is out of your life, you'll acquire a line of suitors in no time."

Sorrow took hold of Julia, and she walked to the wardrobe to hide her distress. Was she alone now too?

❀ ❀ ❀

Julia stood at the door to Dempsey's, holding it open for Martin, Patrick, Anne, James, and Ned. "Hello, everyone. It is grand to have you."

"Good evening, folks. Welcome, Martin. It is good to have you with us." Walter led the little party to the dining room, where the Dempsey regulars waited. "Find a seat, now." He held a chair for Anne. "Here you go, Martin, sit here beside your future sister-in-law."

"Good to see you, Martin." Eddie sat on his other side. "Your presence is an answer to our prayers."

"Grace and Cara made your favorites." Ellen placed a basket of biscuits before their special guest.

Walter began the prayer. "We thank you, Father, for the fine meal you have provided for us...We offer our prayers for the poor immigrants who arrived at the mission this week... And, we give thanks that our friend Martin is with us tonight."

"Amen," echoed around the table.

"Tell us about your new position, Martin." Walter placed a bowl of green beans on the table before him. "What are your duties at the shoe factory?"

"I will be responsible for ordering the materials for the new building under construction." Martin's eyes beamed.

"Will you be able to do it all?" Mary handed Martin the salt. "Will the hard work cause pain to your poor dear arm?" She covered her face with her apron and lowered her head. Silence descended upon the room.

Julia's heart reached out to Mary. She held Martin in high regard. Her intention had surely been to show how much she cared for him.

Regaining her composure, Mary pulled the cloth away from her face. She addressed Martin again. "I am truly sorry. My concern for you loosened my tongue. I should not have said such a thing. Forgive me."

"Mary, dear, please do not even worry over it," Martin said. "I am learning to live without the lower half of my arm. To ignore the loss will not make me whole again."

Julia's heart swelled with pride. How she loved him.

"Would you rather we change the subject?" Walter's countenance held compassion enough for Martin and for Mary.

"Ah no, I prefer we address the matter of my missing arm with frankness and honesty. There should be no uneasiness between my dear friends and me."

"Aye, Martin, we will just ignore your presence altogether, if you prefer?" James's eyes twinkled, and the room erupted in laughter.

Martin laughed himself. "I have encountered enough awkwardness at work this past week to last my full lifetime. Not only did I stand out as the new man, but here I was with a stump for an arm. Thankfully, there are only a few employees at the place for now. Most are builders and workmen, and they spend little time with me."

Julia cleared her throat. "Sure, and there's always some discomfort with a new position."

Martin nodded to Julia then raised his arm to demonstrate his new shirt. He bowed to Kate. "You did an amazing job. The sleeve conceals the lost lower part of my arm, but the absence of my hand screams out for anyone who draws near to see.

"When I arrived the first day, everyone hesitated to approach me. Of course, they had all heard about the accident. Once they realized I was that fellow, I must say, I became notorious around the place. I am gradually becoming no more than another of the workers." Martin eased over toward Mary.

"So, you see, I am learning to handle the stares and the questions. But you all are family to Patrick and me, and there should be no restraint among family." Martin lowered his head a moment. "Please do not speak softly around me or choose your words carefully. I wish our friendship, all of our friendships, to be as they were before the accident. I want you all to experience my recovery and this new chapter of my life along with me."

Julia's grin caused her cheeks to ache. *He speaks easily of his loss. He is accepting it.*

He turned to Mary again. "Will you promise you will say what you wish, or ask me anything?"

"Does it hurt?" Mary smiled shyly. "'Tis what I really wished to know."

"It does hurt, Mary. When I try to sleep at night, it aches something fierce, even the part that is gone. Can you imagine such a thing? During a wonderful meal such as this, however, with loved ones gathered around, the pain subsides."

"You are the bravest man I know." Ellen rose from the table and bowed deeply.

"I agree," and "Hear, hear," came from all around the table.

Martin shook his head. "I must also mention the fine meals I have enjoyed at Anne's table. I owe my life to the Duffs, and Julia, and Patrick. I am indebted to my nurse, Patty, who taught me to care for myself." He helped himself to another biscuit. "I believe I am in danger of becoming spoiled."

"You know, you are always welcome at our table, Martin." Anne wrinkled her nose at him. "If anything I served or entertainment I provided would ease your pain, I would rush to do it."

Mary rose and headed toward the kitchen. "And I welcome you for a Dempsey supper on any evening."

Tears welled in Julia's eyes. With Martin's grave injury, nothing would surely ever be the same again. Yet, he had pieced his life together. She gripped her napkin with clenched fists. If only, he would include her in that life. Or, with only three months until their wedding, if he would at least discuss the possibility.

❁ ❁ ❁

Julia waved to Kate and Ellen, as they returned to their shop, and followed Lizzie to the attic room.

"Lovely dinner." Lizzie rubbed her stomach. "But Julia, dear, something else is on your mind."

Julia hurried to the top of the steps. "There is nothing for it, but Martin and I must talk. We must decide if our wedding should be postponed, or the marriage will be called off altogether."

"I know Martin loves you, Julia. It will be all right." Lizzie sat at the desk, pulling out a sheet of paper and opening the ink bottle.

"If he asks to postpone the wedding until he gains more confidence that he can manage his new job, of course I will agree." Julia gazed out the window, but darkness had fallen. "But, he must say something. I feel as if I am dangling from the highest branch of a tall tree."

Lizzie walked over to sit with her. "My poor Julia."

"Father Burns has begun a search for a replacement for me in the parish office. I cannot afford to lose my position, if we are not to be married. I must also discuss the matter with Walter and Mary. They have already begun talking of arrangements for the wedding supper they so graciously insisted they would provide."

Julia moved from the window and pulled a nightgown from the wardrobe. "It is a simple matter. We must either postpone the wedding or make the decision to proceed."

Lizzie patted her arm. "You must have this talk with Martin. Do not allow any more time to pass, while you worry and fret. Seek time alone with him and discuss your entire situation. He is a kind man. He will understand your concerns. Speak with him tomorrow." She grinned. "And, be sure to come back here tomorrow night and tell me all that happens."

They hugged, but when Lizzie turned away, tears filled her eyes.

"What is it Lizzie?"

"Aw, nothing really. I am feeling a bit homesick. We never receive a letter from them." Lizzie sat down at the desk again." I know Michael is living at the farmer's place and has no time to write. It is only a few months since I left Blackwater, though. Have Father and Mother forgotten me? Has our Maggie abandoned me altogether? I write to them every week."

"I write to them each month, and Anne has been faithful in her correspondence, as well. I, too, wonder why they do not write. I'm sorry, Lizzie, I forget you are only recently torn from home. Perhaps, we will hear soon."

Julia reached under her bed and drew out a small package. "Meanwhile, we must make do with the old letters. With Kate working late in the shop tonight, we could read one or two of them without upsetting her."

"'Tis a grand idea," Lizzie sat next to Julia, her smile restored.

She would not mind a distraction herself. "You may take these letters out and read them at any time." She chose a thin envelope.

Checking the postmark, she sighed. "Here's a letter Father sent Anne and I, after I had been in St. Louis for a few months. The war, with all of its terrible sadness and hardships, had already spread a cloak of misery throughout the city. Ah, it was a terrible time, Lizzie. The grief Mrs. Flynn and her family suffered when her dear boy did not return home…I feel her pain still." With a shake of her head, she pulled out the single sheet and began to read.

Blackwater

12th Dec. 1861

My Dear Children,
I received your most welcome letter of the 9th. It gave us great pleasure to hear you were well and in good health as we are all at present, thank God.

This has been a hard year in Ireland. The crops were bad and greatly short of the usual compliment in every kind of grain which leaves a great many distressed and will for this winter and in consequence of same my crop being so bad I was not able to pay my rent.

We are happy to hear of you being in good health and good situations and that all dangers of the war appear to be removed from you, at least you say nothing about it in your letter. We got the slip of paper sent in James Dempsey's letter and also the two newspapers. You may tell Grace Donahoo that her father is just alive and I believe not much more.

Let me know if you delivered the slip I sent in my last letter to Mr. Fortune and if you received any kindness from him or how he treated you. Your brother Jimmy's health is just the same as ever. We wish to be remembered to Walter Dempsey and his sister and also wish you to thank them in our behalf for all their kindness to you.

William Doran is now stark staring mad, and roving about night and day. He and his wife are living still on the same stretch and he has given her a broken bone. Kitty remains home still and Mr. Stapleton has lost his senses and turned fanatic.

I conclude by praying for God to protect you, and remain your affectionate father,
   John Carty

"Do you wish me to read another?" Julia looked to Lizzie, but her sister had already drifted off to sleep. She placed the letters back under the bed. She needed rest herself.

Chapter Fifteen

Julia and Mary walked to the mission, warm breezes tugging at their bonnets. "Such a beautiful day, and it is not yet spring." Julia struggled with a large ungainly package that contained a cake Mary baked earlier in the day. "I'm sure the folks at the mission will be pleased to taste one of your fine creations."

"Ah, Julia, haven't I always said you are my favorite of all the girls who worked in the bakery?" Mary leaned toward Julia and shifted the box she carried, as they turned the corner into Park Street.

"Ah, go on with you. Would we not think that silver tongue God gave you is exaggerating a bit?" Julia nudged Mary's arm. "You do say the same to each of the Carty sisters."

"Sure, you are right. I did treasure Anne's company when she lived and worked with us, but she is in her own grand home now, with her fine husband." Mary nodded to an elderly gentleman, who stepped back to allow them to pass. "You girls are all special to Walter and me, partners in the shop more than employees. We never had such fine help in the bakery, until the Carty sisters came to us. Know that I speak from my heart. It is the truth."

Julia stopped and helped Mary rearrange her package. "Thank you, Mary. We will be forever grateful to you and Walter for all you've done."

"Well...our bakery operation plodded along some seven years ago, making a good living, true enough. In the war years, when Anne served as our shop girl and assumed our bookkeeping work, our business flourished. And when you and Kate arrived, you each offered a unique ingredient to our lives at Dempsey's."

"That is kind of you, Mary." Julia blew aside the light brown curls that escaped from their pins.

"You know, these past years could have found us presiding over a reasonably successful bakery business and boarding house, fulfilled to some extent. But, Walter and I were lonely, and that's the truth of it." Mary blinked several times, but a single tear rolled down her cheek. "You may think we took you in, but you see how life has tossed things about. Because of the Carty sisters our lives have been blessed. You girls allowed us to become part of your warm, loving family. Our place is now a true home."

"So now, what is all this fine praise? Are your kind words an attempt to soften me, before you tell me how wonderful Lizzie is?" Julia winked. "Are you saying there is no need for me to hurry home from the church to help you in the shop?"

"You know I meant it all. I cannot find words strong enough to express my appreciation for your years of excellent work at Dempsey's. And, Walter and I have enjoyed your friendship." Mary faced Julia, a guilty little grin spread across her face.

"You are right about Lizzie, though. She is the finest girl I've ever known and the happiest helper I can remember. She is a Carty sister, that's sure. You are talented and hard-working, each one of you."

"Lizzie delights in everything about the bakery." Julia had been bouncing along, but now the sidewalk ended and they moved to the uneven paved road. The lovely weather, Lizzie in St. Louis and doing well in the bakery...ah, how wonderful.

"Indeed, she has grasped the workings out in the shop and she attempts to learn every facet of the oven room operation. With your help and the time Anne spent with her, she has taken over our bookkeeping work." Mary's expression turned serious. "Your father provided a fine education for you girls, I must say.

"I remember the pleasure you brought us with your laughter and stories. In that respect, Lizzie is a copy of you." Mary slowed while they crossed the busy intersection and headed for the church. "Wherever she is, she causes a stir. Rolls are shaped with huge bellies. Bread is stacked at precarious heights and removed to a more even arrangement only when Eddie and George place cloths all about the floor and plead with her to stop."

"Your story sends me back to my years at home." Julia rolled her shoulders slowly, stretching her muscles. "Lizzie, Maura, and Maggie were always giggling and playing tricks... those dear little girls...even our mother could not be vexed with them."

"Lizzie has adopted Grace as her special project and succeeded where even you could not. The two have become great friends, and she makes the poor, sad girl smile with her singing. They often persuade our shy, little Cara to join in their fun."

"Lizzie sings?" Julia frowned. "Did I even know that? My word, I have neglected her."

"Remember how you would beg and plead, before Grace would sing?" Mary bobbed her head. "She often instigates the business now. The change in her is remarkable. She finds little time to be unhappy these days.

"While they work, Lizzie and Grace sing church songs and ballads. Grace is even teaching Lizzie some of the patriotic tunes of our new country." Mary imitated a drumming sound with her lips. "It reminds me of the wartime nights when you girls sang while you sewed uniforms, the sound of your voices soaring throughout the building."

"Perhaps her friendship with Eddie?" Julia chuckled.

"Of course, we must credit Eddie somewhat." Mary's eyes twinkled.

"And, perhaps, the dresses Kate made for Grace?" Julia stood tall and swung her free arm, demonstrating Grace's new, confident walk. "And, the new hairstyle she told me Ellen helped create for her?"

"Certainly so."

"And, you are so right about the singing. So many times, I begged Grace to sing for us. She made endless excuses. It is grand to hear of these many changes she is experiencing."

"Her voice is lovely," Mary nodded. "A true gift it is. We all stood by and watched, helpless, as Grace wasted her young life buried in sadness, pining over that foolish lad back home who cast her aside to marry another girl. We rejoice to see her beautiful smile and hear her wonderful singing."

"Mary dear, before we reach the mission..." A block away. With each step they took, the white cross stretching from the church roof toward the bright, blue sky grew taller. "I must speak with you about the wedding."

"Ah, my dear, is there a problem?" Mary eased herself to the left, preparing to cross the road to the mission. "I noticed distance between you and Martin at dinner the other evening. Whatever is it?"

"It is difficult to say, but I must admit the truth of it. Martin considers himself unworthy of me." Warmth crept along Julia's cheeks. "I have told him again and again the loss of his arm did not diminish my feelings. He should know that. Still, he is honor bound to prove he can provide for me before he can speak of marriage."

"But his new position? From his talk of the work he is doing, I assumed he is progressing well." Mary drew her brows together.

"I pray his success with the new job will change his mind," Julia said. "The wedding date is rushing toward us, though. I do not wish you and Walter to incur any expenses for the wedding supper, until I know we will go forward. Will you bear with me for a while? I have not given up hope."

"We will bide our time." Mary inclined her head toward Julia. "Martin will triumph with this new work, and in the next few weeks, his outlook will improve. I am convinced of it. I can understand, your difficult position, though. My poor Julia. What more will I do to help you?"

They reached the church and descended the steps to the mission. Mary balanced both cakes on a ledge at a side wall, while Julia pushed the heavy door open. Holding it wide with one hand, she wiped away a tear with the other. Then, she took her carton back from Mary.

"Thank you for listening." Julia whispered, as they entered the mission. "Sharing this burden with you has relieved my worry. It's been heavy on me—"

"Ah, Mary and Julia, we are grateful you are here." Bridget Rice burst forward. "With this huge crowd gathered and more certain to arrive, Mrs. Flynn and I prayed you would be free to come soon."

"Well, of course, we've come," Mary removed her cake from its carton and placed it on the counter, and then turned to take Julia's box from her. "Where shall we begin?"

"We can do nothing, until we've taken a moment to admire these splendid gifts." Mrs. Flynn stood before the cakes for a moment, her hands folded. Then, with a curtsy to Mary and Julia, she went off with Bridget to gather vegetables from the storage room.

Julia moved to the sink to help Mary peel potatoes. "Your news this afternoon and your praise of Lizzie are all grand. It does ease my mind, to know you are happy with her. Though I am envious of your time with Lizzie and all the fun I seem to be missing while here at St. Vincent's."

"I do hold one worry." Mary arranged the peeled potatoes in a row along the counter. "While Lizzie assures us she is fine, she still bears the cough she brought with her from home. At times, she appears weak and short of breath. I advised her to consult the doctor, but she has never found the opportunity." Her expression turned grave."I am concerned. I believe you should insist she see Dr. Gallagher."

"I noticed she coughs in her sleep." Julia placed a hand across her forehead. "I have spent so much time visiting Martin, since his accident, I am afraid I have neglected her. I will pay close attention from now on. I'll also talk to Anne, and we will insist she see the doctor. We will tend to her at once—"

"And did you finish your task while I gathered these vegetables?" Mrs. Flynn sidled next to Mary to inspect her long row of peeled potatoes.

"Of course, we did. You remained in the storage room just long enough." Mary gestured toward the tables. "Sit yourself down now. Perhaps you would like a cuppa, my fine lady?"

Mrs. Flynn's giggles sent a shiver of delight through Julia. Though the dainty woman wore a simple blue dress today, the rest of her ensemble far exceeded plain. She wore a matching cap, but where an ordinary bonnet would end at her neckline, this particular one held blue striped streamers attached to the back edge. When she walked, long, starched ribbons floated around her bodice, sleeves, and skirt, extending from the edge of her hair all the way to her shoes. Her dear friend had worn mourning attire for so long it was wonderful to see the return of her extravagant creations.

"I am happy we have this chance to work together today." Julia moved over to Mrs. Flynn and took up the rough cloth they used to clean vegetables. "I miss our conversations in the bakery."

"Sure, I miss seeing you at Dempsey's," Mrs. Flynn said. "And now, I miss my Janey, my great grown girl who has won a position for herself."

"Is Janey happy with the sewing work?" Mary walked up behind them and placed one of the huge potato pots on top of the stove. Then, she stood beside Julia and chopped carrots.

"Kate and Ellen are delighted with her." Mary answered before Mrs. Flynn could speak. "Their business continues to flourish, but now with Janey's assistance, they worry less about finishing their orders on time. On a few of our recent warm evenings, they joined us for a visit on the porch or a short walk. It is grand, indeed, to see Kate and Ellen taking some time out to rest and enjoy the company of the other girls."

"And Janey likes the work." Mrs. Flynn pushed her cutting board across the sink, sending Mary's carrots flying.

"Ellen believes Janey is quite talented," Mary gathered the carrots in her apron and dropped them into a smaller pan. "Even our grand seamstress Kate admires her work. She proclaims your girl possesses a gift for the design of garments. You can be proud of her, Delia. Janey is a fine, pleasant girl. We have all enjoyed her time with us."

Tired immigrants streamed into the mission, and the women hurried to finish their preparations.

"I'll set the tables." Julia covered each one with a fresh cloth, and then organized the silverware. In no time, Lizzie arrived with the day-old goods.

She finished the place settings, the other ladies stirred vegetables and tended potatoes, and Lizzie sliced bread. While the poor, weary folks enjoyed their meal, the women continued to work, cleaning the kitchen, scrubbing dishes as soon as they were emptied, and putting things away in their proper places.

"Ah, Julia, I did not realize you were at the mission still." Father Ryan entered the kitchen. "May I interrupt your work here and beg your help for a short time?"

"Of course, Father." She followed along after him to the store room, finding several cartons of supplies lined up just inside the door. They worked quickly together. Father Ryan unpacked the cooking utensils, cutlery, and dinner plates and placed them on the counter. Julia checked things against the list of items she ordered. She added the supply of mismatched silverware, donated by the mercantile down the block, to her inventory. Then, she fetched a pail of warm water and washed each utensil before the priest dried and stacked the goods on their proper shelves.

"How is Martin?" Father Ryan handed her a clean cloth for her hands. "I am astonished at the progress he has made, in spite of the pain the work causes him. I questioned him at length about the turnverein. His description of the exercises he does there has roused my interest. I may join him one day."

"The discipline he applies to the body building is amazing." A warm rush spread across Julia's face. "Of course, I would say that. But, the hard work has proved beneficial. He seems to have the stamina to manage his new position."

"I suppose the establishment of a new business must be exciting." Father Ryan collected the empty boxes and placed them in the hallway.

"He talks of little else."

"About the wedding?" Father Ryan raised an eyebrow.

"There is no mention of the wedding." Julia grimaced. She'd reveal no more about the sad state of her marriage plans. She must first talk the situation over with Martin.

"Julia, are you ready to leave?" Lizzie bustled into the storage area. A grand smile spread across her face, as she turned to Father Ryan. "Are you finished with your work back here, Father? I would like to steal my sister away."

"With Julia's help, the chores are completed." Father Ryan brushed his hands together. "And, it is time you girls were heading home."

Lizzie nudged Julia's arm. "I've been bursting to tell you, we received a letter from Blackwater.

"It is the first word from home, since I arrived here, Father." Lizzie smothered a cough in her sleeve. "I was beginning to think they had forgotten me altogether."

"That is grand, Lizzie," Father Ryan waved them off as they headed back to the kitchen. "I know receiving that letter is a comfort to you."

"I cannot wait to read it." Julia buttoned her coat. She should have paid attention to Lizzie's cough. She pulled her sister's shawl around her shoulders, as Walter arrived to escort them home.

❀ ❀ ❀

Riding along in the carriage, Lizzie talked of Julia's wedding. "Mary's early plants are already spouting, Julia. By June, their blooms will be perfect."

Embarrassed, Julia lowered her head. She had confided in Lizzie about Martin's reluctance to discuss the wedding. Why would her sister even mention it? Unsure of how to respond, she remained quiet.

"I did as you asked, Julia, I mentioned to Grace that perhaps Ellen would sing with her." Julia had worried this matter could be a sensitive one, but the challenge had not deterred Lizzie.

"Grace likes the idea. Rather than harboring any injured feelings, she now talks as if the idea had been her own all along."

"That is grand." Lizzie's success surprised her, and for a moment, she forgot her reluctance to speak about the wedding. "Your skill and tact have brought this problem of the singing to a magnificent conclusion. You have created an extra job for yourself. I can see I will need your assistance with the entire business."

Julia's attention wandered as the talk of music and singers went on around her. She remembered her invitation to supper at Anne's the following evening. Of course, Martin would be there.

As they went along toward Dempsey's, she reaffirmed to herself the pledge she had so recently made to Lizzie. She would speak to Martin and insist they come to a resolution about their wedding. These uncomfortable situations could not continue.

She had been inventing excuses not to push him into an answer. Perhaps, she was afraid to hear his response. It would shatter her heart, if he still considered it his duty to withhold his commitment to her. Her family and friends could no longer be misled, though. She and Martin must come to a decision.

Only Mary seemed to understand her plight. As they rode along, she gave Julia's arm an understanding pat.

❀ ❀ ❀

That night, with Kate and Lizzie already sleeping, she nestled in her bed in the attic room. Since her candle still flickered and the faint bit of light did not seem to disturb her sisters, she retrieved the letter from home and began to read.

Blackwater

March 2, 1867

My dear daughters,
We received your welcome letter yesterday. We were happy to hear you all were well. I hope this letter will find you all in good health as this leaves us all here at present, thank God.
My dear daughters, the times are bad. We are praying for a successful crop this year, or we will not be able to pay the rent. I am sorry to say, we are heavily in debt. Your loving father,
John Carty

Dear Lizzie, it is a great comfort to us to hear from you. Tell Anne to send a picture of herself in the next letter.
Dear Lizzie, I want to let you know the way we are circumstanced here. Michael is in

the one place, his time will be out short of three years. His wages are small, only #12 per year. He is a good boy. Anything he has to spare he gives us. He would like to go to America but we won't give him consent and the reason is your Father has been helpless. He is scarce able to do anything. We are striving to help him in every way for it is hard to pay a man now the men are scarce. I am posting a letter to Anne today. I hope you will get them in due time. Aunt Mary wishes to be remembered to you.

Write soon and I will send you a longer letter. Please let me know if you have any account of James Brien. Also, Johnny Doran of Ballinard is dead, may the Lord have mercy on him. No more from your mother,
Mrs. Carty

Julia folded the letter. Poor Michael. For so many years, they had been saving money and sending it home for his passage. For so long, they had been planning for his coming to America. Now that he had been indentured to a farmer, it would be nearly three years before they could expect him. It seemed a lifetime.

Her eyelids grew heavy. She returned the letter to its hiding place under the bed, and blew out the candle. Her dear brother still held her thoughts. How could she help him?

Chapter Sixteen

April, 1867
Julia sat at her work table in the back corner of Father Burns' office. Determined to finish before she left for the day, she bent to her work. She checked lists of the supplies ordered and matched them with the proper invoices and receipts. She arranged them in a neat stack. The accountant, Charles, would come in on Wednesday of the following week. Anything Julia could do to help his work progress smoothly would save money for the parish.

Distracted by a movement, she looked up from her work to see Anne standing in the doorway. "You are lovely." Julia walked around the desk for a closer look.

"Thank you." Anne's smile matched the glow that seemed to surround her. "So, you like the dress…or cape, I suppose…or whatever you would call this creation of Kate's. She designed it for me."

"You've been able to disguise your condition through most of the winter months, but you have flourished with the sprouting of spring blossoms." Julia gestured to Anne's usually petite, slim waist. "Neither apron, nor robe, nor any other garment will hide the fact that your time approaches."

Anne gathered her shawl around her. "I am afraid you are right."

"This frock is the most beautiful hue I've ever seen. At first glance, I thought it to be dark blue. Now that I've moved closer, I believe it to be a gorgeous shade of deep purple. The beautiful color and Kate's clever design provide you with a look of grace and elegance such as I've never seen before."

"Thank you dear." Anne sat in a chair beside the door.

"It a shame the time is near when you will be forced to retire from public and confine yourself to your home until the baby's birth." Julia bent her head for a closer scrutiny of the many tucks in the sides of the dress. "In the coming weeks, your wonderful new garment will only be seen at the early Sunday morning service."

After a quick, insistent rap on the door, Grace Donahoo rushed into the room, wearing a bakery apron over her dress. Around both, in place of her own grey cloak, she had wrapped a worn black shawl. Julia recognized it as one left behind months ago by a bakery customer and never reclaimed.

Grace shifted her gaze between them, her stricken eyes and stiff awkward motions causing the hair on Julia's arm to stand on end.

"Grace? What is it?" Concern registered across Anne's face. "Why are you trembling?"

"Come sit down." Julia walked toward Grace, her arms outstretched.

She opened her mouth, attempting to speak, but no words came.

"Take a slow, deep breath." Julia took the girl's arm, intending to guide her to a chair, but Grace stood firm.

Finally, she managed to speak. "It is our Lizzie, you see. She has fallen ill."

"Cara has gone to fetch you, Anne." Graces voice trembled. "We didn't know you would be here, true enough. You must rush home with me, both of you."

Julia hurried back to her desk, and with one sweep of her arm, she pushed her work into the top drawer. "Father Burns is out of the office. I'll write a note for him."

In a few moments, she and Anne followed Grace down the steps and out the door. They headed across the church yard to Park Street. "Now, tell us what happened, Grace." Julia attempted to keep her impatience from her voice, but she could not push back her sharp tone.

"You know, Lizzie's cough improved some, after you girls convinced her to consult with the doctor." Grace brushed her hair back from her eyes. "Mary hovered over her until she swallowed each dose of the remedy he prescribed. These last few days, her cough all but disappeared.

"This morning, the cough flared up again. Lizzie tried to hide it from us, but I noticed her sad state. Mary insisted she swallow more of the syrup, but the medicine seemed to lose its effectiveness." Grace rubbed at her eyes and pushed back her hair without success. "She appeared overcome by weakness, and she toiled for each breath."

Julia increased her pace. When she heard Anne's slight whine, she took her arm.

"While we worked together in the shop, Lizzie insisted she would be fine." Grace also breathed with some difficulty. "Try as she might to conceal her illness, Lizzie became more flushed than she ever has been. A short time later, she collapsed on the floor. We attempted to lift her to a sitting position, and when we failed, Mary called for Walter. As I left to fetch you, Walter sent Eddie for the doctor and he carried Lizzie to Mary's room."

"Perhaps Dr. Gallagher will prepare a strong medicine for her." Julia led them across the road. "Something will help her."

Grace shook her head. "I am worried. She appears to be extremely ill."

"But, she will improve. She must." Julia held off the distressing thoughts threatening to invade her mind and heart. Grace did forever see the worst of things.

"I watched my mother die." Grace's grim expression brought back Julia's apprehension. "I do not wish to alarm you.

I could be mistaken, but I am so worried. Lizzie brings the sad sight of my poor mam to mind."

"That cannot be, not our Lizzie." Anne's head swayed back and forth. Tears appeared in her eyes and filled her voice.

Julia kept moving, Anne's quivering hand grasping her own. And then, her sister stumbled, tugging Julia forward.

"I am so sorry."Looking down at her feet, Julia concentrated on reducing her stride, measuring each footfall. "Grace, please take Anne's other arm."

"I am fine, Julia." Anne attempted to match her pace. "We must hurry on to Lizzie."

"No, we will ease our steps. I apologize for rushing you, dear." They proceeded at a measured gait from then on.

When they reached the bakery, they encountered Walter, pacing back and forth in front of the bakery window.

"I'm watching for the doctor."

Julia patted his arm. "He will be here directly. We must hurry in to Lizzie. Do not worry."

He continued his patrol.

The girls ran through the doorway to the shop, and Grace hurried behind the counter to help out. Julia and Anne headed for the steps. "I'll go first." Julia moved up toward Mary's room, proceeding slowly, holding Anne's arm.

They found Kate already there, removing Lizzie's shoes. Julia settled Anne into a chair and went over to help. "My poor little sister, what will I do for you?" She untied Lizzie's apron, slipped it from her shoulders, and folded it. While Kate covered Lizzie, they all three looked down at her pale, still face.

"How are you faring, Lizzie?" Julia took her hand, frowning as her eyes remained closed. She did seem to hear Julia's greeting, or recognize her touch.

Mary entered the room and joined their efforts. She arranged soft pillows all around, as Julia placed a cool cloth on her forehead.

Keeper of Trust

They worked together to push Anne, chair and all, against the side of the bed. Standing next to Anne, Julia gazed down at their dear little sister. She remained so still. Had she slipped into a deep sleep?

"Did you girls run all the way?" Mary asked. "Poor Anne."

Julia felt her cheeks burn with shame all over again. She should never have made her sister run home. "I am so sorry I rushed you." She leaned in close to Anne and tugged at one of the many tucks in her beautiful dress. "James would never forgive me if I caused harm to his precious wife and child, would he?"

"Stay right here now and rest." Mary headed out the door. "Should I bring you water? Or, would you prefer tea?" She bustled away without waiting for Anne's answer.

"I will be all right." Anne shook her head, a plea in her eyes. "Do not give it another thought. We must turn our concern and our prayers to Lizzie now."

"It comforts me to have you here, Anne." Kate sat on the arm of the chair and rubbed Anne's back. "We need you with us."

Julia understood Kate. She, too, was thankful for her dear sister's presence. Anne would calm them all. She would know what to do.

"Lizzie seemed fine when I left this morning." Kate moved away and paced the small space along the side of the bed. "I believed she had improved a little, since she began to take the cough medicine the doctor prescribed. What could have happened?"

Heavy footsteps sounded on the stairs. In a moment, Walter entered the room with the doctor, who promptly ushered them all out in the hallway. Julia leaned against the wall, outside of Mary's room, turning her thoughts to Lizzie, searching for any ray of hope.

The doctor came out of the room, after what seemed an eternity. His worried look betrayed his apprehension. "I have done everything possible, but her fever alarms me. I suggest you summon Father Burns."

Julia's last reserves of optimism slipped away.

They filed back into Mary's bedroom. The white islet spread had been folded and placed on a chair. Matching white curtains fluttered at the open window. Two small chairs, a desk, and a bureau were the only other accessories in the room. Lizzie, still sleeping, looked tiny in the great four-poster bed.

When Julia fell to her knees beside her sister, Anne attempted to bring her bulk down beside her. She landed prostrate on the floor, pulling Julia and Kate down along with her. Julia, Kate, and Mary, working together, lifted Anne from the floor and guided her back into the chair.

A giggle escaped from Anne, as she settled back. "If Lizzie were awake, she would laugh with us." For a moment, their worry slipped away.

At a soft knock, Julia opened the bedroom door to find Grace, Ellen, and Cara in the hallway. "We wish to do something for our dear Lizzie," Ellen whispered to Julia. "Please allow us to take a turn at watching over her."

Ellen stopped beside Anne. "You must have your rest." She patted Anne's arm, anxiety wrinkling her brow.

The other girls nodded as they prepared to go back to their work. "We will take good care of Lizzie for you. You must think of the grand baby we are all longing to have here with us." Grace knelt before Anne, and looked into her eyes.

"Ah, not to worry over Anne. You are all underestimating our Mr. Duff. As soon as he learns where Anne is, he will march right here and hover over her. His concern for her well-being will put your anxiety to shame." Julia glanced over to Anne. In spite of her distress, a grin escaped. "Have I exaggerated?"

"No, Julia, you are quite right. I will soon be bundled up and carried home to bed."

Keeper of Trust

"As well you should be." Kate's worry over Anne's condition seemed the fine thread keeping her from collapse. "I will see you home right now, if you wish."

Anne shook her head. "Resting here beside Lizzie is the best place for me right now."

Julia bowed her head, feeling a weight of responsibility. Lizzie ill…Kate ready to crumble…Anne nearing her time. Would she possess the strength to sustain each one?

❁ ❁ ❁

Lizzie fought valiantly for each breath, surprising Julia with her strength. She awakened now and then and spoke softly to the girls. When offered, she took sips of water and attempted to consume the soup Mary prepared for her, but she experienced difficulty swallowing. Even as she rested, her struggle continued.

Julia stood beside Lizzie's bed, listening to her labored wheezing, as she prepared to leave for work the next morning. "Mary, shall we move Lizzie to the attic room?"

"We'll not disturb our poor dear girl. Do not even think of such a thing. It is you and Anne and Kate I'm concerned about." Mary took Julia's hands and held them with a firm grip. "You do know, dear, Lizzie is weakening with the passing of each hour? You understand she cannot hold on much longer?"

"I know, Mary. We all realize it, Kate more than any of us. She held vigil with our little Jimmy before he died back home. Lizzie's gasping for breath is similar to the suffering he bore for so long. We will none of us ever forget his brave struggle." She walked toward the door. "We know. We are just praying for a recovery, is all."

"As we all are, dear, but you are the strong one, now. Anne's time grows near, and the baby is drawing out all of her strength. And, Kate suffers beyond our comprehension over Lizzie's condition." Mary brushed wisps of hair from Julia's eyes. "You must prepare them both for what will surely come to pass. Gather your sisters together and say your goodbyes to Lizzie. Make peace with whatever is God's will."

"You are so right, Mary. I will talk to them right away." Julia turned back for one more look. She ran her finger along Lizzie's arm, now resting under the covers. "I will be gone no more than an hour. I'll speak with Kate first, run to Anne's, and then I must finish my preparations for the accountant when he comes to the office on Wednesday. I know Father Burns will understand my leaving as soon as I complete the work."

A short time later, Julia returned to Dempsey's and joined her sisters at Lizzie's bedside. "Walter fetched Anne," Kate said, "and I came upstairs from my shop just a few minutes ago." They spent several hours sitting there: the four Carty sisters together for what could only be a short time longer.

Quiet settled over the room, Lizzie's harsh breathing the only sound that could be heard. Julia considered Mary's advice about preparing her sisters. Ah my...how should she begin? "Lizzie, dear, Anne and Kate and I were thrilled when you arrived in St. Louis."

Anne picked up the thread of her talk. "We are all so proud of the splendid way you have taken over the shop girl position."

"Remember the grand times we had together back home in Blackwater." Kate sat beside the bed, hemming a thick cotton coverlet made up of pink and blue patches. She leaned forward. "Lizzie, we all love you so."

Lizzie awoke for a few moments and looked at each of the girls. Then, with a smile she drifted back to sleep.

Julia could not hold back her tears. She rested her cheek on the bed beside Lizzie. She felt a touch.

Lizzie's fingers tangled in her hair then slipped away.

Julia turned to Anne and Kate. "Did you see?"

Anne nodded and lowered herself to the bed. In a moment, a smile spread across her face. "Kate, come here. When I inched myself closer to Lizzie, she pressed against me."

Moving around to the side of the bed where Anne sat, Kate folded Lizzie's hand between both of her own. "Lizzie? I love you. I need you with me. Please show you can hear me."

Julia stared at Lizzie's hand, held cradled in Kate's. In a moment, she observed a slight movement. Lizzie had taken hold of Kate's fingers. While they all watched, she tugged at them.

"Kate." Lizzie's voice wavered. But her gaze, aimed directly at Kate, held firm. "Keep yourself calm. Promise me. Love. Forgive."

The girls all leaned forward to hear her words, spoken so softly. Then, Lizzie's eyes closed.

"Lizzie, talk to me." Kate threw herself down beside her. "I will heed your words. I will try." Kate touched her cheek, but Lizzie had drifted back to sleep.

Moved beyond her ability to speak, Julia knelt beside the bed. Anne sat in the chair, with Kate perched on the arm right next to her. They remained that way for a time, all together, gazing down at their sister.

A short time later, James came in to take Anne home.

Julia handed Anne an envelope. "Will you take this to Martin? We were to meet tonight and discuss the wedding. I have asked him to delay it until tomorrow."

❀ ❀ ❀

The following morning, the third day of Lizzie's illness, Julia prepared to leave for work. She searched Lizzie's face carefully. Her usual rosy cheeks appeared pale, pasty. Her breathing, though quieter, seemed shallow, and a bluish tint circled her sweet lips.

How prophetic Mary's words had been. She would ever be grateful for her suggestion that they come together to say goodbye.

The doctor arrived a short time later, and after only a few moments at Lizzie's bedside, he motioned for Julia and Kate to follow him to the hallway. His face grim, he avoided their eyes when he spoke. "It will not be long."

Julia's heart twisted.

Back in the bedroom, Julia gazed at her young sister. "If only, I could help her," she said to Anne, who entered the room behind her. "If I could carry some of her pain and take on those breaths she labors to draw in, I would rush to do it."

"J-j-julia?" Lizzie struggled to turn and face her.

She leaned down, wiping Lizzie's lips with a warm cloth.

"I wish to…I will…" Her voice trailed away.

"Lizzie dear, I cannot understand your meaning."

"Kate, Anne, are you…?" Lizzie pushed away the quilt covering her.

"She seems to wish to tell us something," Anne said.

Julia moved a step closer. Lizzie's speech came out jumbled. She grew restless, tossing and rolling on the bed, her increased movements causing her difficult breathing to commence again.

"Anne, Julia, K-k-kate. Thank you…for w-w-atching with me."

"Lizzie, please be calm." Julia took her hand. "Rest now and soon you will be well. Aye, you must not leave us. We all need you so."

A few moments later, Lizzie lapsed into a light sleep, a faint smile across her face. Pictures of her little sister whirled through Julia's mind: Lizzie arriving at Dempsey's, just eight months ago, exhausted but smiling; Lizzie at work in the oven room, a grin spread across her face; Lizzie in their attic room, giving Kate a good night hug, and then turning her attention to her.

Father Burns arrived then. No more time for fear or sorrow.

Julia, Anne, and Kate moved back to make room for the priest. He prepared to administer the last rites, pouring out the blessed oil and lighting a small candle. Julia straightened the covers and smoothed the pillows.

Mary entered the room. Moving quietly, she propped the door open with a small chair she had retrieved from the hall. A few moments later, Walter appeared, standing just inside the door.

Julia heard movements out in the hallway, and she turned to see Grace, Ellen, and Cara slip in quietly. Standing behind them were Walter's helpers, Eddie and George. How quickly Lizzie had come to know and care for each of them. How they all loved her.

As Father Burns prayed and they followed along with the familiar words, Lizzie gathered strength. She raised herself up on the pillows and favored them with a glorious smile. While the priest touched her forehead, hands, and feet with oil, Julia drew in close to her. She sat on the side of the bed and held Lizzie's hand. Anne and Kate also edged up to the bed. Anne rubbed Lizzie's arm, and Kate brushed her hair back from her brow.

For a moment, Lizzie rested her head on Julia's shoulder, and focused her gaze into her eyes. She turned her head slowly to look at Anne and Kate. And then she spoke. Her voice had grown faint, her words just barely audible: "love…you."

A long sigh escaped Lizzie's lips. Her head slipped back on the pillow, and Julia smoothed her hair.

"Has she fallen into a deep sleep?" Julia turned her eyes to the doctor.

Responding with a slight nod of his head, the doctor stepped back from the bed and watched with them.

The priest's prayers continued.

Then, Lizzie's breathing stopped.

"Lizzie! No!" Kate's scream filled the room, sending chills coursing through Julia. Anne stood so close her shivers penetrated Julia's clothing.

With tears trickling down her cheeks, Julia reached out to fold Lizzie's hands on top of the cover. She stood with Anne and Kate, shock and sorrow closing around her, a heavy cloak that descended along her shoulders and arms. No more words. Silence hovered in the room.

"Please God, not our Lizzie." Too late, Julia regained her voice. Lizzie had slipped off with the angels. "We welcomed her to America so recently. We were coming to know her again. Please God, do not take her from us. We all love her so."

"She was dear to me." Mary hugged Julia. "She brought joy to all of us at Dempsey's. Earlier this week, we discussed the cake we would bake for your wedding. Ah, I cannot bear this."

"I must go." Father Burns packed his things. "We must all move downstairs." Taking Julia's arm, he ushered them out of the room. Once they all stood in the hallway, the doctor closed Mary's bedroom door firmly behind them.

Julia kept close to her sisters, wishing to draw strength and comfort from them.

"I will notify the undertaker." Julia caught the doctor's words to Walter, as they passed through the shop on their way to the dining room. Had Anne and Kate heard?

Grace moved out to the shop to close up for the day. "I'll deliver the day-old goods to the mission on my way back to St. Vincent's," Father Burns said.

Julia roused herself and returned to the shop to help Grace fill the baskets.

After Father left, Julia walked to the dining room. Cara had prepared tea, and the others sat at the table.

"Lizzie..." Her words trailed off. She couldn't even express a full thought. Next to her, Anne bowed her head down to the table.

Julia pushed her chair back, her sister's neediness jolting her to awareness. "Anne, dear, do you need to rest? We could move to the parlor? You could stretch out on Mary's comfortable sofa."

"No, I am well." Anne raised her bulk, slowly. "I am experiencing no great pain. It is only my heart is broken."

Julia helped Anne to a more comfortable chair set back in the corner of the room. While Kate went in search of a footstool for her swollen feet, she rubbed Anne's shoulders. "I should

Keeper of Trust

never have pulled you along the way from the church the other day."

"I feel comfortable here, Julia." Anne held a pillow across her swollen stomach. "You must not fret over me."

Once Anne had been settled, Julia found a soft cloth and rubbed the dining room table, until the dark wood shone. Then she moved a pitcher and glasses from the buffet and polished the surface briskly. She'd welcome any exertion that would keep her thoughts from the sadness.

Father Burns must have alerted Bridget Rice, for she arrived a few minutes later.

"I am so sorry, Julia. Lizzie was a lovely girl."

"Thank you for coming. You are so kind." Julia attempted to take Bridget's basket, but she squeezed her hand and turned away.

Bridget went to the kitchen with Grace, to prepare supper for them all, and Julia headed back to the dining room.

She had just passed through the archway leading out of the shop, when she heard the bang of the bakery door. Moments later, heavy footsteps stomped up to the second floor. A thump, likely the stretcher hitting the wall, caused Julia's head to jolt backward.

"Julia." Kate came up beside her and reached out to her. Without speaking, they clung to one another. After another few moments, the footsteps retreated along the stairway. She longed to move back to the shop, to gaze upon Lizzie one more time and say one last goodbye. No, it would be too painful.

She held tightly to her sister's hand. The door of the shop banged closed, and in a few moments, the clip-clop of the horses announced the departure of the hearse.

Julia linked her arm though Kate's and led her away. "Let's return to the dining room. We will be surrounded by people who love us." They found everyone milling about the room, heads shaking. Mary sat in the corner beside Anne, her arms wrapped around her shoulders.

"Julia, what's happened?" Martin entered the room through the bakery, his expressive eyes wide, questioning.

With Martin beside her, Julia's terrible ache subsided, but it would not be pushed away entirely.

"Our Lizzie..." A new wave of anguish gripped Julia. She dropped into a chair.

"These past three days, we all struggled to accept how ill she had grown." Walter stood beside Martin, his eyes sorrowful. "As each night came, we did not think she would survive it. As the new day dawned, we held hope..."

"Julia sent me a note. I knew the girls worried...I should have..." Martin knelt beside Julia. "I am so sorry, my dear. What will I do to help you?"

Wiping away her tears, Julia started up from her chair, nearly toppling Martin. He'd come, finally, to discuss their wedding.

Martin gathered her close. "Forgive me, Julia. I should have heeded Anne's words. I did not understand how ill Lizzie had grown."

"We did not understand it either." Julia leaned against him. His touch brought a small measure of comfort. "I still cannot believe she is gone."

Grace, Cara, and Bridget placed food on the dining room table. "Eat something, please," Grace said.

Mary pulled up chairs. "Yes, come and sit at the table. We will all need our strength."

Julia and Martin helped Anne move back to the table then took their own places.

The wonderful aromas should have awakened her hunger. Julia drew a deep breath. When had she last tasted food? She attempted a few spoons, but she could not manage to swallow more than a few morsels. They all must feel the same.

Walter began their prayer. With her mind wrapped in a flood of anguish, Julia could not make out all of his words. One brief sentence, words she would remember through all of her life, pierced the depth of her being. "We thank you Lord, for allowing us the gift of Lizzie's brief time with us…"

All sound in the room ceased, when James arrived and moved quickly to Anne. "Our dear little sister…" Her words, though softly spoken, pounded at Julia's heart. Lizzie's death must be experienced all over again.

"I cannot fathom this. Last Friday night, she came to supper with us." James's shock brought strength and force to his voice. "I'm attempting to absorb what you are telling me, but 'tis beyond belief. Lizzie seemed well enough last week. Ach no!" He pounded his fist on the table. "I remember now. She did cough some. I also recall she refused my offer to escort her home." He collapsed into the chair next to Anne. "She convinced me she would be fine walking home alone. I should never have permitted it."

"We had no inkling of what would come." Julia reached out and squeezed James's shoulder. "On Monday morning, she bustled about and sang."

"I, too, am troubled," Mary said. "I allowed her to perform her usual duties in the shop, lifting trays, and carrying filled baskets out to customers' wagons. She worked so hard, and all the while, she was hiding her struggle from me. A few hours later, she collapsed right out in the shop, and began to slip away from us. Now she is gone. It is too much to take in. I believe I would feel better if I could cry, but there are no more tears."

Grace moved to Mary and hugged her.

Martin placed his hand on Julia's arm. "Arrangements must be tended to. If you wish, I will do what I can for you?"

"Aye, thank you." Julia rose from the table. "You are right. We must see to things."

"You stay here." James confident voice commanded their attention. "You girls are barely capable of speaking. Let Martin and I do this one thing for you. Walter, will you come along?"

Walter nodded and went to fetch his hat and coat. As the three men prepared to leave, Martin turned back to Julia with a questioning look.

"Do what you think best." She glanced at her sisters.

"Yes, I agree," Anne said.

"Of course," Kate walked toward the three men. "We trust your judgment."

When they had gone, Julia sipped her tea. "We waited so long for our Lizzie to come." Though she thought she had no more tears, they poured forth again. She wiped them away and lifted her chin. "Now, she has left us. Ah, I do not know what I am saying. How will I…no…how will we all go on?"

Chapter Seventeen

Dempsey's closed the next day. In the oven rooms, Walter and his helpers baked only enough to fill the orders they already held. Gus Mueller delivered bread and pastries to supply the mission. Likewise, Kate and Ellen sat quietly in their shuttered dressmaking shop and finished the work they had promised to deliver.

Julia stretched to place a bushel basket of potatoes on the highest shelf in the storeroom. "It is fortunate there is plenty of space back here."

"And, shelves, too, thanks to Martin's skill and the work of James and the others." Mary pushed two large boxes closer to their worktable.

"You are holding up well, my dear." Mary examined the fruit at the top of a sack of oranges. "Leftovers...they've been around awhile. Well...we will find some use for them." She handed the sack up to Julia.

"Keeping busy is the only way I can go on." Julia stepped down from the ladder and rubbed her aching arms. "I cannot think about...what happened. But, there are no tears today." She retrieved another basket and placed still another carton on the highest shelf. "The generosity of our dear friends amazes me."

"They wish to offer what solace they can." Mary pulled heavy brown paper from another carton. "Whew...onions."

She passed the box up to Julia. "Well that's the end of it." Mary surveyed the shelves. "We have more food than we can possibly eat. I will ask Walter to deliver some to the mission in the morning."

"That is a grand idea." Julia closed the door and linked her arm with Mary's as they made their way to the dining room. "We must hurry. Grace has been putting supper together, using what our friends sent in for us. She wishes to offer us consolation with her meal."

"Ah, good, you are here." Walter drummed his fingers on the table, as he sat at the far end of the room with Eddie and George on either side of him. "We are ready to offer our thanksgiving."

Grace and Cara placed bowls of potatoes and turnips on the table amidst an array of steaming platters.

When they all sat, he bowed his head. "Lord, we thank you for this bountiful array…We seek your blessings of peace and consolation…Please help us accept Your holy will."

At his "Amen," a low, sorrowful whisper echoed around the table.

Julia sighed, squeezing back tears. Poor, dear Walter. Was he avoiding saying Lizzie's name, as she had throughout the day?

"Thank you for the wonderful meal, Grace." Mary said.

"Yes. You did a grand job of blending these dishes." Julia glanced around the table as everyone nodded their agreement.

"You are welcome." Grace spoke quietly.

Conversation trailed off. They ate with reticence, little sound save the scraping of forks against porcelain plates.

"That was delicious." Julia stood, her shoulders lifting. It was over, finally.

Working in silence, the girls cleaned the dining room and the kitchen.

Later, Julia caught up to Kate as she headed for the stairway. "With our chores finished for the evening, perhaps, we could visit Anne?"

"A fine idea, Julia." Kate retrieved their coats. "I worried about Anne all through the day."

❋ ❋ ❋

"Julia, Kate, you are so good to come." Anne called to them through the open kitchen window. "How are you both faring?"

Julia studied her sister closely. Anne's red eyes and raw nose betrayed her distress. Thank goodness they had come. "Have you spent the day crying? Perhaps Kate and I will distract you from your sorrow."

As they entered the kitchen, James and Martin strode through the opposite doorway, carrying dishes from the dining room. Julia moved to the sink where Anne stood, her hands immersed in soapy water.

"How is everyone at Dempsey's?" James stacked plates on the counter.

Martin stopped beside Julia, a basket of silverware tucked under his right arm. "How are you?"

"It has been a sad day." Julia shivered, feeling Martin's breath on her neck. "We tried to keep busy, but with the shop closed, time hung suspended, a long dismal winter rather than a single day."

When Julia poured tea for everyone, James headed for the door. "I'll take my cup to the parlor and leave you girls to talk."

Martin took a cup from Julia. "Goodnight. I will meet you at the church in the morning." His hand lingered on her arm then he followed James out of the kitchen.

Julia's skin tingled. Did she dare hope?

When the kitchen had been put in order, Julia sat with her sisters. They sipped their tea, and took turns releasing sighs.

Kate tapped her food against the chair leg. "Remember when Lizzie opened the attic window to chase out the fairies?"

Julia chuckled. "She persisted in saying 'paddy' for boy, and she giggled when I corrected her. We settled on 'lad.'" Her eyes filled with tears. "Last evening, as we sat together and composed the letter to our parents, informing them of the sad news, I was dry-eyed and calm. I suppose I was in shock."

"We all were." Kate eased a few inches away from them, her arms folded.

"Since early this morning, the truth of losing Lizzie has overpowered me." Julia dabbed at her eyes with her handkerchief. "I cannot speak of her, or even say her name, without giving way to a rush of tears." Ah now, what was she thinking, burdening her sisters? Their visit was meant to cheer Anne. "I'm sorry. I will halt my weeping."

"Are there things we must discuss?" Kate's eyes met Julia's for the first time that day.

"I believe the arrangements are complete." Julia dragged her chair over, until her elbow touched Kate's. "According to Father Burns, everything is in place for the funeral tomorrow. Did we do the right thing, not holding a wake?"

"We three are in a sorry state." Anne had been sitting back from the table, head bent, fingers interlocked. Now, she looked up and cleared her throat. "I do not think we could endure such a vigil without our dear ones in Ireland to mourn with us."

"I suppose Walter's suggestion was a sensible one." Kate reached for Anne's hand. "Lizzie lived in St. Louis only a short time. She knew few people outside of Dempsey's and St. Vincent's."

"I believe we will all be relieved when the rituals of public mourning are over and we are left to make peace on our own." Anne's voice quivered. "Nothing will bring our Lizzie back." She bowed her head as her tears poured forth.

Julia squeezed her shoulder. Her sister's delicate condition caused concern, but an enduring strength rested deep within Anne. She would suffer, true, but she would survive.

Keeper of Trust

Her true worry rested with Kate's unsteady state of mind. Could she rise above the loss? Chills raced down Julia's spine, as she watched Kate stroke Anne's arm, her eyes hollow. Since Lizzie's death, she shed few tears. She spoke sparingly, and the few words she did utter came out bland and lifeless.

"Stay calm, dear." Kate drew as close as Anne's expanding bulk would permit. "We will take care of you. We will come through this together."

Julia joined them in the hug. She needed comfort herself.

When they settled back in their chairs, Kate slipped over to the corner of the kitchen and returned with the bag she carried from Dempsey's. She drew out the length of white lace Julia had seen earlier and held it up for their inspection.

"Oh my!" Julia's breath caught. "That is the most exquisite gown I have ever seen."

"I made it today for Lizzie." Kate lifted the long flowing garment high and draped the hem across Julia's knees.

Julia examined the dress, taking care not to soil the wonderful creation. Only the intricate lace pattern adorned the gown. The sleeves, strips of the same lace interspersed with panels of white muslin, narrowed at the shoulder, widening gradually to a generous balloon at the wrist. "The lace is as soft as it is lovely."

"I wished to express my great love for Lizzie. Sewing is what I do best." Kate's cheeks grew damp, but she made no sound.

Julia offered her a handkerchief, and hid her smile. Finally, the poor girl. Kate had been holding back.

"Surely, this is the best work you have ever done." Julia helped Kate fold the dress. "It is a magnificent gown. Just the thing for an angel. Our angel."

"'Tis lovely, Kate." Anne held a corner of the bag, while Julia and Kate tucked the dress back inside. They stood together, their tears now spent. "It is a wonderful, thoughtful thing you have done."

Julia fetched her shawl. "We must set out for Dempsey's. The time has come for Kate and me to face our second night in the attic room without Lizzie."

❁ ❁ ❁

The day of Lizzie's funeral dawned amidst an outburst of thunder and lightning.

Kate and Julia trudged to St. Vincent's with the Dempsey group gathered behind them as if a cocoon, shielding them from their pain. Anne and James followed along in the carriage. Julia tucked her chin low. Could there have been a time of darker, gloomier skies or greater sorrow?

The funeral at St. Vincent's shone with beauty and simplicity. Their friends filled the church. Father Burns and Father Ryan offered petitions for the soul of their beloved Lizzie and prayers for peace and consolation for those left behind. Between the prayers, Ellen and Grace sang without accompaniment, their lovely voices soaring to every corner of the church.

When the service ended, their friends left them. The early morning rain now poured down in torrents.

Julia joined Martin in the bakery wagon, pushing back thoughts of the mission ahead. "Neither the coverings of the vehicles nor the umbrellas will protect us from this deluge." She drew her shawl over her head and shoulders, but the dampness seeped in all around her. "Have you been to Calvary Cemetery? The ride seems interminable."

"I have been there for several military funerals." Martin scanned the road ahead "It is a long way. An hour's ride, I believe. The cemetery is located at the northernmost edge of the city."

"I do not believe I have ever been this far from Dempsey's since I arrived in St. Louis." Julia leaned against Martin's shoulder as they passed rows of houses, a few small farms, and vacant, flooded fields. He did not pull away.

She grasped the wooden seat, as the wagon bumped and swayed. The sad little procession entered the cemetery gates, at last. The wagon trailed behind the hearse, along a winding, tree-lined road. Would this ride never end?

The horses pulled off to the side and the vehicles lined up on the grass. Julia rested her eyes on the coffin as the men lifted the coarse wooden box and carried it the short distance to the gravesite. Mourners moved along behind them on foot. The rain continued without any lull, thoroughly soaking everyone's clothing. The chill coursing through Julia felt more akin to the dead of winter than the spring day it was.

She and Martin fell into step behind Anne and James. Walter held the arms of Mary and Kate, and the Dempsey girls and Walter's helpers followed behind them.

"Lizzie is resting with God. She no longer must cough or struggle for each breath."

At Mary's words, Kate's snuffles lessened.

"Think how happy Lizzie would be Kate, wearing that lovely dress you created for her." Julia turned back to face her sister. If only she could find the right words to ease her pain.

As they proceeded onward, Julia leaned toward Martin's ear. "Since sharing a few moments of closeness at Anne's, last night, Kate has withdrawn again." No need for her to whisper. The constant blasts of thunder blocked out all but the closest conversation. "She insists she is bearing up, but I am not convinced. She appears lost and forlorn."

"I pray time will heal her." Sadness filled Martin's eyes.

Julia and Martin huddled with the other mourners in the chilling rain at the gravesite. She felt their bond of shock and sorrow, as Father Burns uttered brief prayers. When he ended with the final benediction, "…May the perpetual light shine upon her," a strong chorus of "amen's" followed.

Mary draped her arm over Kate's shoulder. "I loved her dearly."

Kate took Mary's hands between her own. "I know, I know. She loved you too." Kate's voice trailed away. She stood motionless, her face pale, and her expression pained and angry. When Walter took her arm, she seemed not to notice, and he sorrowfully stepped aside.

Even when Julia pulled Kate close and held her with a strong grip, she stood rigid. Could she accept no comfort? "Please, Kate, allow me to console you. I need comforting, too."

No answer.

Moving away from her sister, Julia knelt with the others to retrieve a clump of dirt...a bit of mud actually...to toss on the coffin as the men lowered it into the grave.

Kate raised her arm high over her head and attempted to crumble the soil. As the small bits of dirt trickled down, she cried out, in a loud, clear tone laced with bitterness. "I hold you all responsible. The Hogans, the British, my parents..." Her tortured cry rang out through the wind and rain. "The cruel treatment Lizzie endured at the hands of the Hogan's surely caused her illness. Her death is on their heads."

The pouring, blowing raindrops sliced at Julia's cheeks as she met Kate's wild stare. "Please, dear, calm yourself. Each word of condemnation tears at my heart and pounds at my spirit." Julia trembled. With Lizzie gone, would she and Anne be capable of helping Kate? Did they possess the strength to sustain her?

Without warning, Kate lunged near the edge of the gaping hole. "Lizzie, my sweet Lizzie!" Her voice weakened, but desperation filled her cries.

"Kate, be careful." Julia stepped closer and took a firm hold of her hand. "Watch your step."

Martin braced Kate from the other side, with his strong right arm.

Kate pressed forward. Losing her balance, she tottered precariously at the edge of the grave. "Lizzie!" Her strangled cry pierced the air.

Julia gaped in horror, as Kate's foot slipped in the mud. She fell from her grasp and stumbled toward the open hole.

"Allow me." James edged Julia away and he and Martin seized the sobbing Kate. They placed her on firm ground, and led her from the edge of the open grave.

"Let us move back to the wagons." Arms spread wide, Father Burns ushered them away from the gravesite and headed them back to the carriages.

Julia held Kate's hand as they stumbled along, with Martin on the other side nearest to the road.

"When I saw Lizzie alight from Walter's carriage that first day, she smiled at me and my heart filled with happiness." Kate blinked rapidly. "I worried about her, when our parents sent her to work at Hogan's. I thought she had recovered from her illness. She recuperated from her trip well enough. And then, she grew to love the bakery so. The work energized her. In her brief eight months at Dempsey's, her joy spilled over everyone who lived and worked there."

Kate turned toward Walter and Mary and bestowed a small smile upon them. "She sure did take over the place, did she not?"

A sob burst forth from Anne. When James placed his arm around her shoulders to steady her, Julia exhaled and bent close to Kate. "Anne has been blessed with a caring husband who will watch over her. Still, she will need us. She grows near to her confinement."

"Aye, I cannot return to the bakery without Lizzie. I cannot go on without her." As they reached the carriages, Kate whirled and darted back toward the grave.

Walter and Martin grasped Kate's arms and held her firmly, and then handed her, Anne, and Mary into the carriage.

Julia sighed. "At last, we can move away from this sad, frightful place." She accepted Martin's good hand, allowing him to help her into the Dempsey wagon. She slipped into a side bench and he sat beside her. The rest of the Dempsey group joined them.

Of course, they must go back to the bakery. What else could they do?

❦ ❦ ❦

Back at Dempsey's Julia pressed shaking fingers against the door jam and gazed into the shop. For the first time since she had come to St. Louis, the bakery stood bare. With the shelves emptied and silence replacing closing oven doors and banging trays, the eerie quiet brought a new rush of trembling. Only a faint aroma of fresh bread and pastries remained from two days before.

"Let's rush upstairs for dry clothes." Julia took Anne's hand. "I'm not sure what we will find for you, but we will try."

Once they had changed, Julia glanced at her bed. How comforting it would be to stretch out on the mattress and hide from the cruelties of the world. Would she dare? Even for a few moments? But their friends waited for them in the dining room.

When they arrived downstairs, Mrs. Flynn poured tea into cups and passed them around. "Here's a nice hot cuppa for you. Ah, 'tis such a terrible day to be outside."

"I warmed some towels." Mrs. Rice handed one to Anne. "Perhaps, if you fold this around your head and shoulders, it will soothe you."

Her eyes aching from lack of sleep and extensive weeping, Julia gazed around the room. What a difference from the bare shelves of the shop. An enormous array of covered dishes filled the shelves and the massive breakfront at the back wall. Friends from the neighborhood had carried in platters and trays, piled with steaming food. The women from St. Vincent's, under the direction of Mrs. Flynn, had assembled a meal for them.

"We appreciate all you've done for us." Julia nodded to Mrs. Rice, who poured water into their glasses from a pewter pitcher.

The aroma of the freshly prepared meats, vegetables, and salads filled the dining room. Though her body craved nourishment, she could force only small morsels of the food into her mouth.

When Bridget stepped up behind her and offered a serving of meat from the steaming platter she held, Julia shook her head. "We are so grateful for your care." She smiled at her dear friend. If only, these wonderful dishes and the kindness of their friends could ease their grief.

When the meal ended, at last, the men headed for the oven room to inspect Walter's latest project, his month's long attempt at building a rotating fan. "I remember when you demonstrated the fan for Lizzie and me," Julia leaned back in her chair and spoke to Walter as he passed. "You turned the blades around with your thumb and explained how you were attempting to make it rotate on its own."

"I am still attempting it." Walter grinned and followed behind the other men.

"You girls go off and have a rest. You must watch over our Anne." Mrs. Flynn extended her arm to help Anne from her chair. "We will clean up and store away this mountain of leftover food."

With nothing left to do, Julia joined Mary, Anne, and Kate in the parlor. Mary nodded her head, shaking it a little, and adjusted her cap.

"What is it dear? You seem to have something you must say." Julia wrapped her arm around Mary's shoulders, and their tears began anew. "You can tell us. Whatever has upset you so, we want you to share it with us."

Kate straightened in her chair, remorse spread across her face. "I am so sorry if I caused you pain, Mary. Please forgive me. I did not intend to make a scene at the cemetery. I know not what force came over me and caused me to act in such an irrational manner." Kate buried her head in her hands. "And, I have shamed our dear, sweet Lizzie."

Julia rushed over to sit beside Kate. "There is nothing to forgive. And, our Lizzie would have understood. Was she not the dearest, kindest girl in the world? And did she not love you above anyone else?"

Mary sat on the other side of Kate. "Now, you are not to have a care. You did not upset me, Kate. It is Lizzie I wished to talk of." She wiped more tears from her eyes and blew her nose. "Could there have been a sweeter child than our Lizzie? Though almost twenty years separated us, I felt a close, tender bond with her."

"We understand what you are saying, Mary," Julia said. "I know I speak for Anne and Kate. We were all aware of your steadying influence on Lizzie and of the comfort and confidence she drew from you."

"I do not wish to appear presumptuous. I know how you all loved your little sister. But Lizzie arrived here a mere child, and she missed her home and your family desperately." Mary lifted her shoulders. "God has been good to me. I have been blessed with a fine life. But when Lizzie came, she brought joy to this place I had never known before. In the few short months we had her with us, I grew to love her like my own daughter."

"She had begun to mature under your sweet direction." Julia embraced Mary again. Her dear friend must not hold any feelings of guilt for loving Lizzie. "We assure you our little sister loved you in return."

"You do not understand." Mary drew away from Julia and waved her hands at the girls. "At times, I pretended she was my own child. Sure, I only dreamed, but I have betrayed your own poor, dear mam. Aye, she will be grief-stricken over losing her wonderful girl." She stood and faced them. "I would not for the entire world wish to take her place. I would not cause her any more sorrow than when she receives your letter. Ah my, I am guilt ridden."

The scene at home, when the family received their letter, passed before Julia's eyes. Father would bring the envelope into the cottage and everyone would gather around to hear the news. She could not even think about the grief their message would bring her family.

"Oh, the thought of them reading our words..." Anne raised her bulk from her chair with a great effort. "I can picture their faces, when they learn Lizzie is gone. It will be the saddest thing in the world."

Tears flowed again. Perhaps their weeping had lost all restraint. Kate bent her head way out over her knees, shaking.

"What is it dear?" Julia placed a finger beneath Kate's chin and lifted her face upward. But...there were no tears.

A mischievous grin spread across Kate's face. "Our mother...we were never allowed to call her mam, Mary...will continue to sew." Kate pretended to hold a piece of cloth in her lap. With her right hand, she mimicked a deep, swooping sewing motion. Then she snickered.

"Mary, do not think for one moment your love for Lizzie will hurt or disturb our Mother. She will suffer over the loss, surely. You must believe what I am saying, though. She behaved toward her children like no other mother I have ever known. She loved Lizzie, but in her own way." Kate appealed to Julia and Anne for agreement, and when they both nodded, she continued. "She will mourn, but she will continue to sew. With her, the stitching will never cease."

"Remember how Lizzie loved to giggle?" If only Julia could prolong this bit of lightheartedness. They needed a respite from their overwhelming grief. "She especially loved to make Kate laugh. Remember when she told us about Lizzie learning to sew...?"

The others joined in, one by one, each telling their favorite Lizzie story. For a moment, they forgot their tears. Mary smiled along with them. They would hold memories of Lizzie in their hearts forever. But, could they find the strength to go on?

Chapter Eighteen

April, 1867

One afternoon, a few days after the funeral, Julia arrived at Anne's door a bit later than her usual walk from St. Vincent's. "I've not much time." She followed Anne into the kitchen, but did not remove her shawl. "After missing so many days last week, I have worked hard to catch up with my tasks. I will visit for a moment then I must rush home to help Mary. It's been sorrowful in that dreary bakery without Lizzie's laughter and singing. And, Kate and I are lonely in the attic room without her giggles and her hugs."

She shook her head when Anne reached for the teapot. "Not even time for tea. I only sought to gain a hug from you."

"I could use a hug as well. I've been thinking of Lizzie all day." Anne stretched her arms toward Julia, but released her as soon as they embraced.

"I had almost forgotten. I have a note for you from Martin." Pushing aside her roomy apron, Anne pulled a slip of paper from her pocket and handed it to Julia.

A note from Martin! He had not sent her a message like this in months. Unfolding the sheet, she read the few sentences.

"He wishes to speak with me tonight after supper." She stared down at the floor. Would this be a joyful discussion or a sorrowful one? Raising her eyes to meet Anne's, she shook her head. "We must talk, certainly. Our wedding is less than two months off. Pray for me, Anne. Pray for us both. I'm not sure what will be decided."

"I will pray, Julia." Anne folded her hands in front of her. "And please, promise me you will return tomorrow and tell me everything."

"Sure, I will come." Julia hurried toward the door. "Let us hope tomorrow I will burst in with shouts of joy."

❀ ❀ ❀

Just after supper, Julia heard footsteps in the hallway. She trembled. Her future, whatever it may be, walked toward her.

Martin strode into the kitchen. "Good evening, Kate, Ellen, Grace, Cara—"

"Sure, and we might finish up here without the assistance of Princess Julia." Kate pushed her toward Martin. The girls all joined in the laughter at Kate's folly.

"You must go," Ellen cried.

Grace placed a hand on her shoulder. "We will manage here."

Julia raised her hands in defeat and removed her apron. She couldn't subdue a grin as she turned to Martin. "Will I need a wrap?"

He held up her shawl. "When I walked through the dining room, Mary handed me this." He wound the wrap about her shoulders, and they went out through the hallway toward the back door.

The girls in the kitchen bowed and waved, calling out "princess, your highness," and "your majesty." Julia turned back and fluttered her hand at them. Even without her presence, Lizzie's teasing habits lingered.

❀ ❀ ❀

Martin steered her toward the park, as he had so many evenings before the accident. In the fading light of the lovely spring evening, they walked wordlessly along for a time. He held her arm a safe distance from her hand, and her fingers, which she ached to interlock with his.

While they strolled along the outer edges of the park, Julia bounced and squirmed. Did he plan to say anything at all?

Martin cleared his throat. "I scarcely know where to begin. I suppose with Lizzie. Can you bear to talk of her?"

"I love to talk of Lizzie. It soothes me, somehow." Feeling a slight flutter, Julia placed her hand across her heart. "The mention of her name keeps her alive. Of course, the tears come at all unexpected times. If you will tolerate a few unbidden tears, please do not hesitate to speak of Lizzie."

"I am so sorry you lost your little sister. She was a dear girl. I will miss her." Martin's probing gaze touched deep in her soul. Since the day of his accident, he had never looked directly at her. Was this now a return of the endearment she could not live without?

"Your kindness helped to sustain me these last few days. I could not have endured the grief without you." Julia struggled to hold her breaths even. Perhaps they could regain the extraordinary connection they once held. Perhaps...

Martin's intense blue eyes darkened. The deep lines drawn across his forehead and cheeks betrayed the gravity of his thoughts. "I do not wish to cause you any more distress, but we should talk about our plans. Could you bear it?"

"Yes, we must come to some resolutions. Whatever is to happen between you and me, however we proceed, we cannot delay any longer." Julia dropped her arms to her sides, grasping her skirt in tight fists. Did he intend to end it all? He must tell her.

"Do you still love me?" Martin faced her, interlocking his fingers with hers. "Could you possibly love a fellow with but one arm?"

Julia pressed closer. "Oh, my dear. Of course, I do." Love filled his words, of that she was certain. What a glorious sound.

Her heart pounding, she slowed her pace. "I have never stopped loving you. Your bravery in the face of your terrible pain and perseverance in rebuilding your strength has made me love you all the more."

But yet...had she spoken too soon? He had made no mention of his love for her.

"Julia..." Martin cleared his throat. "There are matters we must address before we continue our talk of love."

His strained expression did not waver. What was he thinking? Julia's original quiver turned to a shudder.

"You know, my memory of the weeks I spent in the hospital is blurred. I am aware you sat beside me every possible moment. I recall waking each afternoon to find you there." He removed his jacket and placed it across her shoulders. "What I'm asking is, were you there when the doctors and nurses worked on my arm, what's left of my arm?"

"The nurses were very proper, of course." Julia stroked her chin as she gathered her thoughts. "They usually asked me to step outside, but if I sat at the window reading, they sometimes allowed me to remain in the room." She turned to face him. "What is it? What are you asking me?"

Martin's voice trembled. "Did you see the arm? The stump? The hideous wound? Have you had a clear view of the damage?" His face blanched.

Understanding dawned. Her answers mattered deeply. Julia offered him a reassuring smile. "In the hospital, they kept you well covered. One afternoon, though, a young nurse came in alone. She permitted me to help her bathe your arm and change the dressing. I believe I am a bit of a nurse, you see. I am not squeamish at all." She reached out and patted Martin's wounded arm. "I have seen your injury, Martin. Is that what you wish to know?"

He jerked away. "And still, you say you love me, a man with only half an arm, a man who walks through life now a cripple?"

"Oh my dear, I do love you. Do not ever doubt it." How could she convince him? "While I am sorry for your injury and I mourn the loss of the hand I so loved to hold, I do not ever think of you as a cripple." If only she could find the right words. "You move with ease and balance. Your carriage is erect and confident. Unless someone stood right before you, they would never suppose you have sustained such a serious loss. Do not suggest to me that you are diminished."

Martin's eyes still questioned, but Julia noticed a hint of a smile at the corners of his lips.

"I look at you and I see a vigorous man, filled with strength of mind and body and courage beyond any I've ever known. I am proud to be standing beside you."

They turned onto a diagonal path that led across the park, Martin's gaze never leaving hers. New spring blossoms and greenery sprouted all around them, their sweet, fragrant scents filling the night air. Julia saw only Martin. Heard only his breathing. Felt only his light touch on her arm.

Moments passed. Time hung suspended. Martin's stiff, hesitant smile relaxed and grew until it beamed. "Oh, Julia, I love you. I cherish you with every breath I take. I have worked to recover my strength and succeed at my new position for you alone." Deep within the park, with no one else in sight, Martin stood straight and spoke firmly. "My goal has ever been to rebuild my life and become worthy of your love."

"Say it again." Julia stamped her foot. "I have not heard those precious words for such a long time. Repeat them, please."

"I love you. Is that what you wish to hear?" Martin's furrowed brows eased. His eyes twinkled. "If you permit it, I will spend my life repeating the words. I love you, Julia Carty."

When she raised her arms to embrace him, he held her away. What was he thinking now?

"I apologize for my manner toward you since the accident. While you supported me and tended me through this entire ordeal, I held myself cold and distant."

"Well, not cold, exactly." Julia rolled her head from side to side. He mustn't feel any remorse. She did not like his pushing her away, that was sure, but she did understand. She inclined her face toward him, offering a slight smile. "Perhaps, a little breezy."

He chuckled. "Nevertheless, you remained constant in your devotion toward me. In my worst moments of pain, I could feel your love soar above and around the wall I placed between us." Martin touched her hair. His fingers clutched a straying curl. "I am sorry for that reserve, Julia. I regret hurting you. I apologize for causing you distress. Will you forgive me?"

Edging a little closer, she ran her fingers along his firm jaw. "I do forgive you, and I love you. I will always love you." Julia knew she should allow him to finish, but she must know his intentions. "Please continue, Martin. What are your feelings about our life together? I have been so worried you had changed your mind about our marriage. Do we have a future?"

"Oh, my lovely girl." Martin rested his eyes on her.

Was this Martin Tobin, tossing propriety to the winds and showing no concern about who observed them? My word, if he didn't reach out then and pull her close.

"After the accident, I presumed I had no right to love you, to have you love me. With my strength returning, my confidence grows that I will be able to perform each facet of my new position. I consider myself able to care for you." Martin shifted away and glanced down at the path. "I have begun to hope."

Julia leaned her head on his shoulder. "I gained the impression you considered me an immature, silly girl, unable to love you because of an unfortunate injury." She probed Martin's eyes. Had she, indeed, touched the core of his concern?

"I worried you thought of me as flighty, interested in amusement and adventure only. I supposed you no longer wanted me for a wife."

"I am sorry I misled you. I am so sorry for pushing you away." He touched her cheek. "You know, when I first met you I believed you a lovely young girl. Since we became acquainted, you have lived through a war, the loss of a young brother and two sisters, and then my misfortune. I have watched you emerge into a beautiful, wise and mature woman. I have loved you all along the way."

"You called me your butterfly." She trembled…was that it? Was she, indeed, as jittery as a moth?

"I was thinking of your beauty then. Like the butterflies I once studied in my nature classes." He grinned at her. "I see you now, transformed, ready to soar out into life. I pray…will it be… with me?"

"Of course, I wish to spend my life with you." Julia willed strength into her meek voice. "And, thank you for your kind words."

"I love you, my Julia." He drew her close.

Her hands rested against his chest, the rough, bumpy wool comforting beneath her fingers. "I love you too, Martin."

She exhaled with a deep sigh. Had she pulled her breaths inward since Martin's accident? Now, warm spring air moved through her with an ease she had missed, not just tonight, but for months.

"Are you ready to discuss our plans? Will we move forward together?" Ah dear, was she being too bold again?

Martin led her on, to a far corner of the park. "If you will have me, my love, I will be the happiest man in the world. I am overjoyed to be talking about our wedding, our life together." His steady eyes reflected the serious thought and consideration behind his words. "Two concerns held me back. Once I began to recover and move on with my life, I worried because I treated you shamefully. I left you alone to face the embarrassing questions about our wedding. With the date approaching quickly and some of the arrangements already made, I refused to discuss the matter."

Julia leaned against a wooden fence beside the path. Was this a beginning?

Martin placed himself directly before her. Intense blue eyes searched hers. A strand of dark, curly hair slipped across his forehead. "I was afraid I had hurt you so deeply you could not forgive me. Then, Lizzie died, and I worried it was too soon to speak of our marriage."

"We have already settled that you are forgiven." Julia could not control the smile exploding across her face. "But we must promise that in the future we will talk things over, no matter the subject, and all will be forever forgotten."

"I hereby promise I will talk everything over with you in the future." Martin bowed to her.

"I, too, promise to speak with you about each and every problem that arises." When she heard his chuckle, she laughed along with him. "You are right. It is unlikely I will fail to share my every thought."

He reached out and tweaked her nose. "I would expect nothing else."

She shifted away from the fence. "Let us move on." After Martin's declaration of love, how could she not forego her bruised pride? "If we decide to marry as planned, we must inform Father Burns and the Dempsey's right away. Or, should we postpone the ceremony?"

"What are your feelings?" Martin asked. "Will your sisters consider June too soon after Lizzie's death?"

A light breeze tickled Julia's face and stirred her clothing. "I feel certain it would make Lizzie happy if we proceed, and Anne and Kate will support whatever we decide." An unexpected jolt of pain struck her heart. Lizzie would not celebrate with them. "It is true, Martin, we are all bent down with grief.

"Perhaps we should postpone the wedding for a time, perhaps another three months."

Martin nodded. "I think you are right."

A new rush of sadness threatened. To hold back the tears, she leaned against Martin's shoulder. "I do not believe we will rise out of this overpowering sorrow in a few weeks. Would you agree to a September wedding rather than June?"

"I will do whatever will help you and your sisters pass through this terrible sadness." Martin offered her a handkerchief.

"Thank you." Julia blew her nose and managed a smile. "I believe time will remove this veil of grief."

"I am proof of time's healing power." With a grin, he stretched his arms wide. "Look what it's done for me."

"My sisters may protest a postponement." She nodded. "Once they have an opportunity to consider the idea, I am sure they will be relieved to hear we will have a September wedding."

"Julia, I would be the happiest man in the entire world, if you consent to marry me in September." Martin chest shook with laughter. "Shall we speak with Father Burns…again?"

"I'll arrange it with him." Julia inched closer, touching his cheek. Could she read his thoughts? "Are you feeling confident about this decision?"

"Oh, Julia, I am sure." The kiss, his lips brushing hers, softly, surely, brought sparks rushing through her, and at the same time, a sensation of tenderness she had never before experienced.

"I love you, Julia. I do not deserve you, but I am grateful you persevered in your love for me. This is the happiest moment of my life. Are you happy, too?"

She blinked her eyes shut for a moment. What new bliss she and Martin had been granted. "I love you too, Martin. And, yes, this is the happiest moment I have ever experienced."

Keeper of Trust

When they headed for home, Julia removed his jacket and handed it to him. "For some reason, I've grown warm." She giggled.

They moved together, shoulders touching. When Martin placed his arm around her, it slipped down to his side. "Ah no...I cannot..." He lowered his head.

"It is all my doing. Flushed with your loving words, I shifted to your left side." Julia gazed up at him. Had her thoughtlessness spoiled this wonderful, loving moment? "I will move around you."

"It is all right, Julia, Do not worry so." He slipped into his coat, and entwining her fingers with his, placed them in his pocket. "It is just a new skill I must learn, strengthening my shoulder and my elbow. I will practice tomorrow. By our wedding, I will be capable of embracing you with two arms."

"If you will allow me, I wish the privilege of practicing with you. Meanwhile, I'll settle for walking along, as we are, with our hands joined in your pocket." Julia grinned. Martin smiling...his calm reaction to this small setback...their wedding proceeding. What a wonderful night. Their love had endured.

❦ ❦ ❦

While visiting Anne the next afternoon, Julia couldn't help but smile at her. Her plain grey dress, covered with a bulky man's shirt, had been wrapped in an apron she could barely tie around her waist. Such unusual clothing for a warm, spring day? Her hair appeared neatly coiffed, as usual, but her flushed cheeks and puffy hands and feet revealed her discomfort.

"Anne, you are looking done for." Julia rubbed her hands together. "Are you well?"

"I am fine, Julia." Anne's laugh held a sharp edge. "In spite of my present appearance, I am quite healthy."

Are you certain?" Julia slowed her impatient toe-tapping. Though she yearned to talk of her coming wedding, her excitement waned. Would it be well received? Anne appeared as if she'd spent her day bowed down with grief. She would not appreciate her urge to twirl about the room.

"I have been thinking about Grandmother Doran and her silly superstitions." Anne took up her mending and set to work on a torn sleeve. "Do you recall her dire predictions of what would come from walking over a stick that had been snapped in half, or touching a newborn chick? Do you remember how we all laughed at her foolishness?"

Julia searched her memory…she must find something cheerful. "I do recall Grandmother saying Mother should be calm and think pleasant thoughts when she carried a baby. Otherwise, she insisted, the child would be troubled all its life."

Anne dropped the sewing work in her lap. "I do remember Grandmother's words. And, I will attempt to find a cheerful topic."

"Sure, if her predictions had any substance, we children would all have been doomed to a lifetime of melancholy. Our poor mother was morose as far back as I can recall, including the times when she carried our young brothers and sisters." The unkind remark, an unfortunate truth, flew from Julia's mouth, before she could restrain herself. But this subject would not do at all. She must alter their train of thought.

"We all miss Lizzie so. Sometimes I cannot believe she is really gone." Anne's face had already darkened. "While I work about the house during the day, or I walk to the bakery or the market, I turn aside to whisper something to her or ask a question. Each time, it is a shock when I discover she is not there beside me."

"Lizzie would not wish us all to move about with gloomy faces. I promised myself I would thrust aside my sorrow and move through the days with a smile. You see, I am trying, too." Julia pulled a stocking from Anne's basket. Could her limited skills manage this small mending project? "You are right. It is just so hard."

"The mending?" Anne's shoulders shook with laughter.

"At last, I've made you smile. Now, hold on to the thought of my poor sewing skills. I have something I must tell you, and my grand story cannot be related while we are in the depths of sorrow."

A nervous giggle escaped, as she grasped her sister's arm. "I bring you the most wonderful, exciting tale of my life. Martin has declared his love. He explained his concern that his injury rendered him unworthy of me." With new determination, she slipped brown cotton thread into her needle. "Our wedding will go forward. You must celebrate with me."

"Oh Julia, I am so happy for you." With Anne's face beaming, Julia grew more confident.

"Before I leave, there is something I must ask. Martin and I plan to meet with Father Burns tonight. We have decided to push the wedding back to September. I wish…no, I need… your agreement before we proceed."

"James and I did not postpone our wedding after we learned of our dear Maura's death." Anne's lips quivered.

Julia let her mind slip back to the past year. Three weeks before Anne's wedding to James, word came from Ireland of Maura's passing. Their dear little sister. Grief-stricken over the loss of the child she had cared for until the day she left Ireland for America, Anne had been thrown into a quandary. After much advice and many consultations, she proceeded with the wedding.

"It was a different circumstance altogether," Julia said. "The time for your wedding was upon us. Every arrangement had been completed. James had readied this fine home for our family. And, poor Maura had been in heaven a few weeks before we even learned of her death."

"Yes, but—"

"Please, Anne, I need your agreement on the new date." Julia rubbed her hand across her forehead. She must find the words. "I also seek advice on experiencing a joyful wedding in the midst of our sorrow. You know, we are none of us ready for a celebration. And I do long for my wedding day to be an occasion of joy."

"Of course, you are right," Anne pushed the sewing aside. "Proceed with the September date. You and Martin have my blessing."

Judging by her quick and ferocious hug, Julia suspected her sister felt some relief.

"I support you with all my heart." Anne released her grip. "I am thrilled for you. Go forward with a smile. You and Martin deserve some joy. Kate and I will make it our mission to see that you have a happy wedding. And you know Lizzie would have been thrilled for you."

"Aye, she would." Julia tossed the stocking in the basket. Nothing for it, but her mending would need practice.

"Have you talked to Kate? I know she will agree with me." Anne twisted her loose-hanging apron strings.

"I planned to tell her tonight." Sobered by the thought of the coming talk, Julia rose to take her leave. "Poor Kate, she remains so quiet and sad. I hesitate to approach her with my marriage plans. I cannot be sure of her reaction."

"Kate loves discussing your wedding, particularly the dresses. Knowing you are moving ahead will bring her pleasure, you can be sure of it." Anne rubbed the growing mound beneath her apron. "Your wonderful news has brought me such happiness. I would skip if I could."

The girls laughed together.

"Thank you for your kind words." Slipping her shawl around her shoulders, Julia headed for the door. "I must hurry off to help Mary and Grace in the shop. I cannot allow my wedding plans to keep me from my duty."

Anne followed her. "Do not be concerned. Your grand news will cheer Kate."

"As we set out with our new resolutions of cheerful thoughts, consider the baby soon to come. Fill your dreams with the joy you and James will soon be experiencing." Julia squeezed her sister's cheek. "And if you can spare the time, add some thoughts about my wedding. I can see I should have insisted we begin our visit with talk of my marriage. Our conversation about the wedding has caused a glow to spread all around you."

Would talk of the wedding bring the same happiness to Kate?

Chapter Nineteen

Blackwater

April 15, 1867

Dear Julia,
    We received your sorrowful letter on the 4th. It leaves us all here sick with trouble. Dear Julia, the death of Lizzie leaves us a very unhappy spring. It was the first bad news we ever got from America. Dear Julia, let us know was it with you she died and the name of the priest with her and also the name of the churchyard she was buried in. Dear Julia, my father and mother are not able to say anything this time, they are too sick with trouble.
    Dear Julia, excuse this small letter, but I am not able to write a large one. Remember me to Kate and Anne, and to Anne's husband, and to all the friends. I was happy to hear Lizzie had so respectable a funeral. I expect to see her grave yet with the help of God. Everyone was sorry for Lizzie. I cannot say more at present. I remain your affectionate brother until death. Michael Carty

On the first Friday in May, two weeks after she and Martin renewed their intentions to wed, Julia finished her work at St. Vincent's and rushed back to Dempsey's. When she arrived at the shop, she found the bakery empty.

"We've had only a few customers this afternoon." Grace spread her arms across the abundance of goods remaining on the counter. "It is nice to see your smiling face, but there is not much work to be done."

"Well, I see I am not needed here." Julia pretended to pout, but her lips eased into a grin. An idea had already occurred to her. "I believe I will run to Anne's. Since her time draws near, it may be my last opportunity to look in on her before the baby comes."

"Fine idea." Grace pulled a broom from the closet. "Perhaps you could persuade Mary and Kate to accompany you."

"Thank you, dear," An easy smile spread across Julia's face as she headed back to the baking rooms to find Mary. What a good soul Grace was. As she hurried along, her smile deepened. Lizzie had wished to be left on her own in the shop. Grace probably held the same desire to impress Walter and Mary with her ability to handle the bakery on her own.

She stopped to see Mary first.

"Of course," Mary said. "I would love to visit Anne."

Kate, on the other hand, shook her head.

Julia pulled her facial muscles downward, attempting her saddest expression. "Oh, please come with us, Kate. I worry Anne does not take time for a proper rest. Perhaps, together, we could persuade her to slow her pace."

"I cannot." Kate held up a strand of black thread and slipped it through the eye of her needle. "We have dress orders we must finish. I shall remain here and work."

"I also wish Anne to see this letter we received from Michael." Julia waved the envelope before Kate.

With a great dramatic swirl, Ellen rushed over and handed Kate her shawl. With a laugh, she eased her through the doorway toward Julia. "You must visit your sister. I'll be sewing with hands and feet until you return."

A tiny grin caused Kate's lips to turn slightly upward. "You two have overpowered me."

Shaking their heads over Ellen's silliness, Julia, Kate, and Mary started off for the short walk to the Duff's house. Little conversation passed between them. The exercise worked wonders for Julia, though. The strong rays of the sun soothed her soul. The soft breezes pushing back their bonnets also appeared to diminish the lines of distress drawn across Kate's brow.

❦ ❦ ❦

Her sister had pushed the door only half open, when Julia called out to her. "Good day to you, Anne!"

"How wonderful to find you on my porch!" Anne relieved Mary of her armload of baked goods, and they trooped inside.

"Ah, my dear, it is good to see you," Mary helped Anne arrange the bakery cartons across the kitchen table. "Our little Grace is making a grand effort in the shop, trying so hard to please. She insisted she would care for everything on her own while we paid you a short visit. There was nothing for it, but we must come away and show her we trust in her ability."

Julia chuckled. Mary also suspected Grace wanted them to leave her alone in the shop to prove herself.

"We had encouragement from Ellen, as well." Mary's eyes twinkled. "Now, what could her reason be for pushing Kate out the door?" When they all laughed, Mary turned to Anne. "I pray you approve of the idea? Is this is a proper time to come calling?"

"It is a perfect time for a visit." Anne urged Julia, Kate, and Mary to sit at the table.

"Well, what have we here?" Julia's eyes wandered around the room. With no coverings shielding the windows, the bright sunlight shone right through the sparkling panes. Each chair in the room held a panel of freshly ironed, white curtains. "Anne, what have you been doing? You should not be taking on any strenuous tasks right now. Will we help you hang these curtains?"

"I could use some assistance." Anne waved off Julia's concern. "James worries over me, as you do, and I would surely be relieved to hang these curtains before he comes in from work. Somehow, I cannot manage to reach high enough to put them up." Anne edged over toward the back wall, attempting to block their view of something near the window.

"Aha, the stepladder." Julia removed a curtain panel from the chair nearest Anne. She placed an arm around her sister and led her to it. "Sit."

"Mary, will you put the tea kettle on, please?" Julia waved the fluffy white curtain in the air then handed it to Kate. "Shall we rescue Anne?" She pulled up the stepladder and they went to work.

"I am making myself at home in your kitchen." Humming, Mary placed the teapot on the stove. She moved the bakery boxes to the sideboard and set a hotplate on the table then she took a platter from the cupboard and arranged the pastries in an intricate pattern.

"You are all doing a grand job." Anne sat back and stretched out her arms. "I must admit resting in this chair feels wonderful."

Julia worked quickly, pushing the ladder from window to window, while Kate held each curtain high for her "I suppose we would not even wish to learn how you removed the curtains from this height?" She shook her head. "Would our Mr. James be upset to know you climbed on this wobbly thing?"

"Oh please, spare me." Anne raised her arms high, as if begging for mercy. "There must be some service I could perform for you in exchange for your silence?"

Mary frowned. "Will he not notice the sparkling, clean curtains?"

"Not likely." Kate's answer drew laughs from the others.

"I realize Anne's husband is dear to your heart," Julia said, "but I'll guarantee our James did not know there were curtains in this kitchen to begin with."

Anne giggled. A delightful sound.

With the curtains hung to Anne's satisfaction, Julia returned the ladder to its place on the back porch. The kettle whistled, and they began their teatime in a happy mood. Julia considered the lighthearted talk the best medicine for Anne, but it proved impossible to sit together for long without thoughts of Lizzie.

"On any day the sunshine appears, Walter insists I must go about and keep active." Mary poured tea, as they all settled in around the table. "I wish he would do the same."

"Your words are a gentle reminder to us, Mary." Julia passed around the pitcher of milk, and then the sugar. "I worry about you and Walter and everyone at Dempsey's. While we sisters have been enveloped in a cloak of kindness and comforting, we are not the only ones suffering. Our little group at the bakery lost a dear and beloved friend. The shroud of sadness surrounds us all."

"Just yesterday, I gave myself another lecture about being cheerful and going on with life." Anne shifted in her chair. "I offered this same advice to Julia the other day, but still, I find it difficult to put into practice. I pray God will soon favor us all with some peace of mind."

"I would not have survived Lizzie's death, without the compassion you girls showered over me." Mary paused and took Julia's hand. She reached out to Kate and Anne with the other. "When Walter and I arrived here, our parents were gone, and we had been torn from our home. We built a good life. Though we were working hard and fulfilling our dream of success in America, we suffered dreadful loneliness. Then, you came,

Anne, and in the years that followed, Julia, Kate, and Lizzie, and you made us part of your warm and wonderful family."

"Ah, Mary, I could not love you and Walter more if you were my own sister and brother, and Anne and Kate feel the same." A chorus of agreement exploded from her sisters as Julia passed around the tray of Mary's fine currant rolls. She couldn't suppress a giggle. "It is your splendid icings we really care for." Her words brought smiles, but the relief was short lived.

"If only our Lizzie survived." Mary cast her sad gaze down toward the table. "But, God planned things His own way."

Julia tapped her fingers on the table. Their opportunities for visiting together were rare. "Lizzie loved tea time. She would not wish us to waste a moment of our visit being sorrowful."

Julia wiggled her finger at Anne. "You, little mother, must take any opportunity to rest yourself. We will have no more curtain laundering."

"Or, anything that necessitates climbing a ladder." Kate rubbed Anne's arm. "I will come help you, whenever you need me."

"Thank you, Kate. I appreciate your concern, really I do, but there is something I need more than a rest. I am too large to even wrap my cloak around myself and pretty well confined to home." Anne stood and favored them with an awkward curtsy. "I am eager for news. You must provide me with the happenings of the neighborhood. Let us begin with Grace. You say she is faring well in the shop?"

"She is busy in her new position, and doing well, indeed." Julia held Anne's chair steady and helped her ease back down. "In just these few short weeks, Grace has all but taken over in the shop. I worried losing Lizzie would return the poor girl to her old, sad self. Praise be to God, it did not happen. She wasted so many years, pining over the foolish Will Stapleton and working at that thankless cleaning job at the mission. She has straightened herself around, mastering the cooking position at Dempsey's, and now, proving capable of handling an even more respectable station in the shop. Sure, I rejoice for her."

"Of course, after the loss of our wonderful girl, we knew Dempsey's would never be the same." With Julia tugging at her collar, Mary lifted her chin. "Grace puts forth a tremendous effort to maintain a friendly cheerful manner with our customers. She faces an impossible task in attempting to replace our Lizzie, though. She was special, and our customers loved her. Still, I believe Grace is being more successful than even she expected. I have watched her smiles come easier each day."

"Remember the Grace who arrived in St. Louis with me?" Anne tilted her head toward Mary.

"I do remember the day you and Grace came to live at Dempsey's. Clothed all in grey, Grace's mood matched her attire." Mary retrieved the steaming teapot. "The change in her is marvelous. She has always been a sweet, kind girl, in spite of her melancholy. Now, her new happiness is a pleasure to behold."

"I award the credit for Grace's turnabout to Eddie." Grinning, Julia stood and saluted. If only her foolish gesture, any silliness, would help them forget. She would march around the entire house to be rewarded with a smile from Kate.

"I agree." With a chuckle, Mary poured hot tea into each cup. "Grace counts the change well enough, but you know, she has not received the education that would enable her to handle the bakery accounts. That pesky chore has returned to me."

"I would consider it a privilege to help you with the books." Pulling a pencil from the shelf behind her, Julia mimicked writing on the tablecloth.

"Thank you, my dear, for your kind offer, but your days are filled with your work at St. Vincent's. Your position has certainly grown in the past year." Mary nodded to each of the girls. "If only your father would come. He would provide grand help to us at Dempsey's."

"Perhaps someday, he will come. I have not given up hope." Drawing a deep breath, Julia glanced at Kate. Would the mention of Father upset her?

Kate met her gaze with a shrug.

"Father Ryan promised to find someone with knowledge of accounts from among the immigrants arriving at the mission." Mary tapped her spoon on the table. "If I fall into a badger's hole, I will call on you. Otherwise I'll leave you in peace."

"And now, it is your turn, my little mother." Julia stood behind Anne's chair and placed a hand at either side of her sister's face. "We must have a report. Tell us, besides exhaustion from climbing ladders and ironing curtains, how are you faring?"

"I feel just wonderful." Anne favored each of her visitors with a smile. "As my time draws near, I suffer the constraints of this confinement. James and I take short walks in the evening, but it is not the same as venturing out on your own whenever you please. It is grand to have you all here with me."

"Perhaps, we could borrow a cape or raincoat from James." Julia snickered.

"We have talked about everything but the wedding." Anne squeezed Julia's hand, still resting on her cheek. "We are all thrilled to hear you will proceed. I understand postponing the ceremony until September, and I support your decision."

"I heartily agree with Anne." Kate straightened her slumped shoulders and spoke in a strong voice. "I assured Julia she must go on with her plans."

"You know, you have my best wishes." Mary offered Julia a second slice of chocolate cake.

"Thank you. Since Martin and I decided the wedding will take place in September, we are at peace with our resolution." Julia took a healthy bite of the cake and swallowed. "Lizzie, always the romantic, would be happy for us. I hold no reservations on that score."

Kate folded her arms. "A good decision."

"My childish dreams of a perfect wedding, my entire family gathered around and a handsome, charming prince by my side, were foolhardy. Of course, Martin is handsome and charming." Julia raised her napkin to cover the warmth she could feel spreading across her cheeks. "But, have we Carty sisters not learned a grim lesson in these last sad years?"

Meeting Anne's gaze, she searched her eyes. "You faced this same dilemma over our little Maura's death. Have I done the right thing?"

"I began my wedding day overwhelmed with sadness and worried about everyone at home." Anne's expression turned wistful. "While you and Kate helped me dress that afternoon, you both encouraged me to set aside my sorrow and focus my attention on my husband-to-be. Once I saw James waiting at the altar, I easily concentrated on him. From that moment, the day took a blissful turn. Your day will be the same. We will manage."

Julia addressed Kate, her words coming unevenly. "Our wedding is a little more than four months away. Will this postponement allow enough time for you to heal?"

"Your wedding may move me and everyone away from the sadness." Kate banged her cup on the table. "A deadline of just over four months will encourage us to push aside the grief and remember Lizzie with joy."

"There is something more." Julia paced back and forth between the table and the stove. "Martin located a house he believes will make a good home for us. He noticed the place was vacant when he passed it last week on his way to Dempsey's."

"Have you seen it?" Mary spoke over the joyful cries of Anne and Kate.

"We walked along the outside of the building. Martin contacted the owner and obtained a key from him, and he asked Walter to inspect the place with us tomorrow evening." Julia's excitement grew as she spoke. She pressed her hands together to hold them still. "I cannot wait to discover what's inside."

"Is it any distance from here?" Kate rose and gathered their plates.

"On Henrietta Street, a few blocks south of the bakery." Julia snatched the last bite of cake, before Kate could take it away.

"Oh my, I will be missing out again." Anne attempted to move toward the kitchen sink.

Kate nudged her back in her chair. "You stay put."

"You must all come for another visit after you have seen the place." Anne remained seated, her eyes aglow. "I will need details, Julia."

"Martin has been concerned that you would not approve of the brief, three-month postponement. He will be pleased to hear you all support our plans—"

"I must return to my shop." Kate pulled her shawl across her shoulders.

"Only wait a bit, and Mary and I will accompany you." Julia frowned. Why the sudden mood shift? "I will be but a moment longer here."

"I cannot wait. I must go. But first, I have a challenge to place before you." Kate focused her attention on Anne. "You and James will welcome a fine baby, a new member of our Duff-Carty-Dempsey families into our midst."

She turned to Julia, determination blazing from her eyes. "Then, in some four months, we will celebrate a joyous, long-awaited wedding. We will add the name of Tobin to our family group."

Julia nodded. "Yes, but—"

"Lizzie loved you all. She adored Walter and Mary." Kate took Mary's hand. "I charge you to honor her memory."

Julia gasped. What had prompted these strong words from Kate, who hadn't spoken so much in weeks?

"I give you this commission. Think of the good times we were privileged to share with Lizzie. Proceed through the occasion of the birth of the baby and the celebration of the wedding with peace and joy in your hearts. That is the best way to bring honor to our girl."

"I will remember your brave words." Anne stood and hugged Kate.

"I, too, will try." Mary glanced over to them, bobbing her head as she packed the leftover sweets in the box for Anne.

"We must continue on, somehow." Julia clutched Kate's arm. Could this resolve for peace and joy her sister proposed move them away from their grief? "We must certainly attempt it."

Kate spun around and stalked out the door. Julia, Anne, and Mary stood together, watching her descend the steps, her heels banging all along the way.

"I suppose we have our orders." Julia furrowed her brow.

Rising from her chair, Anne chuckled. "I suppose we do."

Mary gathered her hat and hand bag. "I believe we have been put in our places." Her little giggle grew into a huge, hearty laugh. "It pleases me to hear such strong words from Kate. I pray it means she has begun to heal."

"If only that is the case." Julia held the door for Mary, bracing it with her hip against a strong gust of wind. "I long to see Kate returned to her former confident self."

Chapter Twenty

On a Monday evening, two weeks after visiting Anne, Julia helped Mary and Grace pack the baked goods for the mission.

James rushed into the shop, deep creases marring his usual cheerful face. His disheveled hair and clothing made him resemble a street rogue. "Julia! Hurry! Anne needs you. Her time is here!"

Julia trembled, her excitement mixed with alarm. She passed the baskets to Grace. Thank goodness it was now her task to deliver goods to the mission. She turned to Mary. "May I go?"

"Of course, go to Anne. Rush home with James right away." Mary headed to the back of the shop. "I'll fetch Kate. We will place supper on the table here and come in all haste."

She latched on to James's arm. "Are you in need of anything? Shall I send supper along with you?"

"Just Julia for now." He eased out of Mary's grasp. When he reached the door, he gripped the heavy iron frame. "You and Kate come too, please, when you are able."

James ran the three blocks to the house. Julia hurried alongside, holding fast to his arm. Finally, he slowed his steps, allowing her to catch her breath.

"Anne has been in pain all day." James's words came quickly, agitation in his voice. "She determined she would persevere alone until I returned from work."

"She is the brave, fearless warrior she always has been." The wind whipped her bonnet and Julia clutched it. "She should have sent for me. Has the doctor arrived?"

"I waited for him to come before I left her. Doc tells me Anne is doing well." He rubbed his hand along his jaw. "She just looks so tired."

At last, they approached the house. "Why don't you sit on the front porch and rest a bit?" Julia sighed. Poor James. So worried. She wished to help him, but what could she say to soothe his concern?

"I cannot rest." James held the door for her. "I must speak with the doctor before I can be relaxing."

Doctor Gallagher stood at Anne's bedside, in complete charge. "James and I have already carried in the iron kettle. Peggy brought a few cloths, but she is occupied in the kitchen, preparing supper. I will count on you to keep your sister comfortable, Julia." He favored her with a kind smile.

"What will I do first?" Julia scrutinized the room…the sturdy bed and dresser James found at an auction house…the quilt Anne brought from home…everything neat as could be.

"Give your sister a hug. Then keep the kettle filled and supply me with clean cloths."

She dropped to her knees and took Anne's hands. "How are you dear?" Julia winced to see her sister in pain. Could she provide the comfort and reassurance Anne needed? Could she help her through childbirth?

"I'm happy you are here." Anne offered the tiniest smile. "I will be fine. Do not worry."

Julia ran to the kitchen. Water and towels. If only she could do more. She shook her head in wonder. How different this was from a birthing back home, where a midwife attended, and at times, family members alone. How fortunate Anne was to have such care.

Too busy to worry, Julia rushed to do anything that would bring her sister relief. In the distance, the door closed.

"How is our Anne?" Walter's words and James's response faded. They were likely headed to the kitchen.

"Anne, dear." Kate entered the room, knelt beside the bed, and buried her face in Anne's shoulder.

Mary stood with Julia, clutching her arm. "What does Doctor Gallagher say—?"

"Anne!" James burst in from the kitchen and pushed through the band of women standing guard around the bed. He knelt beside his wife.

"I am fine, dear." Anne patted his head. "Please try not to worry."

"One last kiss then it's off to the kitchen for you." Kate eased him out of the room.

Julia's heart ached for James. Wishing to reassure him, she followed as Kate and Mary guided him through the hallway. "Mary, Kate, and I will care for her."

"She is in pain—"

"Anne will bear it. Off with you, now." Mary's firm push belied her gentle voice. "It will not be long. You know you cannot be in the room with Anne, unless you wish for a house filled with wee sprites in place of a sweet baby."

"That is a barrelful of nonsense, Mary Dempsey." Kate chuckled.

"Sure, I know it. I only wished to give the poor, sad fellow something to think about."

James lunged toward the bedroom. "Julia...? The doctor...?"

"He left to check on another patient about to deliver." Julia attempted to take James's hand, but she could not draw close enough. She settled for casting him a reassuring smile. "He promised us he will be right back. Stay calm, James. Doctor Gallagher says Anne is a strong girl and will manage this in fine fashion. And, I will be right here. I will not leave her side."

James's voice faded as Mary nudged him toward the kitchen.

Anne shifted in the bed, causing the springs to squeek. "Poor James. I would like to reassure him."

"Do not worry, Anne." Kate knelt in the spot James had just left. "Walter, Martin, Ned, and Patrick are all in the kitchen. The entire Dempsey group will be here at one time or another to offer James comfort and support. They will tend to him."

The back door slammed. Heavy footsteps crossed the porch.

Anne raised her shoulders then dropped back to the pillow. "What is the ruckus?"

While Julia wiped Anne's face and arms with a warm cloth, Mary stationed herself at the window. "Walter has an arm around James's shoulder. They are headed down the alley, and Martin, Ned, and Patrick have joined them. Wait...James turned around, and...Oh my...he's started back to the house with the others trailing behind him. Now, he's arrived back at the gate.

"Ah, here comes the good Doctor Gallagher."

"I must say, Anne, since I came to America, I have not longed for our mother more than I do at this moment." Julia held a cup to Anne's lips. "Small sips only, dear."

"We do not have Mother," Anne said, "but I admit I will be happy to see the doctor come through the door."

A few moments passed. Doctor Gallagher spoke with James outside the bedroom door then took up his post at Anne's bedside.

"Thank you, doctor, for giving our sister such fine care." Julia bobbed her head at Kate and Mary. "And we helpers are all happy you have returned."

"Delivering a baby is the greatest joy of my life." The doctor smiled.

Over the long night, Julia made many trips out to the kitchen to give James reports of Anne's well-being.

"Is he all right?" Anne's voice sounded weary.

"He is fine, Anne. The kitchen is filled with folks who wish to comfort him." Placing a stack of towels on the dresser, Julia bent to kiss her sister. "And I must say your Peggy is a wonder. Before I even ask, she produces towels."

And then...a healthy baby boy arrived in their midst. A hush fell over the room. Julia held her breath...glanced at the clock...inspected her sister and nephew. "It is three thirty, Anne, and you and James have a fine son."

Anne cried softly. "Thanks be to God."

Doctor Gallagher handed the wailing baby to Julia. "Clean him, please. His mother will want him soon." He turned his attention to Anne.

"Oh how beautiful." She wrapped a blanket around him, gently. "He is perfect, Anne...so tiny...so precious. Oh, my dear child."

"I'll help you." While Julia held the baby, Kate washed his rosy skin with a warm cloth. His strong cries softened to whimpers.

"Rub softly now." The doctor instructed them while he tended Anne. "Use a circular motion. Be gentle." He turned to Mary. "Will you find clean linens for the bed?"

While they worked, an aura of reverence filled the room. Julia could not speak...no words could describe the joy and awe of the past few moments.

Kate came up behind her and took the baby. "Julia, you go on out to the kitchen and share the news with James and the others."

She sighed. How empty her arms felt. "I'll hurry right off. At last, I can take him the word he has been waiting to hear"

"Well, walk slowly. Try to hold James back as long as possible." Mary unfolded a clean nightgown. "We need time to prepare our new mother to greet her husband."

All eyes immediately turned to Julia, when she entered the kitchen. "James, I have a grand announcement." A fresh wave of excitement seized her. "Thomas Duff has arrived, the first baby of the family born in America."

"Congratulations, James! I am happy for you and Anne." Walter slapped him on the back.

A subdued cheer resounded around the kitchen. For a few minutes, the proud father shared the joyous news with the folks gathered in the room and received their congratulations.

Julia eased around the swarm of folks talking to James and leaned against Martin. "He is so beautiful. 'Tis truly a blessing."

Martin glanced at her, a little shyness in his eyes. "A blessing that will surely be ours one day."

James's firm grasp of Julia's arm forced her to turn away from Martin.

"I must go to Anne. I must see my son."

When Julia and James entered the bedroom, the place had been returned to perfect order. "This beautiful sight takes my breath away," she said. Anne, looking lovely and serene, held the precious baby in her arms and smiled up to his father.

James pulled up a chair and sat beside Anne. "How are you, my dear?" He pulled aside the baby's cover. "My two little dears."

"Congratulations." The doctor took the baby from Anne and handed him to James.

A wide grin spread across his face.

Julia laughed. No trepidation from this new father.

Complete and perfect bliss shone from Anne's eyes. Julia had never seen such a look of joy in any person before. "It is not magnificent, Kate?"

Kate nodded. She pulled a tiny blanket from her bag and placed it over the baby.

Julia helped her smooth it around him. "I have seen you working over this cover." She touched a blue square. "Where is the pink?"

"We'll save it for another time." Kate's grin widened.

Julia hugged Mary. "It is so beautiful watching Anne and James, huddled together with their fine, healthy son." She should

Keeper of Trust

be allowing them these few precious moments alone with their baby. But...she could not pull her eyes away.

After the doctor left, James took Julia's arm. "I will manage Anne and the baby by myself tonight. I've already sent our helper, Peggy, to her room. She will need rest in order to care for Anne in the morning."

Julia nodded as Anne unwound the many coverings Kate wrapped around the baby. She caressed his soft baby skin and then pulled him close. His dark hair jutted out in every direction and his strong arms and legs punched and kicked the air. His face settled into a scowl. When Anne wrapped him in the blanket again, he grew quiet.

Julia's breath caught. Had she imagined it...Had she observed a flicker of a smile cross his tiny face?

James walked to the window, cradling the baby in his arms. "Your grandfather could be outside, looking up at these same stars." He gazed down at his son, bending his head low and rubbing his nose against the tiny baby nose and lips. "Of course, I'm being foolish. It's already well past daybreak in Ireland. No matter." He looked out toward a cluster of stars.

"Well here's a splendid grandson for you, Da. You would be pleased with this fine, robust boy. Only you being here with us on this night could make it more perfect. I pray you will meet him before he is too well grown."

Grandson. Julia shivered. How pleased and proud James appeared...and yet...so sad. She shared his sorrow. If only her family had come to America. They would be here to welcome their grandson and bask in Anne's happiness.

Anne stirred in the bed. "James?"

"I am...we...are right here." James crossed the room and sat on the side of the bed. He surrendered the precious bundle, and then taking great care, he gathered them both in his arms. "I am proud of you, Anne, and of my son. You have managed a fine job of it. Doc assures me our boy is hale and fit."

"Does his name suit?" Anne appealed to James and then to the girls hovering in the doorway.

"Thomas Duff." James chuckled. "It is perfect. He looks like a Tom."

"We must leave you to your happiness." Julia waved to the little family. "Goodbye, Anne, James. Goodnight, baby Tom. I pray you will sleep tonight." She moved out with Kate and Mary, pulling the door shut behind them.

"With Anne performing the work today, the first half of our pact has been fulfilled." Julia wished to shout and sing. With the late hour, she settled for a sigh. "She delivered a beautiful, healthy baby boy, in an atmosphere of peace and joy."

Kate nodded, her eyes blazing through the darkness. "Now it is your turn. It is time to prepare for a glorious wedding."

❦ ❦ ❦

In their attic room a short time later, Julia rested her head on her pillow, reading one of Anne's old letters from home.

Kate placed a hand on her shoulder.

Julia scrambled up, her heartbeats drumming in her ears. "I thought you were already asleep. I did not wish to upset you."

With a genuine smile, Kate lowered herself to the edge of the mattress. "Move over. I will read with you."

"Oh…well…of course." Wrapping a quilt across her shoulders, Julia shifted over to make room for Kate on the bed. "This letter was written shortly before Maura died."

> *My Dear Children,*
> *We received your welcome letter on the 28th. We were happy to hear you were all well, and we are all well here, with the exception of Maura. She is poorly in health these three months. She has fallen into consumption. Dr. Sheridan told us she would not do any good. She is short on her breathing. I have to be up with her sometimes*

by night. She is reduced very much. We also received a cheque of #4.0.0 for which we were thankful to you.

Remember us to Grace Donahoo and tell her all friends here are well.

No more at present from your loving parents,

John and Nell Carty

Kate sighed. "I have been thinking of Maggie. If only we could bring her to America. How I long to have her here with us."

"We will, one day, Kate. We will." Julia held out a corner of her cover, and Kate scooted beneath it.

"And, I am sorry about raising the matter of traveling on to Oregon, a few weeks ago." She couldn't repress the yawn that broke through. "Now that Martin and I are proceeding with the wedding, I am going back on my word."

"It is all right." Kate ruffled Julia's hair. "I believed all along you would marry. I felt certain you would not consider leaving the wonderful Martin Tobin."

"No. I do not think I could do that right now." Julia bowed her head. Would Kate see her blush? Of course she did, but on this night of wonder and awe her only response was a squeeze.

"Besides, we have a precious new nephew." Kate swung her folded arms, as if she rocked a baby. "It would prove difficult to leave him. Perhaps I will go one day, but not now."

Kate moved closer, linking her arms with Julia and laying her head on her shoulder.

Julia stifled a gasp. Had her troubled sister's heart softened? Perhaps, their tiny nephew was all she'd needed? If only she could remain awake and savor this rare moment of closeness with Kate, but it had been a long night. Her eyelids protested.

She awakened the next morning to the sound of Kate's heels pounding across the floor. Her heart full, she swung her feet over the edge of the bed. "The last I remember, we were snuggled together. It reminded me of old times."

"Nah, Julia. I moved to my own bed after you fell asleep. You roll and toss too much." Kate marched through the doorway and hurried down the steps.

Julia stood, her shoulders slumping. The warmth and neediness she shared with Kate in the wee hours of the morning had been only temporary. How could she sustain that unity?

Chapter Twenty-One

September 24, 1867

Julia's wedding day dawned amid a profusion of thunder and lightning and torrents of water slashing against the bakery building. She hummed over the incessant pounding of rain against the walls. It would take more than a little moisture and gloom to diminish her joy.

A tiny stream of happiness as light as a soft, cool breeze rose up within her. She donned her work dress and sturdy shoes. Spinning and twirling, she headed for the laundry room.

"Is it not a glorious day?"Julia circled around the smiling Cara, who fumbled with her brush. "And how is it you are already at work? Have you never gone to sleep at all?"

Cara shook her head, her thin brown curls spilling from their net. "I thought I'd be without a helper this morning. Scrubbing shirts is no task for you on your wedding day. Aye, and 'tis no fit day for a wedding. While I work here now, I'm praying the rain will stop." She clucked her tongue as Julia knelt beside a wash tub.

"I will burst into pieces if I do not keep moving, Cara." Julia selected her favorite brush, and after dipping it in the soapy water, she attacked a dirty shirt collar. "I am filled with such an abundance of joy the happiness may come dripping through my fingertips."

"Well scrub away then. I would not wish you to lose one ounces of happiness." Cara's smile peeked from behind one of Walter's coarse, tan work shirts. "It is a lucky girl, you are. You and your fine young man deserve every ounce of bliss in the world."

"Thank you." Julia leaned toward Cara and bumped her shoulder.

"You know, I have always held your sister Anne in high regard. She is a fine girl, and she provided great help to me when we worked together on Saturday mornings." Cara snickered. "Ah now, I remember the foot races we had. I would never admit it to her, but she outpaced me a time or two." She moved away from Julia to retrieve a pail of water heating on the small hearth across the room. After pouring warm water into her wash tub, she added the rest into Julia's.

"Since you came along, the Saturday morning laundry chores have been a constant round of excitement. I will miss you and your stories and games." Cara shook her scrub brush at Julia, sending a shower of suds her way. "You must come by of a Saturday morning to cheer me."

Julia offered Cara a wet, soapy embrace. She could not resist one more whirl around the room before she returned to her vigorous scrubbing.

She and Cara worked on, washing, rinsing, and hanging garments on the clothes line inside the dreary room. "I'm just thinking that by this afternoon, I will be a married woman. It is all so thrilling." She shook off the daydreams and folded the few already-dried things then helped Cara set the place back to order.

With the laundry door shut behind them, Cara headed for the kitchen. Allowing her happy thoughts to return, Julia ambled through the long hallway toward the shop.

❊ ❊ ❊

Keeper of Trust

When Julia entered the bakery, her first glance out the window confirmed what the thunder and lightning warned. The heavy rain continued.

"Mrs. Hennessy, Mrs. O'Brien, Mrs. Dolan, hello." The women milled about the shop, waiting for Mary to serve them. Julia moved behind the counter. "What will I help you with?" she asked the woman nearest her.

Mrs. Hennessey sidled over to Julia. "A few cinnamon biscuits." She shook her head. "Are you worrying about the rain?"

"I do not believe in any silly superstitions." Julia laughed. Was Mrs. Hennessey more concerned about rain on her wedding day than baked goods? "Your stories are wasted on me."

"A bride walked to church in the rain." Mrs. Dolan stepped between them planting her shopping bag on the counter. "Lightning struck her and her new husband on their way home."

Mrs. O'Brien took her two loaves of bread from Mary and edged closer to Julia. "A young bride allowed the rain to soil her veil, and—"

"Ladies!" Mrs. Flynn burst into the shop. She marched across the room, her umbrella held high above her head.

Was the gesture a threat or a game? Julia grinned…but… Mrs. Flynn sometimes proved unpredictable.

"You'll not be frightening our lovely bride." A smile peeked through Mrs. Flynn's scowl.

Giggling, the women pretended to duck away and hide.

"The divil is after me." Mrs. Dolan took up her purchases and ran out the door, holding her bag in front of her, as if protection from an assailant.

Just after the door closed behind the last of the customers, Kate marched through the archway at the back of the shop. "I am here to collect our fair bride." She placed an arm around Julia's shoulders and led her away from the counter.

"Is there anything I can do for you, my dear?" Mrs. Flynn rushed after them, the same bridal veil she wore to Anne's wedding trailing behind her. "I am headed back to the kitchen to help Grace and Cara with your wedding supper. Will I be of service to you before I leave?"

Julia eyed the delicate ecru lace attached to the base of her neckline. So much more daring than how she'd worn it at Anne's wedding, tucked into a belt and draped across the back of her dress. Julia tried not to chuckle as the beautiful veil billowed out around the woman like an enormous fluffy cloud.

"Mrs. Flynn, you are so kind to help. Kate will take fine care of me, thank you. I will see you at the wedding, will I not?"

"Of course, I'll be there." She patted Julia's arm, and turned her attention to Kate. "Take your sister upstairs, and bring her back to us a lovely bride. We will expect to see you gliding down that center isle of St. Vincent's in all your glory and splendor in just a few hours."

"Hurry on up and dress, Julia," Mary said. "We will be waiting."

"Go on now" Mrs. Flynn called out.

Julia and Kate ran for the stairway, waving to Mary, giggling all the way. "Seeing Mrs. Flynn drawing some joy from life again adds to my already abundant happiness."

She reached the attic room right behind Kate. Sitting at the desk, watching her sister at work, she grew quiet. Her thoughts drifted to the afternoon to come…and to her dear Martin.

Kate took down the dress that hung from the top drawer of the wardrobe and spread it over her bed.

"Oh, I had forgotten how beautiful it is." Julia reached out a hand…and, oh so gently…touched the beautiful ivory satin, enhanced by delicate lace trim at the neckline and sleeves. The cloth shimmered as the folds of the wide skirt cascaded across the mattress.

Kate arranged the floor-length veil across her own bed. "The lace is exquisite, is it not? The sisters at St. Vincent's do such lovely work." She moved to the wardrobe once more and returned with the white slippers Anne had worn on her wedding day. Helping Julia tug them on, she frowned. "Do the shoes fit?"

"A little tight, but I will manage."

"Once you become Mrs. Tobin, you won't feel your toes." Kate smiled at her.

Julia giggled. "Mrs. Tobin. Oh my."

"One more thing." Kate pulled a sack from beneath her bed, and pushing aside the veil, she dumped out a mound of silky, lacy undergarments.

"Oh, Kate. How lovely." Julia threw her arms around her sister. "What a wonderful surprise." She ran her fingers through the array of frilly things scattered on the bed. "Thank you so much."

"Now that your apparel is organized, let's see to your hair." Kate pulled out the pins. "I'll get my brush."

Sitting still, Julia allowed Kate to comb and pin until she was satisfied. "I will miss being here with you in our cozy little space."

"No sadness allowed for my bride." Returning the brush to the shelf, Kate pounded her heels across the floor. "Our Lizzie would wish you only pleasant thoughts on your wedding day. And, remember our pact. Anne has already accomplished her part of the bargain." She winked at Julia. "A joyful wedding is next."

"It will be a happy day, Kate." Julia grasped her sister's hand. "I am as determined as you to make it so."

"I had near forgotten." Kate pulled a small item from beneath her mattress. "Lizzie brought this ring with her from home. It appears to be gold, but is likely an inexpensive imitation. I discovered it when I dusted her bed." Kate held the tiny ring out to Julia. "You must carry it with you and remember Lizzie with joy today. Perhaps, we could pin it… ah…somewhere?"

Julia traced her finger along the tiny shamrock etched across the top. "What a thoughtful thing to do, Kate. I will treasure this always." With Kate's help, she secured the ring in the small pocket in the side seam of her dress.

Kate stood before Julia and held her arms with a firm grip. "No tears now, you must promise."

"You sound just like Lizzie." Julia inhaled a deep breath, while she searched for a handkerchief.

"I mean it. No tears allowed."

"I promise." Julia brushed her fingers across the ring. Lizzie would be with her...she would keep her strong.

"Will you be all right here in the attic room alone?"

"I will be fine." Kate stepped back and inspected her with a critical eye.

Julia took the opportunity for a long look at her sister. While Kate had been helping her, she had also readied herself. How had she not noticed the gorgeous dress? "You look beautiful. When did you find the time to create this exquisite blue gown? With this new empire waist, you appear tall and elegant." Julia kissed her forehead. "The entire creation is marvelous. God willing, you'll be our next bride."

"Perhaps, one day, but it will be none too soon. Do you see suitors loitering all about?" Kate waved her hand, as if brushing away her concern. "Do not worry, Julia. It will be lonely here, but perhaps our Maggie will come soon. Now, let us move you and this elegant gown down the stairs."

Together, they raised the hem of the skirt and train from the floor. Watchful that not a speck of dust collected on the cloth, Julia descended one step at a time, moving slowly, cautiously. Oh, if Lizzie could see her now.

At Kate's prod, she shook away the thought and continued down the steps. When they reached the second floor landing, Mary and Grace approached.

"We will help you the rest of the way." Grace held the front of the dress high, and Kate followed along behind, raising the back.

"I should have dressed on the first floor." Julia giggled as they bumped and jostled one another along the staircase.

Passing through the parlor, Mary waved Mrs. Flynn, Ellen, and Cara over to join them. "We have assembled a supply of umbrellas and blankets to hold over your head and spread out in the carriage."

When Mary pushed open the door, she gasped. "Oh, what a grand surprise! The rain has stopped, and the sun is peeking through the clouds. A weak ray, 'tis true, but sunshine all the same."

"Wait. I'm coming." Walter sprang forward and helped Julia into the carriage. "I have never seen so much material. Or, is this another person?" His laughter boomed, though he handled the cloth with great care.

"'Tis called a train, Walter." Ellen assisted him with arranging the yards of cloth around Julia. "I know you've seen a bride or two. You likely helped Anne maneuver this very dress less than two years ago."

"Perhaps." Walter closed the carriage door gently.

"Thank you so much." Adjusting the folds of material draped on the floor, Julia leaned toward Mary, in the back seat. "I believe I could become accustomed to this attention."

An unfamiliar rumble sounded behind her. She glanced back through the rear window, to a sight she would remember forever.

"Oh my, it is James, Anne, and baby Tom, in the front seat of the buggy they hired for the day." Turning full around to wave to them, her breath caught. Wedged in the back of the carriage, between his brother, Patrick, and James's brother, Ned, sat her wonderful Martin. She clutched at her chest. "My dear."

He grinned at her and waved.

"It is a good thing our bakery customers are not here to see you ignoring all their superstitious decrees." Mary shook her finger at Julia. "Not seeing the groom before the wedding is surely their most important rule of all."

"You are so right, Mary. I am indeed taking a grave risk." Julia waved and favored Martin with her best smile. Lightness and joy filled her spirit, with a hint of butterflies.

Once she had been escorted into the vestibule of St. Vincent's, the Dempsey folks hurried on to find seats, leaving Julia, Anne, Kate, and Mary standing in the back of church.

"Allow me to take one last look at you." Kate arranged her skirt and train and veil. She then inspected Anne and Mary and made final adjustments to her own dress.

"We will leave you now." Anne squeezed her arm. "Be happy."

And then she stood alone.

The organ music reached a full crescendo as Walter appeared and offered her his arm.

Julia grinned. "Thank you for supporting me, Walter dear."

"The pleasure is mine." He bowed low before her.

They moved slowly along the middle aisle. The church glowed as never before, with new gaslights gleaming from the side walls. Ahead, on the simple white and gold altar, candles glowed. Julia blinked. Was she suspended in air? Her feet were surely not making contact with the floor.

Martin stood at the altar...straight and solemn...waiting. She rested her gaze on her handsome husband-to-be. As she approached him, a wave of calm and peace settled over her.

Grace and Ellen joined their voices in a magnificent song. "Joyful, joyful, we adore You...."

A catch formed in Julia's throat. Dear little Lizzie had made the arrangements for the two girls to sing together.

She and Martin stood together at the altar. At Father Burns' prompt, they joined hands.

"I, Martin Tobin, take thee, Julia Carty, to be my wedded wife..." love shone from his eyes. A lump appeared in Julia's throat.

Thinking only of Martin, her voice held steady. "I, Julia Carty, take thee, Martin Tobin..." She pledged her love...her life...to this wonderful man.

The priest blessed the ring then handed it to Patrick, who stepped forward and placed the gold band between Martin's thumb and forefinger. Patrick stood with his hands cupped beneath theirs. No need. Without hesitation, Martin slipped the ring on her finger.

Julia's smile wavered. Martin and Patrick practiced this... for her.

Standing with their hands clasped, they offered a prayer of thanksgiving together. After the years of waiting, planning, and anticipating, the marriage ceremony flew by."I wish to slow the time and savor this moment," she whispered to him.

They moved back down the aisle, and when they reached the vestibule, Martin placed both arms around her and kissed her soundly.

"You worked at this." Julia whispered in his ear. His poor injured arm held her firmly, the elbow hooked over her shoulder. "You could not have given me a grander gift. I would be happy to practice this strong hug with you forever." And then, their private moment vanished.

"Congratulations, Martin. Julia. Long life and happiness!" Good wishes rained over them.

They joined hands, and in no time, stood outside in the now bright, sparkling sunlight. Martin helped her into the back of the carriage and arranged her dress and veil.

Along the short ride to Dempsey's, he sat close and whispered in her ear. "I love you."

Julia's heart fluttered. Was her new husband not amazing? First his practicing with the ring...the two-arm hug...now the vanishing of his reserve. "I cannot believe we are married. Pinch me, so I will know it is real."

He kissed her fingers instead.

"Well, I'm not above a pinch." She lifted his left arm and pinched the stump, lightly. "Did you feel it?"

"I did, and I will be pleased if you do not often pinch me."

"You must kiss me frequently, if you wish to avoid it." Their laughter filled the carriage.

❦ ❦ ❦

Back at the bakery, Julia and Martin moved through the parlor and entered the dining room. "The place looks beautiful, Martin...my husband..." The words tickled her tongue. "The girls did all of this. They ironed the long, white tablecloths, gathered flowers from Mary's garden, and arranged the masses of candles all around the room. It is spectacular."

"It is indeed wonderful." Martin whispered his agreement as they took their places at the table.

"Such enticing aromas, don't you agree? But with excitement filling every speck of my being, I know I will not be able to eat a bite." Julia waved to Ellen and Cara as they hurried to the kitchen. She called out to Grace and Mrs. Flynn who had begun to place bread and butter on the table and nodded to Eddie and George who had been enlisted to carry the heavy platters, laden with beef, ham, and turkey to the table.

"What a grand feast." Martin moved his chair closer to Julia. "I have attended many suppers here, but Walter and Mary, Mrs. Flynn, and the girls have outdone themselves today."

Julia tasted a morsel of each of the many delicacies spread out before her. She must show appreciation. "I admit, I was wrong. My first mistake as a married woman." She wrinkled her nose at Martin. "Everything tastes wonderful."

The guests raised many toasts to the health of the bride and groom with glasses of cider or water. Cries of *"slante'!"* "best wishes!" and "long life!" resounded from every corner.

280

Julia's family, the entire Dempsey group, the priests from St. Vincent's, Mrs. Flynn and her family, and Bridget Rice and her family filled the dining room. "I am so happy your uncle Joseph is here." Julia smiled at Martin's uncle who sat across the table from her. "Though we had time for no more than a few words, he seems a fine man."

"I am pleased you were able to persuade Gus Mueller and his wife, Tilda to come." With the conversation around the room and the clinking of glasses and shifting of plates making it difficult to hear, Martin leaned close. "He has been so helpful to me, introducing me to his turnverein."

"I begged Officer Quinn to come with his family, and I pleaded with Mr. Collins to bring his wife and son. I am disappointed they did not attend." Julia turned to Martin, a brow raised. "I have already decided they will be our first dinner guests."

"You've planned a Tobin supper already, have you?" Martin's eyes glowed. "I'm teasing. It is a fine idea."

Cara and Mrs. Flynn entered the dining room bearing Walter's special wedding cake and some desserts from the ovens of Gus and Tilda Mueller. Julia seized the moment and turned to Anne. "I am thrilled to have you sitting beside me on my wedding day. You look healthy and fit."

"Do not give it a thought, Julia. I feel grand and I am enjoying every minute of your celebration. I assured you I would not miss your wedding." Anne and James each took a turn holding their chubby, smiling baby, proudly introducing him to everyone around the table.

"Perhaps Tom would come with me for a nap?" With Anne's nod of approval, Mrs. Flynn carried the baby upstairs.

Walter's fiddler friends appeared in the dining room and struck up a tune. "We are here to collect the bride and groom," the three men shouted.

"May I escort you to the ballroom, my princess?" Martin took her arm as a cheer went up from the guests. They followed along behind the musicians to a vacant area Walter had readied for dancing.

"And, will you dance with me, my dear?" Alone in the center of the room, they moved together...awkwardly at first. "Another thing we will practice." He smiled.

"That is a wonderful idea." Julia eased closer. "I look forward to it."

Folks entering the room behind them clapped and cheered. Julia grinned. Of course, their dear friends would take no notice of their few missteps.

"I am floating along atop a magical, fluffy cloud." Julia held Martin's injured arm with a light grip and they finished the dance. "A dream I held in my heart for so long, is unfolding, more glorious and romantic than I could ever have imagined." When the song ended, she could not bear to move away and they stepped into the next dance.

They stopped to rest, leaning toward one another. "Just look at our dear, serious little Anne, dancing a furious reel with James," Julia whispered to Martin. "And her with a baby no more than three months old."

After they shared one last dance, Anne and Kate claimed Julia. "Let's hurry," Anne said. "I wish to stop at Walter's room and check on Mrs. Flynn and my sleeping baby."

In the attic room, Kate moved with efficiency. "Let us ease you out of this beautiful wedding gown, and into this." She and Anne presented her with a lovely, soft lilac frock. "Here you are. Sewn by the fine hand of Kate Carty."

Julia giggled. "Thank you Kate. It is exquisite." She hugged her sister. "And thank you, Anne, for everything." She embraced her, and together, the sisters started down the stairs.

Martin gave a small gasp as she moved to his side. "My lovely wife."

"She is lovely, indeed." Walter began clapping and everyone joined in.

"It is time to say goodbye." Martin led her to the door, and they dashed out together.

"Thank you, all," she called out one last time as they headed off toward their new home.

❀ ❀ ❀

"I will cherish this memory forever." Julia grasped Martin's shoulder with no reservations. "The first few moments in our new home. The first time we shut the door behind us, locking it just to be sure. And at long last, we are alone, husband and wife."

"I admired you that day we met at the church. My devotion has grown stronger each day since. I love you, Julia Tobin." Martin gathered her close. "For the rest of my life, I will love you with all my heart."

They whirled around to a private melody in their own grand parlor. No fiddles played. Julia clutched Martin with both hands. Finally, her dream had come true.

Epilogue

September 18, 1868
 Dear Julia, we were happy to hear of you being married and to a man from a family we knew. May God send you luck. Remember us all to your husband and also his brother Patrick.
 Dear Julia, I hope you are contented and we will be happy and contented for you. I hope you have made a home for yourself. Mrs. Carty

October 20, 1868

The Dempsey group drew together in the months following Lizzie's death. They each seemed to appreciate anew their precious friendships and how fragile a life could be.

Julia, blooming with the new life within her, had received all their care and attention. The months had flown by, and with her two baby girls, her life had taken a dramatic turn.

On a quiet evening, two weeks after the births, she rested in the parlor with her sweet babies in her arms. With both girls asleep, she read through the letter from home.

She peeked over the page at her sleeping daughters. "Until this brief message, we received only two short notes in over a year. Why have none of them written?"

The babies responded with soft sighs.

Keeper of Trust

Julia let the letter fall to the basket at her feet. "I miss them all. I long for Father, Mother, Michael and Maggie. I ache because they have not met my lovely twins." A tear escaped and she adjusted a tiny pink bundle and wiped the moisture away with her sleeve.

"I will remain calm and tranquil and allow myself no sadness." Julia had kept her pledge to Kate, to hold joy in her heart. She would not permit that happiness to slip away... especially now with so many blessings.

Her thoughts turned to Anne. Expecting again and nearing her delivery date, her sister now endured the same confinement Julia found so intolerable.

Someone knocked at the door. Taking some time, shifting the babies in her arms, she rose from the chair. By then the door closed.

"Julia, I have been longing to see you." Anne paused in the doorway, her eyes wide and smile brilliant. When she crossed the room, Julia wrapped her in a grand, but ungainly hug. Wedged between her and Anne's swollen body, the two infants squirmed.

"What a wonderful surprise. I so wished to see you. But, how did you get in?" Julia adjusted the babies in her arms.

"Ceil admitted me. She said to tell you she has gone on up to bed."

"Walter and Mary arranged for Ceil to come to us for a few weeks." Julia stretched her arms a little, causing both babies to whimper. "She is providing such grand help we are considering asking her to stay on permanently. Rest will be good for her. The dear girl will need every ounce of strength come morning."

Anne groaned. "I remember. I will experience those harried mornings soon again."

"Here now, wait a moment. I'll set the babies down and take your wrap." Julia reached for Anne's shawl.

"No. No." Anne threw her shawl across the back of a chair and drew another chair beside Julia. "Sit here with me. I so ached to be with you, to see for myself that you were recovering from your confinement. I yearned to have my first look at my beautiful nieces."

"Well, James would be no match against all of that yearning and longing, I'm sure." Julia's laugh filled the corner of the cozy parlor.

"When I could not wait another moment, I convinced James to walk here with me." Anne stretched out in the chair. "He and Tom have gone to see Walter. We will have an opportunity for a talk, before they return."

"I wish them a nice long visit." Julia squeezed Anne's arm. "I have been saving so many things to tell you. I have questions, too."

Anne folded her arms across her wide girth, swaying a little. "I must say, you make a wonderful picture, with your sparkling eyes and glowing cheeks and these fine, beautiful babies in your arms."

"Thank you, dear." Julia touched Anne's hair. "I shall return the compliment." Julia bounced in her chair. She had so longed to see Anne...and here she sat, right before her. "Impending motherhood becomes you. And your hair has once again turned a lovely dark shade of red.

"Twins, Julia. Twins! In all our attic room dreams and imaginings, did we ever envision such a remarkable thing would happen? And you, looking so fine." Anne sat erect and gave her a long, slow examination. "Even after giving birth to two babies, you are still the young, beautiful girl who stepped off the ferry some seven years ago. You appear energetic and high-spirited as ever, but motherhood has bestowed a serenity that adds to your charm and heightens your loveliness."

"I have missed you so, and your visit is a wonderful surprise. Martin sometimes works until late in the evening, and Ceil retires early in preparation for the babies' early awakening. On these nights, I must care for our two fine girls on my own." Julia handed Anne a wiggling pink blanket. "Here is our Maura."

Anne cuddled the bundle. "She feels wonderful. Tiny and sweet. Ah, Maura is such a beautiful name. And she is already drifting off to sleep. She is so perfect. Does Elizabeth look just like her?"

"They favor one another." Julia held out the other little bundle, until the two babies were side by side. "I do not believe they are identical. However they develop, Martin and I are caught up in their spell." When she bent to kiss Elizabeth's forehead, Julia felt certain she witnessed a grin.

"Ah, look, Anne, you have come just in time to see Elizabeth's first smile."

"Well now, we cannot let you two outdo us." Anne tickled Maura's cheek.

"I wish to hear all the news of the outside world..." Elizabeth's tiny hand became entangled in Julia hair, loosening her bun and sending her curls flying.

"I brought you a gift." Anne reached for her bag and drew out a small package. "Bridget Rice and her mother received instructions...somewhere or other...on making candied nuts. Of course, nothing would do but Mary must learn. So, they demonstrated the process for us. Here are the results of my first attempt."

Anne unwound the wrapping paper and handed one to Julia. "James pronounced them quite good, though they appear a little...well...odd."

Julia cleared her throat...covered her mouth...gasped. The nuts...or candies...resembled flat, bumpy rocks. "Oh dear..." She couldn't subdue her laughter and Anne joined her.

"Try one." Anne blew her nose. "They taste wonderful."

Julia took a bite. "Oh my. I have never tasted anything so delicious." A fit of giggles prevented her from trying another.

"Thank you, Anne. The treat is wonderful, but the hearty laugh is much more valuable. Why, our giggling has even put the babies to sleep. I will be sure and tell Bridget and her mother how much I enjoyed their new recipe. And, Mary too, of course."

"Well, I suppose we will need another lesson." Anne dissolved in laughter.

"Well now, tell me about James. Does he work long into the night as well?" Julia pressed her lips together…held her eyes shut tight…still, she laughed.

"Some evenings, he does." Anne still chuckled and minutes passed before she answered. "Other nights he attends laborers' meetings."

"Has his involvement in the union organization grown then?" Julia pushed back the curls that tumbled about her face.

"It has. He assures me the intent of these meetings is peaceful negotiations with employers, but I worry about him." Anne's expression sobered. "I offer a prayer of thanksgiving each time he returns home safely."

"Ah now, I have some news for you. A letter…just a short note…arrived yesterday from home." Julia handed Anne the envelope. "I have already read it over many times."

Anne took the sheet, scanned it, and frowned. "If only, our Michael could come. Can you imagine how our brother would relish the chance to be a part of it all?"

"He would, that's sure." Julia folded the letter and placed it back in her pocket. "I wonder if he will come out once he is free of the indenture. It should be at least two years now since he contracted with the farmer. It is fortunate we have been saving for them all to come with James's father and brother."

"I never speak of the subject in Kate's presence, but before long, she will rage and fume over the business." Anne offered Julia another candy treat and took one for herself. "Her anger is justified, but I worry about Kate's state of mind. Until we know when Michael is coming, I do not wish to upset her."

"Yes, I know." Julia frowned.

"Well, here is a different question we may direct our thoughts toward." Anne took her hand. "It is a most important subject, indeed. Are you as well as you appear? I was not able to attend you when you gave birth, and I have worried about you since."

"Rest easy, Anne. I am feeling fine, but it is my turn to be concerned." Julia attempted to pull a strand of hair from Anne's bun, but it held firm. She giggled. "You must remain peaceful and serene. You must set aside all worries about the folks at Dempsey's, and passage money, and the problems back home in Ireland. Kate and I will take your place and fret over everyone for this short while."

"I am well. You know I am healthy." Anne rose from her chair and placed the package with the remaining nuts on the self beside Julia. "I am remembering the dear sister who was never satisfied to remain at home for long. I recall the romantic dreams you held, of adventures and journeys to faraway places. I worried the care of two babies would place a strain on you. Now, I discover you have things well in hand here. I need not be concerned about you at all. Rather, it is you that Kate and I have come to depend on and place our trust in."

Julia settled back in her chair. Could she force the peace and contentment she now experienced into her expression and her bearing? Could she convince Anne with words?

"I know you have put considerable time into worrying over me. I am aware you offered many prayers over my lack of maturity. I assure you I am at peace. With my dear husband to love and care for, our wonderful babies to fill my arms, and our new life together in America, I possess more excitement and adventure than I ever fancied possible."

Made in the USA
Monee, IL
17 August 2020